THE CONFETTI BED

Simone Sancerre, young and impressionable, has left home to work at the
Hotel Delouche, where she finds herself
falling in love with François, son of *la
patronne,* Claire Delouche. Life seems
wonderful, until the arrival of Barbie, a
vividly beautiful English girl, who shatters
Simone's romantic dreams of a happy
future. François becomes obsessed with
Barbie and Simone and Claire can do
nothing but watch from the sidelines as
François sinks deeper and deeper.

THE CONFETTI BED

THE CONFETTI BED

by
Frances Paige

Magna Large Print Books
Long Preston, North Yorkshire,
England.

British Library Cataloguing in Publication Data.

Paige, Frances
  The confetti bed.

  A catalogue record for this book is
  available from the British Library

  ISBN 0-7505-1158-3

First published in Great Britain by Severn House Publishers
Ltd., 1996

Published in Large Print 1998 by arrangement with Severn
House Publishers Ltd.

Magna Large Print is an imprint of
Library Magna Books Ltd.
Printed and bound in Great Britain by
T.J. International Ltd., Cornwall, PL28 8RW.

For Helen

Chapter One

South-West France 1962...

'You were fortunate,' Madame Claire said, 'to find such a good situation as this.'

'Yes, *Maman* has told me that.' Simone was watching the nightly performance of Madame Claire divesting herself of her voluminous navy-blue knickers, exposing at the same time a whale-like white thigh with a sleight-of-hand glimpse of a mysterious darkness beyond.

Madame had not told her that she would have to share this small room with its two bunk beds, its pervading kitchen smells, cat smells (Mou-Mou, the hotel cat, generally occupied it also), mixed with the rich odour from Madame Claire herself, especially when she lifted her arms to undo her hair and plait it for the night.

But guests came first. For *la patronne* to occupy one of the hotel bedrooms would have been the height of idiocy, far less give one to a young waitress, when the English and the Dutch were clamouring for them during the long school holidays.

'Clamouring' seemed a slight exaggeration, Simone thought. The few English who came only did so because it was cheaper here than in the Dordogne and the Dutch, after a year or two, usually bought their own houses, recognizing their cheapness and the possibilities of the region. 'Space,' Mr Van de Vriess had said to her, rolling his eyes over his morning Kir, 'so much space here.'

'They like the space here,' Madame said with a corroborating sweep of her arm round their small cluttered bedroom. 'In Amsterdam they are squeezed like matches in a box into tall houses which are in constant danger of falling into the canals...' Madame, who hardly stirred out of the village all year, who regarded going to Gramout five miles away as a major expedition, was an expert on all things foreign.

Life for Simone since she had arrived at the Hotel Delouche three months ago had been composed of unremitting hard work. Madame Claire neither spared herself nor her old husband, Jean-Paul. Why, then, should she spare Simone, a young girl barely eighteen who came from a farm where she well knew the girl's mother had imposed the same harsh regime?

But Madame was fair. The work was shared, even with Monsieur at his age.

Sometimes when Simone went out to the yard with yet another load of freshly-washed linen, she would find him sitting with a basin on his spindly knees while he peeled the daily bucket of potatoes for the *pommes frites.*

'She works you into the ground, *Mademoiselle?*' he would ask, lifting his shaking head to give her a gap-toothed grin. He suffered from an illness which gave him a permanent tremor in his hands and kept his head wobbling on his thin neck. He had pale blue eyes, watery but shrewd, despite the tremor. 'She tests you, but if you come up to her requirements, she will be your friend for life.'

'Yes, Monsieur.' She would nod, teeth gripped round a clothes peg, sheets flapping round her head as she pinned them...that English child at *his* age, she would be thinking, and his mother not once making an apology...

'The only one whom she spares is François. The apple of her eye. Did you know that?' There was a one-sided smile as he went on with his scraping and peeling. In spite of his shaking hands he was remarkably adroit. The potatoes lying in the bucket of water were white, smooth, skinless globes. Before his illness, Simone understood, he had been the *menuisier* in the village, a respected craftsman with the walnut wood of the region.

François, their only son, was at Toulouse taking a course in hotel management, as Madame had told her many times, even reading to her at night his filial letters when they arrived.

'*Chere Maman, Tout va bien à College. Aujourd'hui j'ai coiffé deux madames et trois garçons. Mis en plis et en brosse.*'

She would heave herself onto an elbow of one massive arm, bending forward to see so that she was in imminent danger of rolling out of the narrow bed. The deep valley between her breasts showed above her nightdress. Her body seemed to Simone to be an interesting mystery of scarcely-concealed dark crevices, perhaps because *Maman* had insisted on propriety at all times, and whose clothes were taken off at night under the sheltering tent of a voluminous nightdress.

'He thinks like me, that one.' Madame Claire looked up, nodding. 'Always we have the same idea, to make the Hotel Delouche into an establishment of the first degree. When he returns from his course we shall begin the improvements. François says the *réparations* must begin in the kitchen, a new stove for me and a fine new refrigerator. The scullery wall will

14

be knocked down for *les agrandissements*. Then for him will come the new bar with imitation stone facing, better than the real thing, with a painted mirror behind. Water lilies are *comme il faut*, he tells me.'

Simone would listen entranced. 'And bar stools with little backs, Madame? I have seen those in a film about Las Vegas at the Cosmo. Very *chic*.'

'Possibly.' Madame Claire gave fleeting attention to bar stools with little backs at Las Vegas. 'He intends to establish a hairdressing salon where the old washhouse was—water is already there—and the ladies who come on holiday, and their husbands and children for that matter, will have no need to go to Gramout at all. We shall, of course, advertise the Hotel Delouche in the foreign papers and they will flock here, those of *bon ton*, naturally. We will engage a chef, François says. All that will be required of me will be to wear a black hostess gown and walk among our guests saying, *"Bon appetit"*.'

'And Monsieur?' Simone had a soft side for the old man.

'Ah, *ma coquotte*, unfortunately there is no place for him in those dreams. He is not the man he was. If he gets a chair in the sun that is all he wants. Once upon a time when he was the *menuisier*, what a difference! Black hair and sparkling eyes,

15

all his teeth. And you should have seen his walnut *étagères!* Things change in a marriage. You live life through it, come to terms. Do not look so sad. That is how it goes.'

'Poor monsieur.'

'I have done my weeping. And you, Simone, if you go on as you are doing, you will be promoted to be head waitress with perhaps two assistants. We will have printed menus and real tablecloths, not paper. François thinks rose-shaded lamps in the *salle-à-manger* would be pretty for the ladies. If you make their husbands think they are beautiful, they will buy some decent wine.'

François, François, always François... Simone began to be curious about this paragon of virtue. She wondered if he would be like Marcel, her brother, thin and wiry and dark who did most of the work of the farm since their father had been killed, and was going to marry a slut called Madeleine Bonnard. That was how *Maman* unfairly described her. *Maman* had been bitter ever since their father had been caught in the threshing machine of a neighbour. The tragic accident had darkened Simone's childhood. 'You get yourself a job away from home,' *Maman* had ordered when Marcel had said he was being married, 'three women in the kitchen

16

would be *insupportable...*'

The day François drove into the village square, parked his white Peugeot at the War Memorial, and ran up the steps of the hotel into the dining-room, Simone knew he was for her. She would never look at anyone else in her life. It was fate. It was why she had answered Madame Claire's advertisement in the *Gramout Presse*, why she had endured the hard work, the smells in the little room she shared with Madame, the lack of privacy. When she had been making up the bed for him in the large airy room upstairs, she had known that some day it would be hers as well. She stood shyly smiling as he burst into the room like a firecracker. *'Me voici! Bonjour, tout le monde!'*

He was not like Marcel at all, her yardstick, nor like Jean-Paul, his father, for that matter. He was shorter and broad-shouldered, he had an infectious smile where Marcel had a straight mouth, his hair was a light brown except above his brow where it was gilded in a smooth wave, a *mèche,* as if it had been bleached by the sun. His skin was warmly golden, and smooth.

But it was the way he went rushing into his mother's arms and then his father's which captivated her. A warm

17

heart. *'Maman!* Papa! I am so happy to be home.' His dark eyes like his mother's glistened with tears. She could never have loved anyone with a heart of cement.

They had a family dinner before the guests arrived, and after she had brought the plates of soup to the table he had invited her to sit down with them.

'Why not?' Madame answered for her. 'This is a happy occasion, our son home again. And Simone has become one of the family.'

'Merci, Madame.' Simone sipped her soup, her head down. When François asked her if she would *faire chabrol* with them, the unaccustomed wine he poured into its dregs made her cheeks burn in pleased embarrassment.

He told them all about the grand city of Toulouse, the restaurants with their awnings in the squares, Place Wilson, Place Saint-Georges, but seemed more impressed by the Sports Stadium than the Basilica. 'Partly built of brick, if you please, not good stone like our church here. But there's a good flea market round it on Sundays. And the discos! Have you heard of the Beatles, Simone? It is an English group. Very *yé-yé.* '

'I suppose you had time for some studies,' Madame Claire cried delightedly, but pretending to be severe.

'Of course! Haven't I shown you my Certificate of Merit yet?' He jumped up and returned with a parchment roll and two packages. He handed the roll to his father. 'There, Papa, we will have it framed and hang it beside the one you got from the Mairie for long service,' and tearing open the larger of the two packages he disclosed a brilliantly-coloured shawl which he shook out and draped round his mother's shoulders. 'That is for you, *Maman*, from Galeries Lafayette, no less!'

Tears were in her eyes as she stroked it. Simone, seeing the writhing purple dragons with their forked tongues did not think it was quite Madame's style. 'It is beautiful, François. Too good to wear. I will put it in my drawer.'

'Put it in your drawer! I ask you!' He appealed to Simone. 'But it is to wear, *Maman!*' She'll never wear it, Simone thought, watching. She had only two dresses, her black and grey striped cotton overall for mornings, bought in the Gramout market, and her rusty black for evenings. She looked at François, touched by the little scene. His eyes smiled when they met hers. She imagined there was a halo round him. It must be his golden skin, his blond streak. 'And for you, Simone,' he handed her the other parcel. 'Some crystallized violets. Maman told me not to forget you. You can keep your handkerchiefs in the box when it is empty.'

'Thank you, Monsieur François.' She was shy as she accepted it. She took off the paper and saw the pale violet of the box, decorated with the deeper violet of flowers. 'It is just the thing,' she said, *'merci mille fois,'* thinking of the clutter already on the little table which separated her bed from Madame's, the hairpins, the night light, the photographs of François in his various stages of development, lying down, sitting up, standing, the glass with Madame's false teeth.

'Don't you think we have made a good choice in Simone?' Madame said coyly. She had *faire chabrol* to good effect.

'Don't embarrass me, please.' Simone shook her head, smiling. 'Your son isn't concerned with me.'

'But he is. You are part of the hotel, one of us now.' She flung an end of the shawl round one shoulder like a Spanish dancer. The dragons writhed. 'We are a team now, François, myself and you. Isn't that so, François?'

'And Papa too, don't forget.'

'There is no need to speak for me, my boy,' Jean-Paul said, his head almost shaking off the stem of his thin neck, 'I know your mother often forgets I'm here.'

'No, no, Jean-Paul!' Madame wiped the corner of her eye with the forked tongue on the shawl. 'You distress me when you talk like that. But I am practical. I know you haven't got the strength now to participate. But to say that I forget...no, that is cruel, my dear husband.'

'And yet you sleep in a bunk bed beside Mademoiselle?' One side of his mouth went up. He had made for himself sleeping quarters in one of the outhouses, or perhaps she had arranged it. There was a single iron bedstead and an empty barrel for his table with a candle on it. The electricity didn't extend as far as the outhouses. He had hung his tools on the wall in neat rows.

C'est la vie, mon cher. Her head was up now. 'Do not unbare your soul in front of this young girl. And you like Simone. You said so. Why not give her a bit of praise?'

'Do we all have to have certificates of merit to frame and hang on the walls?' His eyes were bleak. 'But certainly, I should be pleased to do that.' He spoke to François, his head shaking like an apple on its branch in a gale. 'She is a hard-working girl, quick, but more important, kind. And she sees under the surface of things.'

'Bon, Papa!' François laughed, his eyes meeting Simone's again. 'Did you know

21

my father was a great man for the ladies?' And when she laughed too, 'You like it here?'

'Yes, very much, thank you. Your parents have been good to me.'

'She is one of us now, *effectivement*,' Madame said. 'Now we must eat quickly and clear the table. I see some of the children peeping in. Their parents tell them to do that because they haven't the courage themselves.'

They finished their meal with despatch, then Simone piled up their plates and ran to open the half-glassed doors with the net curtains stretched tightly across them. The guests were sitting in the evening sunlight drinking their aperitifs. As usual, the two English couples were at separate tables. The English always ignored their compatriots until the day before their departure when they acted as if they had just discovered each other. She heard one of the Englishmen say loudly in French, 'Of course the food in some of those little out-of-the-way places is *sensass* at a fraction of the price!' '*Sensass!*' his wife with the tired hair and the dirndl skirt echoed.

A loud banging noise from the dining-room behind was almost drowning their words. Madame was at the small table outside the kitchen door where she cut the bread. A huge, lethal-looking knife was attached by a hinge to a wooden board, and with it nightly she chopped rather than sliced the *tourtes*, the round loaves which she preferred to the more elegant *baguettes*. '*Bonsoir, tout le monde!*' she called. 'Please be seated.'

As she began to serve, Simone realized that Madame, given to flights of fancy in her cooking, was showing more than her usual abandon. Perhaps it had been the wine in the soup. More likely, it was due to her son's homecoming. She was halted imperiously by her on her way out of the kitchen with a tray laden with bowls of soup. '*Un moment!*' With a flourish of her wrists she broke a raw egg into each steaming bowl in a matter of seconds. Simone shivered with a mixture of apprehension and delight. It was going to be one of those nights.

The crudités which followed the soup were a mélange of raw and cooked vegetables, with for some reason, or for no reason, some chopped coriander on top of each serving. Perhaps François had brought a bunch of it from Toulouse.

For the entrée, the *accoutrements* with the usual stringy lamb were magnificent in their variety, from huge jars of pickled onions and pickled walnuts, to jugs of green parsley sauce. There were dishes of beans doused in vinegar, yellow moulds of lentil porridge, plates of wheatmeal dumplings and heaped platters of *pommes frites*. The guests looked delighted but slightly nonplussed. Simone heard the same Englishman say to a Frenchman at the next table, *'Sensass!'* *'Sensass!'* his wife echoed.

As an entr'acte, Madame sent Simone round with tiny anchovy *pisalladières,* the remains of a batch which she had made last night for serving with François' aperitif. The flavour of the anchovy must have fought an equal battle with the odour of pickled onion in the respective palates, judging by the attitude of some of the women guests who were leaning back in their chairs and fanning their faces with their serviettes.

During this diversion, Madame in a new frenzy had whipped up a cheese soufflé which unfortunately had died on entering the world, so much so that Simone felt obliged to murmur an apology-cum-explanation as she laid the flaccid mess before each guest. 'An experiment of Madame's. Cheese soufflé à l'Hotel Delouche. She noticed when she cleared the plates that the Englishman didn't say *'Sensass!'*

But she need not have feared. Hope was stirring in the kitchen. Madame, not one to be easily dispirited by a slight contretemps (and egg-shells cracking under her feet), had grilled a shoal of trout, laid them on a bed of snails, possibly also Toulousain, and commanded Simone with waving arm, '*À la table* while they are still hot!'

When she bore the desecrated and half-eaten fish away again after a discreet interval, she was struck by the glassy eyes of the guests which closely resembled those of the trout. The only happy one would be Mou-Mou who would be licking his chops in anticipation, but again, knowing Madame, she could well set Simone to pound the remains and make it into a *pâté* for tomorrow's *hors d'oeuvres*.

Madame Carrione, the old *pensionnaire,* tapped Simone on the arm and whispered, 'She's off again, that one. What has she thought up next for us?'

'*Ça dépend,*' Simone said diplomatically. She was afraid to think.

But the *tarte's aux fruits* were a triumph, enormous, a fitting crescendo with their circles of sliced apples, strawberries, peaches, oranges, all from tins. Monsieur Delouche was the tin-opener. Simone preferred not to look when he was engaged on that operation, nor to wonder why the juice was tinted pink.

And for those who did not care for the *tarte, les Îles flottantes.* Simone, bearing the plates for the last time—how could one tell—met François' eyes at the bar. He beckoned to her. 'Leave the coffee to me, Simone. I'll have a word with *Maman*.'

She thought she heard him say as he stood at the kitchen door, 'That'll do now, *Maman. Mes félicitations*. A meal to remember.' He had a kind heart.

It was after midnight when Simone finished the washing-up, assisted by François. His parents had retired to their separate beds, and the 'black widows' as he called them, unattached village women who formed a kind of Greek chorus around Madame to help with the washing-up (but only when the spirit moved them), had earlier taken one look at the chaos in the kitchen and fled back to their homes and their knitting. When Claire Delouche was on her high horse, it was better to keep out of the way.

'That's it,' François said, hanging up the last soaking tea towel, 'knowing *Maman*, it will be plain fare tomorrow. You seem to cope with her very well, Simone.'

'It is not a question of coping.' She pushed back a heavy lock of hair. She took her fairness from her father who had come from Alsace before the war to work in the region, bought his own farm and married her mother, a local girl.

'You look tired.'

'Not at all.' She shook her head. 'But

I'm dying for a breath of fresh air.' Sometimes she went out for a few minutes to the wooden verandah before she joined Madame, knowing the stuffiness of their room.

'Let's have a stroll round the village,' he said. 'I missed it while I was away, the quietness, the little streets.' And when they walked down the steps and into the small square, 'You said it wasn't a question of coping. That was a profound remark for a young girl.'

'I'm eighteen. You aren't much older, are you?'

'I'm an old man. Twenty-two. You learn a lot when you're away from home.'

'*I'm* away from home.' She smiled at him. 'What I meant was that I know about your mother's dreams for the hotel and I understand them. She talks to me at night when we're in bed. I like to listen to her. I admire how she plans, how she looks forward all the time.'

'Yes, she lives on her dreams, *Maman*, always has.' They crossed the road and walked past the rounded bulk of the church which was far too large for the scattering of villagers, mostly women, who attended Mass. 'When Papa was the *menuisier*, she was going to have him build houses on the outskirts of the village. She thought the Gramout people who wanted a country

27

home would buy them.'

'Do you mean around the *chateau d'eau?*' She had seen the water tower rearing on its hill.

'Yes, she's always liked it around there. As a child I can remember her pushing me out to it in my little carriage. The grass seemed to be greener there and the bushes thicker. I remember the golden smell of the gorse. A secret place.'

'But the houses were never built?'

'No, it was a dream. She couldn't afford the price for the land, but she did buy one plot, for a house for themselves one day. But then Papa took ill, and she managed to buy this hotel with their savings, a run-down place if ever there was...now her dreams are centred on *it.*'

'And on you.'

'Yes, she always says I was a special gift!' He laughed. 'Some gift.' He stopped to point. 'There's my old school. She adored me so much that she used to come over at playtime just to see that I was all right. My teacher had to tell her not to do it, that the other children were teasing me!' They both laughed.

'Parents are like that. My mother is the same. When I was coming to the hotel to work she told our friends, in front of me, that she hoped I would meet someone and get married...' She was thankful it was dark. Blood rushed to her face. Would he think...?

'And have you?' His voice was teasing.

'No, of course not. I've been far too busy to think of it...' She changed the subject. 'That's where they play *pétanque.*' She stopped beside the flat piece of ground beyond the church.

'Is it?' He was still teasing.

'Well, of course you know. Sometimes I watch them for a minute or two when I go to fetch the evening *tourtes* from Monsieur Grinaud.'

'From Christian? Do you carry those great loaves twice each day?' He sounded astonished.

'Yes. Madame Claire says she will get a *Deux Chevaux* quite soon. She was waiting for you to finish your Course first.'

'And so we shall. We need an hotel car, and for shopping in Gramout. And I'll take over the bread collecting now.'

'There's no need, truly. I'm used to getting up early.'

'Then why not come along with me tomorrow morning and try out the Peugeot? Do you drive?'

'Oh, yes. Marcel, my brother, taught me as soon as I was seventeen. I can drive the tractor. I like it.' She felt proud.

They had reached the corner of the steep road which ran downhill from the main street and then rose quickly up to the old castle, the summer home, she believed, of some rich Parisians.

'Strange, the two *chateaux,*' François said softly, 'the old one there and the new one, a different kind, the *chateau d'eau.* As a child I thought of the old one as Papa's because he talked about the Marquis who used to live there, and the new one as *Maman's,* because she loved it and took me there often.'

'I think I like that one.' They could see it against the night sky, luminously grey, a hidden light from the moon behind the clouds edging its tessellated towers with silver.

'I often thought of that view when I was in Toulouse,' François said. 'I came every morning to the Tabac to buy Papa's pipe tobacco. Magical. Papa used to tell me stories of the Marquis who lived there long ago, how he rode through the village before the war, "a triumphal progress", he called it, with everyone bowing and scraping.'

'Is he still alive?' He burst into laughter.

'He was talking about the Hundred Years' War!'

'Oh!' She laughed with him, thinking that in the heartiness of his laughter he resembled his mother, so different from the quietness of Monsieur Delouche although his shaking head did not blind one to his shrewdness.

'If you've finished laughing,' she said tartly, 'we'd better get back. It's only a few hours until Monsieur Grinaud opens his door.'

'You don't like me laughing?' he said, wiping his eyes. 'All right, we'd better get back.'

'Laugh your head off for all I care.'

The village street was deserted, strange, like a village in a dream. The café tables where the youths pretended they were men were surrounded by their tilted chairs, the shutters in Madame Créon's shop were up, hiding her display of 'Fashions from Paris', just twenty years out of date. Madame bought her espadrilles there to ease her swollen feet, and Simone found faded postcards to send occasionally to her mother. They passed Monsieur Grinaud's *Patisserie* with its giant pink plastic cone outside and its revolving stand in the window for his daily selection of cakes.

'Five o'clock tomorrow morning, then?' François said.

'This morning.' She laughed.

'This morning. You're too smart for me.'

When she tiptoed into the little bedroom, Madame's snores hid the small noises she made as she undressed. Mou-Mou raised his head from the foot of Madame's bed then let it fall again, satisfied. Do you think you would like me for a daughter-in-law, Madame Claire? She must be tired to have such a thought pass through her mind.

Chapter Two

She sat, her hands round the bowl of hot coffee, watching him as he hacked off pieces of sausage and put them in his mouth. From time to time he dunked the bread in his coffee as Marcel did, a manly habit, she thought tenderly. Not for them the daintier ways.

Earlier they had had an enthusiastic welcome from Christian Grinaud who had given François a floury hand-clasp and a whack on the shoulder. 'Back again to set the ladies' hearts on fire, eh, François? A city slicker now, isn't that the way of it? How will you support the quietness of the village after Toulouse?'

'Well, you know my mother. Plans go into operation as from today. It's all systems go.'

'Ah, yes, Gramout will become our suburb! But I'll give your mother credit for working hard. And making others work hard. This young mademoiselle will bear me out on that. Do you know she has been here for bread every morning and evening since she arrived?'

'Yes, but we'll soon change that. I'm going to look into getting a hotel car. We'll put you on the map too, Christian, along with the village.'

'*Bon succès*. Have you heard? Fabrice Hegel has an English job, a Spitfire. He ran it into a ditch the first night he went out in it...' It was the same when any of Marcel's friends had come to the farm. Their conversation was carried on as if she didn't exist. Perhaps Madame Claire had felt the same thing as a *menuisier's* wife when she decided to become a person in her own right, the *patronne* of a hotel.

As if she had conjured her up, Madame appeared at the table, looking down her nose, the calm after the storm.

'So! A *tête-à-tête* breakfast, is it? No time to sit about talking, you two. You have the tables to set, Simone, and I've made out a list of shopping for you, François. It's been taking up too much of her time and I need her here.'

'I'm going to see to another car when I'm in Gramout, *Maman*. We need it. It's a stiff climb up to the fish market on Saturday mornings, and there will be a hundred and one things needed once the *réparations* start. Fortunately Simone can drive.'

'You've found out more than *I* have in the short time you've been home.' She nodded briefly. 'Go ahead, then. We need a hotel car, and we agreed on it when your fees stopped. I should have liked something better than a *Deux Chevaux,* but we must walk before we can run. The *réparations* come first. And you'd better call on Monsieur Cavel when you are in Gramout and ask him to get a move on.'

'Trust you not to waste any time, *Maman.'* His teasing was affectionate, and Simone saw her melt, her pale cheeks crease in a smile.

'No time like the present. Have you finished, girl? This is going to be a busy day. People book in at the weekends. I tell you, François, word is already getting around that Hotel Delouche is the place to be.'

'Especially after last night,' he said, grinning at her and she burst into a roar of laughter.

'*Quel toupet!'* He drew back as she pretended to smack his cheek. 'On you go, Simone! That one gets off with murder.'

All that month, in spite of the chaos resulting from the influx of joiners and builders and electricians and every type of workman known to man—Monsieur Cavel, the architect, had got a move on—Simone found that she and François seemed to spend quite a lot of time together.

There was always a reason. They had to call at the haberdashers to buy rolls of plastic—François, like his mother, was a devotee of plastic, and Simone was the only one who had a note of the measurements for tables and shelves. They had to call at the *cave* at Gramout to buy wine, and Simone was the only one who knew how many glasses they needed and which kind. There were constant visits to the wholesale grocers for bags of potatoes because of Madame's liking for making *pommes frites*. She had no trouble with the second-hand *Deux Chevaux* François had bought, but she pretended a feminine nervousness because he seemed to expect it and she was secretly pleased to have his company.

Indeed since his arrival she was blissfully happy. He was easygoing and affectionate but with his mother's shrewdness for a bargain. She learned how to divert his cost-cutting when it meant a sacrifice of quality. When she showed him the sprigged cotton tablecloths in the new delivery of household linen in the big store in Gramout, he agreed that it made plastic look, well, not *de bon ton*. His eyes had been opened in Toulouse. He was a willing disciple.

The June weather was glorious. The hedgerows were wreathed in dog roses climbing amongst the old thorn, the pink campion underneath echoed their colour, loosestrife, vetch and mallow rioted in between. But above all, she thought of it as an *églantine* summer. The fragility of the pale rose cups seemed in a way to epitomize her own state, fragile with love, open to receive...she saw Madame look questioningly at her once or twice in their bedroom which grew steadily stuffier as the weather became hotter and June turned to July.

'You like my son?' she said to her one evening as she examined one bare foot, swollen at the ankle, purple-lined across the instep with the pressure of her espadrilles. She massaged them each night saying, 'Oh, my poor feet! It's the weight of course. If I could be as slim as you...'

'Yes, he's charming.' She tried to sound non-committal. Then greatly daring, because those warm evenings were the time for confidences, when sometimes they were both too exhausted to sleep immediately, 'You're two of a kind, you know. Maybe that's why I like him.'

'Well, well!' Madame looked up, her

swollen purple toes like miniature sausages peeping out from between her hands. 'You're different from the shy little girl who came here in March! He's a good catch, my François. Not just anyone will do for *him*. When this hotel is one of the show places of the region the girls will flock around—not that they don't do that already.' Certainly there were plenty of giggling girls in the village who came to the bar in the evening, but his impartial friendliness was his safeguard, and hers, she hoped.

'No, not just anyone will do,' she agreed.

'But he's sensible. He wouldn't take a girl who didn't share his dreams...' She looked up slyly. 'Would you pass me that ointment the doctor left? He says it will reduce the swelling.'

'You should take a little more rest, Madame. Perhaps lie down in the afternoon. François and I can manage. I've learned some of your dishes and I could prepare the evening meal. Indeed, why not take a day off occasionally?'

'A day off occasionally, she says!' Her huge breasts heaved and swelled beneath the cotton nightgown. 'Can you see the Hotel Delouche without *la Patronne?* No, I'm not ready to step down yet. Perhaps when all the *réparations* are over, and when François is settled with a good wife...get

37

into bed for goodness sake, Simone, and don't lie awake when you're in it either. Don't think I can't hear you sighing. One would think you were in love!'

'Love!' she said, flipping back the bedclothes and jumping into her bed. 'What's that?' It wasn't time yet to wear her heart on her sleeve.

There was an afternoon when the hotel was quiet and the village was in a deep midsummer dream. Most of the guests had gone for a day's shopping to Brive, Monsieur was nodding in his chair in the yard, and the birdlike chatter of the school children going home was over. Madame had gone to visit Sophie Rivaud, one of the black widows who had promised to crochet bands for holding back the new lace curtains. François' idea (and Simone's) of curtains which slid along their rails at the touch of a cord had been dismissed as idiocy.

'First things first, François,' she had said. 'My kitchen, your bar and salon, after that we'll see. I know you want to make us like that upstart place Le Roy, but we must keep some of our own character, that of a country hotel. We have always had crochet bands for the curtains. I might get Sophie to lace pink ribbon through them...' Simone looked fixedly at

François, trying out a small transference of will.

'No pink ribbons, *Maman,*' he had said decidedly. She hid a smile.

The sun was hot on Simone's bare arm which lay along the side of the open Peugeot. She was wearing a short white dress and open-toed high-heeled sandals which she had bought in the Gramout market from an African of huge stature with a shining black face surrounded by even blacker curls. His smile had been dazzling, so dazzling was it that he had sold Simone the shoes a size smaller, saying they were just right and she had believed him.

The sweetness of the air combined with the smell of the *églantine* in the hedgerows was making her want to weep. She had had that feeling several times since François came home, as if her happiness was spilling over in tears. What Madame Claire had heard when they were in bed was her quick indrawing of breath when they threatened to overflow.

'I think of this somehow as an *églantine* summer,' she said. 'It is so beautiful. And so strange. Other summers, I haven't noticed them at all.'

'I like that,' he said, *'L 'Été des Églantines.* Mmmh!' He breathed deeply. 'I can smell their perfume. The countryside is beautiful today.' He waved his hand. 'Down there, deep in the valley, is the ruined mill. Have you ever been there?'

'No.'

'It's a secret place. Would you like to see it?'

'I don't mind.' She was in an *églantine* dream. The soft wind was on her face. 'If it doesn't take too long.'

'It's only a mile or two. The first turning. Look,' he pointed, 'there's the *chateau d'eau*. Where *Maman* used to take me.'

'Yes, you told me.' She came out of her dream to look. The tower, made of the local golden stone, crowned a grassy hill broken by thickets of yellow gorse and privet which would make secret rooms, she thought, little enclosures where someone might lie hidden. The sky behind the tower was delft blue, cloudless. 'Your mother would have difficulty in pushing your carriage up that slope.'

'I don't expect she did. She would sit and rest at the foot. It's quite a walk from the hotel.' He had slowed down and now he increased his speed. 'It's a strange place. I never see anyone there. Perhaps they think it's forbidden, property of the Water Board,' he was slowing down again. 'Ah, here's the turning for the mill,

40

no, that's to the Marmot farm and our land, it's the next one.' He drove about a kilometre. 'Here we are. Hold tight.' He swung into a narrow rutted road.

'Why?'

'It's bumpy as hell. Every summer when I come down it, it gets worse. I think the road-menders have forgotten about it.'

'Every summer...' It was as if a dart had pierced her heart. She went over the giggling village girls in her mind. Who had been the lucky one? Or had there been many? She had seen him laughing with Marie-Thérèse Brabant at the bar last night, she of the Marie-Antoinette hair-style and short dresses puffed out with petticoats whose lace trimming showed as she whirled. Her bracelets clattered up and down her arms, her ear-rings swung. She didn't like this road much. It was bumpy and dark and growing bumpier and darker by the minute. And it was silent, like being in a tomb.

'Some places give me a peculiar feeling,' she said.

'You don't like this one?'

'It's the atmosphere. It's difficult to explain.'

'You'll like it when you get down. It's like reaching...Eldorado.'

She stole a glance at him. His white shirt was open almost to the waist, perhaps a

Toulousain fashion. His neck and chest were deeply golden. Her eye followed the opening of the shirt. A man's body was a mystery to her. She had seen more of Madame Claire's.

'I wish we had brought a picnic,' he said.

'Is that what you usually do?' she asked, and he smiled a male smile.

The road grew deeper and darker, the *églantine* in the hedges became pinker in the gloom and when they emerged into an occasional patch of light it seemed to have become paler, as if making way for the brilliant blue of the tiny butterflies which swarmed in front of them.

And then, it seemed suddenly, they emerged into the light, the road beneath them was smooth and flat, and François drove the car slowly onto a grassy patch where he brought it to a halt. In front of them was the ruined mill, built of the same stone as the water tower, but older, pitted and bleached white in parts, while behind it was the weir over which the water fell in a solid block of silver. In spite of the noise of the water it seemed very silent, as if by maintaining its silence it would keep its secret.

'Do you like it?' he turned to her, his dark eyes glowing with pleasure.

'It's beautiful, but...'

'But what?'

'It's...brooding, as if it had been waiting for hundreds of years, patiently...'

'You're a funny little girl. Sometimes I wonder what goes on behind those brown eyes of yours.' He took her chin in his hand, came very close for a second. 'Not quite brown. There's a gleam of gold in them.' He took his hand away abruptly. 'Come on! Don't just sit there!' He vaulted over the door of the car, came round and opened hers, and they walked to the edge of the water. Here, in the mill pool, it was a deep, blue-green, except where it ruffled silver at the weir.

'You could bathe here.'

'It's been known.' Again the male smile. 'Let's have a rest.' He threw himself down on the grass, then sitting up, pulled her down beside him. 'That's better. Relax.'

She remained sitting, her arms stiff behind her for support. 'Look, there's a mysterious tunnel of trees...'

'Yes, it follows the river. Lovely, but I'm too tired to walk another step.'

'I'm tired too.' A delicious languor came over her and she lay down beside him.

'That mother of mine...' She knew by his sleepy voice that he was really tired, as she was. She pressed her shoulders into the soft coolness of the grass. The constant carrying of heavy plates from the kitchen to the tables made them ache. Perhaps she could suggest, with all the *réparations* going on, that they invest in a few trolleys. They could also be used for displaying the desserts. She was sure they used them at Le Roy.

'Still, she's fair,' she said. 'She shares the work.'

'I know, but she demands a lot. You have to have an illness like Papa to escape.'

'I wonder,' she said, 'what it is that... pushes her.' The words were out before she could stop them.

'Disappointment, kicking against fate, who knows, but it makes her a devil for work. And I'm fundamentally lazy. Did you know that? I would be quite happy for us to stay as a little village hotel with plastic tablecloths, gossiping behind the bar with the locals, not trying to please strangers all the time. But I've been conditioned by her. Can you understand?'

'Perhaps when you feel like that you're more like your father? I don't mean lazy, but...'

'He's not lazy. Resigned, perhaps.'

'You certainly don't look like him, but it's difficult to know what he was like before...' she thought of the nodding head, the eyes which were sometimes bleak.

'A good *menuisier*, steady, content. I

remember him making me a little wooden cart when I was a child which I pushed proudly all round the village.' He laughed. 'He has accepted his illness stoically, even when *Maman* gets impatient with him. *Maman* again! Why does it always get back to her? You never talk about *your* background, Simone.' Because you never ask me, she thought.

'In a way it's dominated by my mother too. It's more bitterness with her than disappointment. My father went through the war without a scratch and then got caught in a threshing machine. He was killed instantly. And not even his own threshing machine. He was helping a neighbour at *la colte.*'

'No wonder she's bitter.' He put out his hand and clasped hers.

'Marcel was working beyond his strength from fourteen which has made him taciturn, and I don't think my mother would have allowed me to leave home except that he is being married and she thought there would be too many women about when he brought his wife to the farm.'

'So you have gone from one kind of work to another?'

'Is there anything else?'

He rose on one elbow to look at her. 'You're eighteen, for God's sake! There's fun and lightness! I saw it in Toulouse. It was not all work there I can tell you. Have fun when you can. You'll be a long time dead.'

'This is fun,' she said, looking up at him.

He bent and kissed her, a butterfly kiss on the mouth leaving an impression of warm lips, a warm, masculine smell. 'You're so young and innocent.'

'I've lived on a farm,' she said, and then realizing the implication of what she had said, she rolled away from him and hurriedly got up. 'We'd better get back. Your mother will be back and she asked me to put the soup on. There's a chicken to pluck as well.'

'And Monsieur Cavel is calling at five to discuss the hairdressing salon.' He sprang to his feet too.

'It's all going to be very grand.' She laughed. 'You will have to grow a moustache and wax the ends!'

He took her hands, laughing with her, and spun her round so fast that one of the heels of her sandals came off.

'I knew these were rubbish,' she said, bending down and taking off the offending shoe. 'Just wait till I see that African next Saturday.'

'Lean on me.' He put his arm round her and helped her to hobble to the car.

When they were seated, he turned to her, his eyes bright with affection. 'That was fun. Did you know you are very sweet? And you blush. No, don't deny it! You're my...*églantine* girl.' He leant towards her and kissed her, but this time his mouth stayed longer on hers. She trembled, and the tears were in her throat again. Why should she want to cry when she was so happy?

'We're supposed to be in a hurry,' she said, hoping she wasn't blushing again.

'Yes, so we are.' He let in the clutch.

Chapter Three

With the coming of July, the hotel began to fill up. Towards the end of the month the French with their children arrived, and a sprinkling of English, although Madame told Simone that they preferred August. The Dutch came in couples, seldom with children, and usually disappeared during the day, intent on house-hunting. The dining-room, however, was full at mealtimes, and Madame had plans to cover in the verandah to accommodate more tables.

Her kitchen was finished, enlarged and

fitted with a shining cooker, although secretly she preferred her old stove which she refused to have removed, a massive affair of black iron with two ovens. The hairdressing salon had been done before the bar, which could be left, if necessary, until the season was over.

François had invested in a white jacket with stand-up collar for his duties at the bar, but had decided, he said, not to grow a moustache with waxed ends. They had laughed about that. He looked in Simone's eyes, more handsome than ever, especially when the gold flash of hair fell forward on his brow.

The village girls were constantly in and out making appointments, emerging from the salon with bouffant hairstyles which matched their skirts. He offered to do Simone's hair, but she preferred its thick straightness. When she washed it, often last thing at night, it felt like a piece of heavy silk as she brushed it in bed.

'You have pretty hair,' Madame said to her one night as she watched her. 'You are wise not to have it teased up like those silly girls. Have you seen Marie-Thérèse Brabant's? It is like the wire brush I use to clean my stove. A mass of broken ends, ruined! Just as those high heels ruin the feet. Where is the pair you bought from that thieving African rascal at the market?'

'A heel came off.'

'There, what did I tell you? Wear espadrilles like me, let the feet breathe.'

'Yes, Madame Claire.' She spoke dreamily, remembering that afternoon with François at the ruined mill. There had been little opportunity for excursions since then, but sometimes their eyes would meet across the dining-room as she hurried with the plates, and the tenderness in them made her hopeful. It was just a matter of him getting used to the idea of her.

They still made their morning expeditions to Christian Grinaud's, the most precious time of the day to her. François' attitude towards her had changed, she noticed. He laughed less, watched more, there was a new gentleness in his behaviour. In the evenings he came into the kitchen and helped with the washing-up, but usually there was a black widow or two about, which gave them little chance for conversation.

'You haven't been home for a fortnight, Simone.' Madame Claire broke into her thoughts. 'François mentioned it to me the other day. He'll drive you. He hasn't any appointments.'

'I hate to trouble him. I could take the *Deux Chevaux* if you don't mind.'

'He wouldn't have suggested it to me if it were any trouble. I think he would like to meet your mother and your brother.'

'If he just dropped me off I could make my own way back...' Because she was so delighted, she protested.

'You're a silly girl. You should be more like Marie-Thérèse. She wouldn't object. She's been trying to get him to come to their house ever since they were at school together.'

'Do you mean I should be flattered?'

Madame laughed, throwing back her head against the pillow. 'Just when I have decided you are a naïve little thing, you come away with a remark like that. You'll do, my girl, you'll do!'

'What do you mean, "I'll do"?' She bent her head and spoke through the heavy veil of her hair as she brushed it. Of course he was his mother's son, but she wasn't a puppet, was she? She wasn't going to allow Madame Claire to pull the strings. She had her pride.

She said to François when they went for bread in the morning, 'I believe your mother has given you permission to drive me to the farm this afternoon.'

He looked at her, smiling, amused at her sarcasm. 'You would rather go alone?'

'No, it was just...'

'I cancelled an appointment to be free to take you. I know what you're thinking, but it wasn't my mother's idea. It was mine, to try and have a little more time with you. I'd like to see where you were brought up, meet your mother and your brother.' He took a step towards her. 'I'm beginning to feel...' the door of the dining-room burst open. A man in overalls stood there.

'*Salut,* François!' He held a sheaf of papers in his hand. 'A delivery from the brewery. Will you sign, please?'

'*D'accord,* Christophe.' He sighed. 'Come along. Never a moment's peace in this place. I should have been a *menuisier,* like Papa.'

'Ah, you'll never be half the man he is.' They went out together, laughing.

Just before lunch there was an unexpected arrival of guests, an English couple, Monsieur and Madame Sinclair, and their daughter, from Haywards Heath, Sussex. Fortunately they had two rooms vacant, the most expensive ones in the hotel, and Madame Claire was highly delighted. She left the details to Simone after greeting them, since she was busy preparing lunch.

Simone was aware of the daughter as one was aware of the sun even when half-turned from it—a radiance. And there was fear in her soul. 'Do you wish to sign too?' She proffered the pen after her father had scrawled his signature.

'There's no need,' the girl said. 'Is there,

Daddy?' She spoke in French. And, to Simone, 'I'm Barbie Sinclair, free, white, and *not* twenty-one.' She laughed as her father barked in appreciation. Her mother simply looked tired.

'Mademoiselle Barbie Sinclair,' Simone repeated, feeling dazed by the girl's vivacity.

'It's Barbara actually, but I'm always called Barbie.' Her excellent French surprised Simone. The English were the worst, generally, shouting their two or three French words at the top of their voices as if that made it clear. The Dutch spoke French like natives. Well, for them there was no alternative, living in such a little country. 'Maybe Barbie suits me better.' She was as lush as the early summer hedgerows. One could become entangled in her charm as the brambles entangled the *églantines*. Any *man* could. 'God, my hair's in a mess!' She twirled one of its tendrils round her finger. 'No hope of having it done in this dump, I suppose? Sorry!' She put her hand to her mouth. 'You work here. Daddy's latest thing is pre-history so Mummy and I have to trail along. Just look at him. He's examining your pictures to see if there are any caves around.'

Simone looked. Monsieur Sinclair was trailing round the room with his wife at his heels, peering at the garish pictures of the surrounding countryside which François had recently bought, the towering cliffs of Rocamadour, the Pont Valentré at Cahors, the Chateau de la Treyne above the Dordogne. The Englishman looked remarkably like a bull terrier. His lips stuck out beneath a short, bristly moustache. And he barked like a dog. They all seemed to look like animals, those Englishman. Monsieur Robinson, who came every year, looked down his nose like a camel and teetered in and out on long spindly legs. His lips quivered like one when he brayed for a drink.

Except this girl. She was a beauty, a threatening, luscious beauty.

'Our cases.' Monsieur Sinclair was with them again. 'Anyone to carry them up?' He barked at the thin, drooping woman beside him, 'Out-of-the-way place this, dear.' How could such a pair produce such a beauty? 'Don't expect much and you won't be disappointed. It's near the Cro-Magnon set-up. That's the main thing.'

François, who must have been listening, and watching, was coming from behind the bar, smiling, charming, his eyes bright with interest. *Permettez-moi.* And to Simone, 'Which numbers, Mademoiselle?' So formal. No *églantine* summer here.

'Five and six.' They were interconnected

53

but with separate doors to the corridor, what Madame Claire called grandly, 'The honeymoon suite'. 'Please follow me,' she said.

She went ahead with the English couple, François following with the girl. She strained her ears to hear what they were saying, heard the strange English words, 'One-armed bandits,' and François' reply, 'Oh, you mean *le flipper?* There are some in the café in the village, but not in my hotel.' She had never heard him being so grand before.

While Simone turned down the bed in the smaller of the two rooms, the girl was seated in front of the mirror. François had deposited her bag, bowing and smiling. 'Something's got to be done with this mop, Barbie.' Simone never addressed herself in mirrors. Mademoiselle Sinclair took out her hairslides and a black river tumbled round her face. 'We've been travelling for absolutely days!' This time she was speaking to Simone. 'We went to Altimira to see some more blasted caves. Spain, you know. Well, maybe you don't. Daddy has gone mad about the beastly things. Did you say there was a place near here for my hair?'

'Monsieur François has a salon in the hotel.'

'Who's he?'

'He carried up your cases. He's the son of the owners.'

'Oh, he's nice! Though God knows what they know about hair here. But needs must. I'll make an appointment.'

'I could do it for you, Mademoiselle.'

'No, thank you. I'm perfectly capable of doing it myself.'

Simone went downstairs, deeply disturbed. Someone like Marie-Thérèse had never given her any cause for jealousy. She was weightless. But this girl...it was when one felt the attraction oneself that one became anxious. She looked at François behind the bar as she crossed to the kitchen. He was standing, gazing at nothing, a drink in his hand. Before lunch. That was ominous...

'What do you think of that one?' Sophie Rivaud said to her in the kitchen later. She was helping Simone with the washing-up.

'What one?' She rinsed a glass twice, seeing how red her hands were becoming. Mademoiselle Barbie had white hands, dimpled over the knuckles. And yet she was slim. Although her bosoms were a good size. Perhaps that meant she would turn to fat in later life, like Madame Claire.

'The English one. She'll bring the young lads sniffing around in no time, I bet. A strong scent that is, and I don't mean

Chanel. Shall I tell you what she...?'
François was at the door.

'Can I see you for a moment, Simone, please?'

She went outside with him. 'I'll be ready in half an hour. I persuaded Madame to lie down. Her feet were terribly swollen. It's the heat.'

'Yes...er, Simone...' he looked embarrassed. 'Would you mind going home yourself this afternoon? It's impossible...'

'No, of course not. What is it?'

'It's...well, it's this English girl. She says she must have her hair done this afternoon...'

'Why "must"?' She tried to keep her voice calm. 'It's early closing today.'

'I know but that's how she put it. She's a guest after all. They've taken the honeymoon suite, as you know.' Honeymoon suite, she thought bitterly, venting her anger on something else, pink bedspreads and pink *poupées* with spread skirts on the beds. And that bull terrier of a man with his thin, drooping, spaniel-wife were scarcely of honeymoon calibre! But Mademoiselle Barbie was, with her luscious body and her lustrous tumbling hair which *must* be done...'I can't refuse,' he was saying, 'she might tell the others that I had been disobliging and I'm building up my clientèle. I'll phone Claude to come in.

Look, take the *Deux Chevaux.*' He knew he was in the wrong.

'No, thank you.' She still kept calm. 'I'll get the two-thirty bus.' She looked at him, keeping her chin high in case the tears would slide out of her eyes. He might see their glitter but he wouldn't realize how her heart was aching. She could tell by the embarrassed tone in his voice, the excitement in his quick movements, his moist eyes, and yet a certain stubbornness in his demeanour, that he was bewitched.

Unexpectedly she found Marcel, Madeleine and her mother sitting round the kitchen table when she arrived at the farm. Usually they would be out in the fields tending the tobacco plants. Her mother generally took charge of the watering which was essential if they were to produce juicy plump leaves, while Marcel went up and down the rows hoeing and weeding.

'Oh, it's you, Simone.' Her mother returned her embrace, scarcely altering her expression. Marcel's straight mouth hardly moved, Madeleine was warmer in her welcome because that was her nature, but she looked strangely defiant. She was a big, handsome girl, good-natured, but given to sitting around doing nothing while others busied themselves about her. 'Don't you ever sit down, Simone?' she would say.

'How is everybody?' Simone said, joining them at the table. 'It's not often I find you having a rest at this time of the day.'

'You tell her, Marcel,' her mother said.

'Madeleine and I are getting married next month.'

'Because she's four months pregnant, that's why. Don't leave that out.' She spat out the words.

'Is it true, Madeleine?' Simone asked. She was surprised, but it wasn't unheard of in farming circles.

'Yes.'

The girl tittered nervously, making Simone say warmly, 'Well, it isn't the end of the world. You'll get married and live happily ever after. The wedding was planned for Christmas anyhow.'

'I wasn't counting on looking after her and a baby right away,' her mother said. 'I was hoping it would be the other way round for a year or two. Maybe you'll have to give up your work, Simone, and come back to the farm. This is a busy time.'

Marcel stirred. 'No, that's not fair, *Maman*. We'll manage. Madeleine is strong and healthy. Having a baby's nothing.'

'Listen to him!' Madeleine said, looking at Simone. 'They're all the same. Get what they want then blame you.'

'He's not blaming you, Madeleine.' She was trying to imagine her taciturn brother as an importunate lover. She didn't blame him either. In such a thankless life as his, he needed some happiness. Being away from home had given her courage. 'You'll have to make the best of it, *Maman,*' she said. 'I can't possibly let Madame Claire down in the middle of the season. We'll see later.'

'Everybody comes before me.' Her voice rose in self-pity. 'I don't count. I might as well go out and die under a hedge.'

'Oh, God!' Marcel scraped back his chair and got up. 'Simone's right. You'll have to make the best of it. Meantime I've got to get on with my work. Don't cry, Madeleine.' He appealed to his sister. 'Make her a cup of tea.'

She got up. 'Good idea.' She spoke comfortingly to her mother who was black-browed with indignation. 'You'll get over it, *Maman.* It's a shock at first, but you'll see...'

She went into the scullery, filled the kettle and stood beside it while she waited for it to boil. I wouldn't have dared to speak like that six months ago, she thought. I'm growing up. She could hear her mother's complaining voice, Madeleine's snuffles and snorts. I wouldn't like to be in Madeleine's shoes. She would be made to regret that she had ever opened her legs to Marcel, and I shouldn't have thoughts

59

like that either. Perhaps Madame Claire's kindly brusqueness was having a salutory effect on her. And there was one thing about Madeleine's predicament, if it could be called that. It put her own worry about the arrival of Mademoiselle Sinclair into perspective.

She infused the tea, put some cups and saucers on a tray. The English girl would go away, and she and François would be together again with their friendship growing in tenderness each day. It had been a mistake to show her jealousy by refusing the *Deux Chevaux*. It would have been much better to have accepted graciously. She opened a box of *patisseries* she had bought when she changed buses at Gramout. Mother's favourite was a *millefeuille*. Perhaps one would sweeten her, she thought, laying the cakes on a plate and licking from her fingers the rich yellow cream which had escaped from the flaky pastry.

'Have a cup of tea,' she said when she went back to the kitchen, 'and a *millefeuille*. You have to keep up your strength, Madeleine.' She saw the reluctant smile on her mother's face and she put an arm round her. 'You too, *Maman*. Now, cheer up and count yourself lucky you're going to have a nice daughter-in-law like Madeleine.'

'Hmm.' She laughed disparagingly through her nose but accepted a *millefeuille*.

On the way back she told herself she must be resolute. The last thing she wanted to do was to go back to the farm and be a whipping block for her mother. Quarrels would abound, and Marcel might well become bitter like Mother and find his relaxation in the local bar with the other young farmers while Madeleine sat by the fire and wept. You're selfish, she told herself. You want to stay beside François.

On the bus from Gramout to the hotel she met one of the two Marmot brothers, Maurice, who occupied the farm near the *chateau d'eau*. He supplied the hotel with eggs, and when Simone went to collect them he invariably had ready a small collation of boudoir biscuits and a glass of golden Monbazillac. The civilized gesture was at variance with the cluttered kitchen where hens pecked on the floor or a bolder one jumped onto the table itself. So far she hadn't met the other brother who was always 'working in the fields'. Madame Claire had said of Monsieur René, *'Il est un peu simple.'*

'How are you, Mademoiselle Bouvier?' Monsieur Maurice asked. He was thin with sparse grey hair and a harrassed expression.

'Very well, thank you. I've been to see my mother. My brother's getting married.'

'*Bon*. That will be to one of the Bonnard girls?'

'Yes, Madeleine.'

'I had heard it was to be a Christmas wedding.'

'Well, no, they've pushed it on a bit.'

'*Ah, bon.*' He hugged his shopping bags. 'How is François? I hear he's home.' Monsieur Maurice obviously went out to collect the local gossip.

'Yes. A few weeks ago. They are busy with the *réparations*. How is your brother, Monsieur Marmot?' The man's face changed. He shook his head in an irritated fashion. 'I haven't met him yet when I've called,' she added.

'He's fencing our property. Obsessed by it! Every day it's hammer, hammer, hammer, in with the posts, stretch the wire, on and on it goes. You know we have ten acres. Yes, Mademoiselle, that is why you haven't seen him. He hardly takes time to eat.'

'Why does he do it?' She smiled. The man's irritation subsided and his head went on one side as he looked at her.

'Ah, well, you'll hardly remember the war. You would scarcely be born. It's because of the Germans. He wants to keep out the Huns.'

She laughed sympathetically. 'But there are none of them around now!'

'*You* know that. *I* know that. But René...' He shook his head. 'You see, he was in the Resistance. He is tortured now because he was tortured then. He can't forget.'

'That's sad. Very sad.' She looked out of the window, seeing the quiet fields, the copses, the small valleys. There wouldn't be enough cover there for the *Maquis*. But up in the high *causse*, where there were underground rivers and *avens* hidden by thickly-growing gorse one could climb down to the *grottes*, if one were agile. The *Maquis* had used them as hiding places, and she had heard there were networks of underground routes, like rabbit burrows... She heard Monsieur Maurice's voice.

'I don't suppose you would think of leaving the Hotel Delouche now, Mademoiselle?' She turned, looking at him questioningly. 'With young Monsieur Delouche home...' he paused, looking embarrassed. 'A little joke. No, I was thinking of all the *réparations*, and so on. My nephew who is a waiter at Le Roy tells me they are looking for more staff. You could get in there with your experience now. And it would be nearer home for you.'

She knew Luc Marmot. He was an old friend of Marcel's. 'Does Luc like it there?'

'Very much. He will become *maître d'hôtel* before long but he talks of going to Paris.'

'I'm not thinking of changing at present,' she said. It was a thought, nevertheless, to put away in case she should ever want to leave. But why should she? She had grown fond of Madame Claire, and Mademoiselle Sinclair would leave soon and François would look at her with tenderness again...

They would marry and run a shipshape little hotel together, and they would build his mother a house on that piece of land near the *chateau d'eau* where she could put her feet up and entertain the black widows...she dreamt, forgetting the presence of Monsieur Maurice.

Chapter Four

It had been a rosy pipe dream, and Mademoiselle Barbie's arrival, the watershed on which it foundered. She didn't go away and the whole village seemed to have eyes only for a drama which appeared to have been put on for their delectation, a drama with three characters, François, the English girl and Simone.

'I didn't see you at the Catus Fête last night,' Christian Grinaud said to her on Sunday morning when she went to fetch the *tourtes*. 'I took Marie-Thérèse.'

'How nice.' She didn't think it was. Christian was far too good for Marie-Thérèse Brabant. 'I was too busy.' François had slipped away about ten o'clock and she had noticed earlier that Monsieur and Madame Sinclair had dined alone, he with a book propped up in front of him, she eating in her usual tired fashion and from time to time glancing around the room with a long-suffering look. Of course, François and Mademoiselle Barbie might not have been at the fête together, but he hadn't appeared at breakfast time, and going upstairs with a tray to Madame Carrione, she had seen scraps of confetti on the stairs and outside François' room. Confetti and fêtes were analogous.

François had come into the kitchen around eleven o'clock looking pale and heavy-eyed. 'Where is everybody?' he said with an obvious effort at brightness. Even his forelock had lost its gleam.

'Your mother is in the garden getting vegetables for the soup.' Sophie Rivaud from the sink shook her finger at him. 'You are a bad boy. That is *your* job. And Simone had to fetch the bread this morning.'

65

'It didn't matter.' She frowned at Sophie.

'Oh, Simone, I'm sorry!' He looked crestfallen. 'I slept in. Is there any coffee left?'

'Help yourself. I'm afraid it's stewed.' She indicated the pot on the stove. He poured himself a bowlful and broke off a piece of bread from one of the fresh loaves.

'Where is everyone?' he said. 'The place is deserted.'

'All the guests have gone walking or shopping in Gramout except the Sinclairs. They set off for Les Eyzies after breakfast.'

'The three of them?' His face was hidden by the bowl.

'No. Mademoiselle Barbie is still in bed. I think she was at the Catus Fête last night.' She shouldn't have said that.

'Ah!' He drained the bowl and put it down. 'That was good. Must get on now.' He got up and went quickly out of the room.

When he was out of earshot Sophie Rivaud said, her angular chin turned towards Simone, her eyes narrowed, 'Don't wear your heart on your sleeve, *mon petit chou*. Men aren't worth it.'

'I don't know what you're talking about, Madame.' She rubbed vigorously at each plate as she piled them ready to carry into the dining-room.

'And you can cut out the "Madame", if you please.' The woman tossed her head. 'You may think I'm just an interfering old widow but that's where you're wrong.'

'What do you mean?'

'I had a man during the war, that's true enough, but he went off with someone else. I've never been married. So much for promises. And men.'

'I'm sorry, Madame...I mean...'

'Oh, you can stick to the title. Everyone else does. And don't be sorry. Just take a lesson from me. And you'd better get on with setting the tables. She'll be back with her vegetables any minute, spitting fire.'

July became August, guests came and went but the Sinclairs stayed on. Simone began to imagine that mocking eyes were following her in the hotel and the village as she went about her duties. Once when she was in the Tabac buying a paper for Monsieur Delouche she met Marie-Thérèse Brabant and a friend. 'Alone, Simone?' the girl asked, her eyes mischievous. She heard their laughter behind her as she went out. She told herself that it was the brilliant sunshine which made her eyes sting.

Each day Monsieur Sinclair with his wife in tow set off for Pêch Merle or Cabrerets or some other cave, but their daughter never went with them. She hung

67

about the hotel talking to François at the bar, or wandered about the village in her short, stiffened dresses which showed her brown legs, the bodice cut low, her glossy hair piled high, her lips the colour of her hair slides.

She became friendly with everyone, even the men who worked on the roads and came for lunch to the hotel. Sometimes there were roars of laughter from their table when she stopped to joke with them. Her command of the *argot* made their eyes roll in appreciation. She was on good terms with everyone in the village, and Simone had actually seen her chatting to Monsieur Sachet who ran the Post Office and who was known for his surly disposition. She had to admit the girl's charm if she could make *him* smile.

She was just as friendly with Simone, standing at the kitchen door while she chatted, never offering to lend a hand, which was natural as a guest, but holding up the work nevertheless. Mademoiselle Claire was brisk with her.

'Why don't you join the new tennis club at the lake, Mademoiselle? It would fill in your time.'

'No, thanks, I'm not a "who's for tennis?" type.' She pretended to hit a tennis ball with an imaginary racquet. She could be amusing.

When Simone congratulated her on her idiomatic use of French, she said that when she was young her family had moved to Nîmes because her brother had a bad chest. 'It didn't do Peter any good because he died there, but I got something out of it at least.'

'And your father perhaps?'

'Yes, that's when he first became interested in pre-history. And now he's decided to write a book on it, God help us! Mummy's fed up. All she wants is to be back with her cronies in Haywards Heath going to those terrible coffee mornings where they exchange knitting patterns. God knows it's boring here, but that's even worse.'

'Don't you work?'

'Me!' She turned a tendril of hair round her finger. 'Not if I can help it. I trained as a secretary but I was in between jobs when the parents decided to go abroad. It was a chance of a free holiday so I jumped at it. I didn't realize how deadly boring it would be...most of the time.' She pulled her cheeks together and glanced across at the bar where François was serving the village youths.

'Couldn't you knit like your mother?' She wanted to hurt because of that look and what it might mean.

'Knit? Me!' She turned back to Simone.

'You must be out of your tiny mind! No, thank you. I'd rather chat with you. Or François.' Her smile was mischievous. 'He's really quite a poppet, isn't he?'

'What is a poppet, please?'

Un peu noceur, non? Well, never mind. "Sweet", "dishy", "sexy with it"...and ready for it too, if you ask me.' Her lips were shining, moist.

'And ready for it too if you ask me'. That was what made Simone sleepless at nights. Every evening, when the local youths gathered at the bar, Barbie would be there, and Simone would hear François' laughter ringing above theirs. When he had occasion to rush past her, perhaps to get some more glasses, he didn't see her, and there would be the remains of the laughter on his face. The look in his eyes made her think that suddenly the whole world had become exciting for him because of Mademoiselle Barbie. She noticed also that Marie-Thérèse and her friends no longer came in, as if they had been supplanted.

Madame Claire made no comment. She worked Simone harder than ever, and at times was short-tempered as if she had become disappointed in her. Jean-Paul went on with his endless tasks in the yard sunshine, occasionally raising his shaking head. Everything had changed since the English girl's arrival.

'*Eh bien,*' Monsieur Jean-Paul said one day to her. 'Mademoiselle Sinclair has stirred up this quiet pool, eh, Simone?' Nothing escaped him. 'But not to worry. The task nearest at hand...' His neck was like one of the plucked chickens which Madame threw whole into the stockpot for her soups. They would fill up under their skin with water and float on the surface, bloated, oozing globules of yellow fat.

She knew François was taking Mademoiselle Barbie out in his white Peugeot when he had an hour or two off in the afternoon. She would see the girl hovering about, sometimes sitting beside the steadily knitting mother, sometimes getting up impatiently to wander round the War Memorial a yard or two from the hotel, or to sit on one of the benches beside the old men. There would be a roar from the car which Simone recognized, and when she went out to the veranda to collect glasses from the tables, the girl would have disappeared.

She spoke to the sad-eyed Madame Sinclair sometimes, wishing to make some sort of contact. 'You like it here, Madame?'

'*Très bien, merci.*' She looked resigned. 'I get a lot of knitting done while my husband is busy.'

'What is it that you knit, please?'

'I am on a committee in England for

71

orphaned boys, and they need scarves and jerseys. I visit their Home sometimes and they tell me which colours they would like.'

'That is a good thing to do.' She thought of her own mother, whose work on the farm took up all her time. What would she be like now with Madeleine lolling on the sofa all day?

'It gives me pleasure, you see,' the English lady was saying. 'I remember my son who died, as I knit.'

'That was sad for you.' Simone looked at the face with its downward lines, the hair which had no life in it. 'But you still have your daughter.'

'Ah, yes, Barbie.' She sighed, shook her head. 'That is a...problem.' She was counting her stitches. 'Three purl, two plain,' she muttered. Some English incantation, Simone thought, and then, what a strange thing to say about her daughter. Still, everyone had problems.

She saw that when she called later that day at the Marmot's farm. Madame had taken a sudden notion to make chocolate soufflés for dinner, and had discovered that her stock of eggs was low. There was another man sitting at the kitchen table when Maurice invited her in.

'Allow me to introduce you to my brother,' he said. 'Mademoiselle Bouvier from the hotel, René.'

The man got up and came towards her with a wide grin and hand outstretched. A powerful wave of garlic preceded him. But even more off-putting was his appearance. The brotherly resemblance was there except that he was bigger, softer in feature, more loose-limbed, but due to some mad caprice he had had all his teeth capped with steel. He didn't smile. He gleamed, as if his mouth was a lit street. She had to prevent herself from shuddering. *'Enchanté,'* he said, making his untidy background, the ashes spilling from the grate, the hens pecking about on the floor, seem surreal.

'How do you do, Monsieur René,' she said. She held herself rigid.

'Some Monbazillac!' Maurice interrupted. 'A boudoir biscuit? Where are they?' He swept some crusts from the table onto the floor as he lifted the lid. 'Ah, here they are.' He held aloft a dirty tin.

'Please don't bother, Monsieur,' she said, 'Madame Claire is in a hurry for the eggs and I have to wait at table very soon.'

René was at her side, touching her elbow. 'You must come and see my barbed wire.' She saw the sudden gleam of teeth. 'You have time for that, no?'

'Don't worry Mademoiselle Simone with your barbed wire,' his brother said. 'You heard her say she was busy.' And to

73

Simone, 'Since you won't indulge, please sit down while I get your eggs.'

'Thank you.' She was left with René who remained standing. Every time she met his eyes he smiled his terrible smile. She had to school herself not to wince.

'How is François?' He sounded ingratiating.

'Very well, I think.'

'Maurice knows all the village gossip. He tells it to me. About the English girl.' He tittered behind his hand.

'What about her?' She spoke sharply.

'It's a little manly joke between us.' He tapped the side of his nose. 'Maurice would be cross at me if I told you.' His voice became pleading. 'Come and see my barbed wire, Mademoiselle. Please! I have used ten rolls so far. The Huns aren't going to get near us now. We're safe, thanks to me.' He swelled out his chest. 'I intend to protect my brother the way he has always protected me.'

'That's good,' she said. She saw with relief that Maurice had returned with the eggs in her bowl. She got up quickly. 'Please put them on Madame's account, Monsieur Marmot.'

'I entertained her, Maurice,' his brother said. 'I have told her of my plans and she thinks I am quite right. I haven't talked much, just entertained her.'

74

'I really must be going,' Simone said. 'Madame is waiting.' She shook hands. Maurice looked apologetic, she thought, but she was rewarded by a pewter smile from his brother.

'Come again,' he said. 'And do not mind about François. Women like that... Pah!' He made a sound of disgust through half-closed lips. 'Maurice knows.' She turned away quickly.

In the car she tried to rid herself of the memory of the soft face and the terrible smile which contradicted the softness. She shuddered although the sun shone through the glass of the little *Deux Chevaux* making it into an oven.

Madame Claire was tight-lipped when she got back. 'That one needs a good talking to. The bar is due to open at five o'clock and it is five past.' She looked at Simone. 'Do you happen to know where he is?'

'François? No, Madame.' She put the bowl of eggs on the table. She felt strangely exhausted. 'Would you like me to start switching those?'

'All in good time. Fold the napkins first. In fans, if you please, like Le Roy. I want this place to look twice as good, the bar open on time, everyone doing their bit and not skulking about when my back is turned.'

She bristled. 'You sent me to the farm.' And then, remembering, 'That brother René...!'

'Harmless! A harmless fool. You are sure you didn't see François?' Madame was not interested in René Marmot at the moment.

'You know perfectly well where he is,' her husband said. He was sitting at the table shelling peas. Some had escaped his shaking thumb and were rolling about on the surface. 'He's out with the English girl. I saw her getting into his car with him.'

'Don't talk nonsense!' His wife glared at him. 'Now it comes back to me. He will be shopping for goods for the *Méchoui* on Saturday because Simone had to go to the farm. Yes, that's it.' She said to Simone in a patronizing fashion, 'You've never been to our *Méchoui,* have you?'

'No, Madame. I only came this March, remember? Do you do the catering for it?'

'I make the salads and crudités. Christian Grinaud bakes pies and roasts the lambs. He has big ovens. And I have offered *pâté de porc* this time, a new departure. Of course, all the table linen is mine. Madame Rivaud is starching the tablecloths. It's a great day for the village with the Maire there. François will set up the bar. Did you remind him to have plenty of glasses?'

'Yes, I did. We have a *Méchoui* in our village as well. Last year we had barbecued ribs.'

'Burned to a frazzle, I heard. So it is all hands to the plough, Simone. This is Wednesday. There will be three solid days of preparation.'

'You take on far too much,' Jean-Paul said. 'You'll be telling us next that you're supplying the confetti!'

'No, no, I take nothing to do with that, nor streamers, nor balloons. I did, when I was on the *Méchoui* committee. Really, Jean-Paul, you say the silliest things...'

'I was only joking,' the old man said humbly, looking down at his task.

'If you had been abler you could have helped them set up the trestle tables but you'd only be in the way...' Simone saw him stop shelling for a second, his hands trembling as he gripped the bowl, then go on again.

When she was setting the tables in the dining-room for dinner, François and the English girl arrived. Her forearms were burned by the sun, and François looked as if he had caught it across his nose and cheeks. All the Gramout shops were in shady squares.

'*Salut.* Simone,' François said in a strange, polite voice. 'Busy?'

'Busy, busy bee.' The girl stopped beside

77

Simone. She could imagine she felt heat coming from her body. 'You should have been with us. We had marvellous fun.'

'I'm glad.' She laid a fork precisely on the paper tablecloth. 'Dinner is in half an hour.'

'Do you hear that, François? Dinner is in half an hour.' She mimicked Simone. 'Everybody's been working while you and I have been gallivanting down by the old mill.' She sang the words. 'I'm going to have a bath first.' She looked at him, her eyes brimming with laughter. 'You too?'

'No time for that, I'm afraid.' He grinned sheepishly, his eyes went to Simone, came away again.

She said to him, 'Your mother wants you to be sure you have plenty of glasses ready for the *Méchoui*.' Her throat hurt so much that she could hardly speak.

'What's a *Méchoui*, what's a *Méchoui*?' The girl was pretending to be a child, pushing out her lower lip. 'Tell me please, I demand to know.'

'It's a...kind of barbecue.' He spoke shortly, and to Simone, 'I *have* plenty of glasses. I'm not a fool.'

'I gave you a list of replacements last week.'

'Did you?'

'Don't you remember? I gave them to you when you were in the bar. You said...'

He interrupted her. 'You're getting as bad as my mother, Simone. I have a hundred things to do, as well as ordering glasses. I don't want you breathing down my neck as well as her!'

'Don't stand for that sort of talk, Simone.' The girl's eyes were shining. 'He's cross, Mummy's little boy is cross...' Simone looked at her, then at François. She had never felt so unwanted in all her life as she stood between them. Their mutual attraction was almost palpable, making it difficult for her to breathe. She lifted the heavy pile of plates, feeling the weight of them pull at the muscles of her arms.

'*Have* you ordered them?' she said.

'No, I have not. There's no problem. I'll phone right away.'

'And I can have my bath, Mummy's boy?' He turned to Barbie, and Simone saw his face clear, saw the worship in his eyes.

'Of course, silly girl,' he said. Simone walked to the next table with her pile of plates.

She had never known such pain. One should be warned that such pain existed. Her heart was round and hard in her breast like a *boule,* her throat ached. How could she support such pain and go on with her work? But that was the answer. Monsieur Jean-Paul had given it to her. The task at

79

hand. If you couldn't have love, at least there was work to help you to forget.

That night Monsieur Sinclair barked at her after he had nearly scraped the pattern off the dish containing his chocolate soufflé. It had been an inspired soufflé. *'Mademoiselle, un moment, s'il vous plaît.* Damn fine dinner all round. My compliments to Madame. Tell me, what was the *entrée?'*

'Pieds de porc, Monsieur.'

'My God!' he said, turning green.

'I told you, Daddy,' his daughter said. 'Don't you remember we ate them at Cahors?' She smiled up at Simone, her eyes sparkling, 'You're not trying to poison us, are you, Simone?'

'No, Mademoiselle.' She began collecting the plates. 'Not before the *Méchoui.'* Suddenly they were laughing together. If it weren't for François, we could be friends, she thought.

Chapter Five

The day dawned perfectly for the *Méchoui.* From early morning the sun shone golden, the Romanesque tower of the church cut squarely into the blue block of the sky.

The shadowed space behind the church, generally occupied by the *pétanque* players had been cleared and swept, and the children warned off.

By midday the tables were set up on their trestles by the helpers, and Simone was there with Madame Claire and a bevy of the black widows, spreading the starched cloths and laying the coloured paper napkins precisely at each place, anchored by a silver-wrapped and ribboned favour.

The funds of the committee were in a good state, and it had been decided to buy cardboard plates and paper cups. Glasses would be used only for the wine, to be supplied as usual by the Hotel Delouche. François had worked solidly all morning with Simone as if they were back to their former friendly footing. Without the English girl's presence he was the François she had first seen on his return from Toulouse and fallen in love with, eyes bright, his *mèche* smooth and gleaming bright from brushing, his skin golden-brown against the white shirt tucked into a red cummerbund.

'I don't know what *Maman* would have done without you,' he said on one of their trips with yet more supplies. 'She had one girl after another, each worse than the one before. She used to write to me about them when I was in Toulouse.'

'I understand her love for the hotel,' she said, 'her wish to build it up for you to inherit.' She couldn't bring herself to say, 'And your wife and children'. 'It's important to her.'

The English girl was nowhere to be seen. Simone imagined that she had cleared out of the way with her father and mother and would make a spectacular entrance when the work was done. She was right. She appeared precisely at four o'clock when Madame's pâté was being served and the children subdued by their parents so that full attention could be given to the band's rousing opening number of welcome to all.

One could say she stopped the show, flanked on either side by her parents, her father red-faced with his bristling bull terrier moustache and striped blazer, her mother looking tired as usual in a tired flowered dress and carrying a large cretonne bag with tortoisehell handles which held her knitting.

Heads went up, forks were poised, the band seemed to falter. Mademoiselle Barbie stood, smiling and poised like a prima ballerina in a white organdie dress which fitted her body to the waist like a second skin then flounced out over stiffened pink petticoats which gave the white organdie a pearl-like glow. Pink ribbons held back her hair which lay long and silkily dark on her back. Her neck and arms were golden-brown.

The Delouche pâté lay untouched on the plates. There was a hush, a sigh, like the wind. And then Simone heard Madame Claire's voice ringing out. She was standing up in her place at the table, in her black dress, the dragons on her shawl seeming to writhe in the heat. If it had been twice as hot the shawl would still have been worn.

'Monsieur and Madame Sinclair! Mademoiselle!' Her hand was held up imperiously as she beckoned. 'Here, if you please. These are the seats for the hotel guests.'

The English people took their places. Some of the young men who were acting as waiters rushed to serve them, the band increased its tempo, waved on by the leader's baton. People, remembering the excellent truffle-specked pâté lowered their heads again. Bowls of salad circulated. There was laughter and talk.

Simone glanced towards the bar which had been erected beside the *épicerie* which had been closed for the day. François stood transfixed, looking in the girl's direction. She had seen the same immobility in cornered rabbits when she had gone over the fields with Marcel on his shooting forays.

The look told her that she had lost him. She watched him as he filled his tray with glasses of wine and began to circulate amongst the tables. She could not bring herself to sit down although once or twice Madame Claire beckoned to her, patting the empty chair beside her. It was easier to go on serving the tables. Food would have choked her.

The afternoon wore on, and course followed course. François was generous with wine. Young men unbuttoned their shirts, the older men took off their best jackets, people sat back in their chairs surfeited with food and drink. The tables were littered with paper hats and streamers, bowls of limp lettuce, dirty plates, half-empty glasses. Everything had been sampled, but some of the meat and chicken pies had proved too heavy for such a day and were lying untouched. The glass dishes of chocolate mousse had turned into brown pools, one of Madame Claire's less-inspired ideas.

Simone, resting for a moment from serving, sat with Monsieur Delouche who had chosen a place at the end of the hotel table. She knew he was conscious of the clumsiness of his hands. The sun shimmered, the talk and laughter waxed and waned; only the children, now permitted to play round the square, were indefatigable. When the church clock tolled seven o'clock it seemed to draw up into its huge bell some of the heat from the baked ground, so that what had been a cauldron became cooled by a gentle evening wind which had sprung up.

The band, replete now, had resumed their places at their instruments and were strumming up. With the sound the atmosphere changed. Some of the mothers snatched the younger children and ushered them off to bed. There was a blatant queue of red-faced men at the *pissoir* behind the Mairie. Simone saw Marie-Thérèse with her friends giggling near the wooden platform, eagerly waiting to be asked to dance.

She looked around for François and saw him gathering glasses in an exemplary fashion. And, yet, wasn't his back taut, his shoulders rigid, indeed his whole body charged with anticipation? The English girl was still sitting at the table with her parents. Her face was composed, secret, her painted fingernails played a tattoo on the cloth, her smile had a Mona Lisa quality.

'Now for the fun,' Jean-Paul said, head shaking. 'Aren't you going to join the young ones? You've done enough.'

'Later,' she said. 'Madame Claire might want me. Besides,' she smiled at him, 'it's nice sitting here with you in the shade of the buttresses...' Her voice was drowned by a sudden deafening din from the band as it threw itself into a polka. So did everyone else, or almost everyone. People rushed about looking for partners, some reluctant ones were dragged towards the dance floor, laughing. In no time it was a jostling mass of dancers, the steady thump-thump of feet almost drowning the band.

'Last year it went on until half-past one,' Jean-Paul said.

'Did it? No point in going to bed before that, then.' She was feeling relaxed. She had eaten a little but drunk three or four glasses of wine. She couldn't remember. Nothing seemed to matter now, or not so much. The hurt which had been her whole body had subsided.

'They took away twenty huge bags of paper from the square. I don't think monsieur le Curé quite approves, but it is the tradition to hold the *Méchoui* here. He says the confetti is tramped into the church for weeks—and probably into the confession box.' She smiled at his shrewdness.

'It's difficult to sweep up. I know,' she said. 'It will be carried into the hotel as well. What we need is a giant vacuum...'

she saw a huge cylinder, a long nozzle like an elephant's trunk coming from it, swirling paper disappearing...

'I think she's gone deaf,' Monsieur Delouche was saying. She came out of her trance to see Luc Marmot standing in front of her.

'I'm dreaming.' She laughed. 'Were you saying something?'

'I was asking you to dance, but if you'd rather not?'

'I'm dying to dance.' She got up, feeling pleased that she could stand. She hadn't thought of dancing with anyone else, only François. But it didn't matter. Luc was all right, an old friend.

'Enjoy yourself,' Jean-Paul said, his head nodding in emphasis.

She had always known Luc Marmot. As a school friend of Marcel's he had often come about the farm when they were younger. Usually she had been banished by Marcel. 'Clear off! We don't want girls hanging around!' His mother was a widow—'*her* husband died in his bed,' she remembered her mother saying—and they lived in Gramout so that she could be near the delicatessen where she worked.

It was hard to believe that the strange Marmot brothers were his uncles. She had a sudden vision of René's soft face, that terrible smile. Something clutched her heart, a fearful kind of apprehension, taking away with it her floating sense of well-being. She was Simone Bouvier again, hard-working Simone Bouvier without glamour who wasn't going to make a fool of herself nor wear her heart on her sleeve...

'I didn't expect to see *you* here,' she said when they were dancing on the wooden floor which swayed under them. She waved to Marie-Thérèse who had danced past, looking triumphant, with Christian Grinaud. A waste of a good man, she thought.

'I didn't expect to come, to be honest,' Luc said, 'but I was visiting at the farm and Uncle Maurice said I should look in at the *Méchoui*, in his place. I think he would have liked to come but he won't leave René at night. It's becoming a sorry state of affairs up there.'

'Yes, I go for eggs sometimes.' She wouldn't mention the brother, nor even think of him. 'They could do with someone to clean up for them,' she laughed, 'and keep the hens out.'

'They could well afford it. Mother is always telling them. Anyhow, I'm glad I've come. I've seen you.'

'That's not a great attraction.'

'You're wrong there.' He was tall, taller than François. He looked down at her, smiling with his eyes. His pale skin was faintly freckled, his features were waiter-fine, she thought. You could imagine him bending solicitously over an hotel guest.

'I don't believe you.' He was Marcel's friend, not hers.

'All right.' He was urbane, again like a waiter. 'The truth is I came to taste Madame Claire's pâté. I'm a spy for Le Roy. I've to find out what her secret is.'

'I'll be an informer, if you like.' He was easy to talk to. 'She empties a bottle of cognac into the mixture.'

'Ah! Well, I hope they appreciate what I've done for them. They're inclined to cut costs at Le Roy.'

'Do you like it there?'

'Yes, I'm getting a good training. I'd like to be the manager some day, or better still, have my own hotel.'

She looked at him and thought he was cut out for it. He was slim and tall, one could imagine him coming forward in greeting, his fair hair brushed sleekly to his skull. Perhaps his chief attribute for a hotelier was his clean, well-groomed appearance. He would inspire confidence. She remembered he had always been tidier than Marcel, even as a schoolboy. One could say he was the type of person people would like to serve their food. Waiters should be clean-shaven always, and be careful about their nails. She was always scrubbing hers.

They stayed together by unspoken consent. Luc said he had only looked in for an hour, and she knew she would have to start soon and collect the leftover food and get it back to the hotel. Madame Claire had said it must not be left too long, otherwise it would not be worth saving.

She hoped François would see her with Luc. She even had the courage to smile and wave when he danced past with Mademoiselle Barbie. That was unbearable, but the hurt was lessened when she saw him with Marie-Thérèse who was wearing a drum majorette paper hat. Perhaps she could still hope... She noticed the village youths were buzzing around the English girl like bees round a honeypot. She tried to concentrate on Luc Marmot, grateful for his company.

She had always got on well with him. He told her anecdotes about Le Roy, about the kind of people who came there, rich Parisians mostly who wanted to spend a few days in *un pays sauvage*. And he seemed to have a kindly nature because he talked again about his uncles. 'We worry about them. They're both a little odd, René more than a little. He's putting barbed wire all round the place now.'

'I know. He told me. It's to keep out the Huns, he says.'

'And protect Maurice. They're devoted to each other. I don't think Maurice realizes how peculiar he's become...but I mustn't talk about family affairs all the time. How do you like the Hotel Delouche, Simone? Is it better than the farm?'

'It's livelier.' She was glad he had changed the subject. 'My mother...' She didn't have to say any more. He knew about her father. 'And now that Madeleine is there, there's no room for me. I'm better out of it.'

'They're getting married soon?'

'Yes, a quiet wedding.' She decided to be frank. 'She's *enceinte*.'

'Marcel told me.' François danced past, again with the English girl. Their eyes were locked, one of her arms was round his neck. The pain was sudden, fresh, unendurable. She wanted to double up with it, to groan aloud. I didn't ask for this, she thought. I don't want to suffer like this at my age... *'There's* someone who looks as if he wouldn't mind being married,' Luc said.

'Who?' She pretended to look around.

'François Delouche. I don't know who he's with, but she's *ravissante*.' Even Luc was bewitched, she thought.

'She's a guest. English. Sometimes I think I'll leave the hotel.' She heard her own waspish voice. 'I'm becoming a dogsbody. Madame Claire is very demanding...'

'I'm sure there would be a place for you at Le Roy if you wanted it. It's being enlarged.'

'Yes, someone told me. I'll remember who it was...in a minute...' The pain wouldn't go away. Was the pain of love and the pain of giving birth similar? You couldn't have one without the other, she supposed. 'What time is it?' She was suddenly desperate to get away.

He looked at his watch, turning his wrist. 'Ten to nine.'

'Ten to nine! I'll have to go. I promised Madame Claire I'd help with the clearing up. Her legs get badly swollen with standing. I don't think I could bear to leave her, really. I like her, you see. With my mother it's different. I love her, but...' He must think she was mad. She stopped dancing abruptly. 'I'm glad I saw you, Luc. Thanks for dancing with me.'

'Hey! Girls don't thank! It's *my* pleasure.' He smiled at her and she liked him so much, his thin face, his straight nose, the brown eyes like her own. He looked competent, and kind, and predictable. That was the trouble. He would do well at Le

Roy or in his own hotel. 'I'll tell Marcel I've seen you. I'd like to give you a hand but I'm due back to relieve another waiter.'

'There's no need. I'm happier working.' They walked off the wooden floor and kissed because they had always kissed. They had known each other for a long time.

'I'd always thought of you as Marcel's little sister,' Luc said. 'You've changed. You've grown up.'

'Everyone does, sooner or later.' She was abrupt. *'Au revoir.'*

François appeared when she was helping Sophie Rivaud to fold the soiled table-cloths. He spoke to his mother who was busy beside them, carefully packing into boxes any food which had been untouched, earthenware dishes of pate, chicken pies. She was even emptying chocolates and nuts into plastic bags. They were all going back to the hotel to be stored away in the walk-in cold store which had been added to her kitchen. 'Tell me what you want me to do, *Maman,'* he said. 'I've got all the wine and spirits back now.'

'Did you keep the half-empty ones? They'll do for my pâtés and desserts.'

'Yes, *Maman,* I kept them.' He smiled at Simone and Sophie.

'Good.' She looked tired and pale.

93

Simone had seen her legs and been horrified at their size. Sophie Rivaud had nodded grimly and said under her breath, 'Her heart...' 'You and Simone should start getting this stuff back to the hotel now. Simone knows where it has to go.'

'Right. Come along, Simone. What a pile of tablecloths! Are you laundering them, Madame Rivaud?'

'*Comme d'habitude.* I can take my time over them. As long as they're ready for the next *Méchoui.*' She gave him her equine smile.

'I'll drop them off at your house, then. Put them in the wash-house at the foot of your garden. *D'accord?*' He seemed full of energy and good humour, as if something had happened to make him happy. Or could it be, her heart suddenly lifted with relief, that Mademoiselle had told him she was leaving and he had been in fact relieved because she had been pursuing *him?* She told herself she would believe that for a time. She couldn't go on bearing the hurt.

They laughed as they loaded the crates and boxes, the plastic bags, the artificial flowers. They discussed the *Méchoui,* how everyone had praised the pâté, how good the band had been.

'I saw you dancing with Luc Marmot,' he said.

'Did you? I saw you dancing with Mademoiselle Barbie.' She was able to say that, lightly.

'Yes.' He nodded. 'She says our dances are old-fashioned compared with England. She wanted the band to play rock and roll. I don't think the Gramout Five could do that if they tried!'

'They played some John Lennon songs. Didn't you notice?'

'Yes, there was one you could waltz to.' His face went soft, his eyes half-closed. 'Barbie tells me his records are a great hit in England.'

'I wonder that she doesn't want to go back there.' It was too late to keep the sharpness out of her voice.

'She's leaving it to her father.' He spoke calmly. Whatever had happened between them he was no longer looking tortured. Perhaps he had realized an English girl was not for him. Perhaps she had told him there was someone else, perhaps, perhaps...

He kissed her good-night when he kissed his mother. 'Get off to bed, you two. You've had a busy day.' His voice was tender but he smiled impartially on them.

The two women were too tired to speak much as they undressed in their small room. 'You've had a hard day, Madame,' Simone said, 'but your pâté was a great

95

success. Everyone liked it. Luc Marmot is going to steal your recipe.'

'He can't because there isn't one. It's in here.' She put her hand on her vast underbodice. 'Cooking must come from the heart as well as the head.' She slowly pulled off a black stocking, sighing as a swollen purple leg emerged. 'I always like the *Méchoui*. It's good to see the village united, even for one day. Everyone forgets the back-biting which goes on all year.'

'All villages are the same. I expect they're talking in ours about Madeleine being pregnant.'

'They'll talk more about her if she doesn't buckle to and help your mother in the farm.'

'She might turn out to have other attributes.' Men were never blamed, she thought. Marcel was still the apple of their mother's eye. And then, because François was uppermost in her mind, she said, 'François was a good son to you tonight. So willing to help.'

'Too willing, maybe.' She heaved herself into her bed. 'That's enough gossiping for tonight, my girl. You get in too.'

'Yes, Madame Claire.'

She lay down and was on the edge of sleep when she heard her voice, 'I'll give you this, Simone. No one worked

96

harder than you. You're a girl after my own heart.'

She turned on her side, her hand under her cheek, comforted.

In the morning she was wakened out of a heavy sleep by Madame Claire shaking her by the shoulder. 'Simone! It's seven o'clock! You have the breakfasts to do.'

'Oh, sorry!' She sat up, rubbing her eyes. 'I overslept. I'll be ready in a minute.'

'Patrice Tenier called on his way to the roadworks. His wife can't come today. She's *fatiguée*. Probably ate too much last night.' And drank too much, no doubt. She had seen Marie, laughing and red-faced, singing along with the band.

'You'll want me to go upstairs?' Madame Tenier came each morning and tidied the bedrooms during the three summer months when they were busy downstairs.

'Yes.' She was unapologetic. 'Sophie Rivaud won't show up, you may be sure of that, nor any of her cronies. It takes them all a week to recover from the *Méchoui*. You know I can't do it. I'll be busy with the cooking.'

She became a whirlwind, setting tables, serving coffee and rolls, dashing to the storehouse in the yard where they kept the dry goods, the cereals and the sugar. François was bustling in and out the kitchen, up and down to the cellar, storing away the crates of wine and spirits. His father made a feeble effort to help, rising from his chair and tottering after him, but he was soon back in his place, looking discomfited. She hoped François had been gentle with him.

As soon as she had washed up the breakfast dishes she assembled her dusters and polishes together with her hand brush and carpet sweeper and made for the bedrooms. If she rushed through them she would just finish in time to wait the tables. Sunday luncheon was no respecter of *Méchouis*. Many families from quite a distance around regarded it as their weekly treat. They were lucky. They would get pâté with truffles and brandy in it, not to mention various left-overs which would have been reconstituted in some weird and wonderful way by Madame, from her heart, she remembered wryly.

In spite of the heavy work of the day before, she felt full of energy. She was sure there was a subtle change in François, a withdrawn kind of calmness, as if he was living in a happy world of his own. Things would turn out all right for her after all. Mademoiselle Barbie would go back to England and she would be forgotten about in no time. She would never have fitted in here in spite of her capacity to fraternize.

You had to be born and brought up in a village to appreciate what it meant, what was expected of you.

She would clean François' room first, she decided. It was at the staircase end of the corridor in any case, and she might as well be methodical. She was serene and happy as she tidied the sprawl of lotions and gels on his dressing-table. Marcel didn't have such an array as this, she thought, taking off the lids to smell them, but, of course, François would know all about such things. He always smelled nice, not like some of the village youths with their pimples and bad breath. Perhaps he could buy wholesale in Toulouse what he needed. That might be useful for her later on...she permitted herself to dream a little.

She swept his bedside rug free of confetti, using her handbrush, polished the floor with her mop and then began to strip the bed. She should have done it the other way round. She was sure Marie Tenier did, but never mind.

He had navy-blue and white striped sheets and pillowcases, possibly also from Toulouse. Very *chic*. She remembered his mother ranting on about them and saying the dye would run and spoil all her household linen, and how François, catching Simone's eye in complicity, had laughed and said, 'Oh, *Maman*, they think of that nowadays! '

As she turned up one of the pillows, she saw, lying under it, a neat little mound of confetti...yes, she should have done it the other way...a little *fistful* of confetti. As if squeezed together and then released. Her heart stopped. She could feel the blood leaving her lips. She shook the sheets lying on the floor and a pink hair-ribbon tumbled out.

She closed her eyes, swayed, opened them again and sank down on the bed, feeling deathly sick. A girl, rosy as the dawn in her pink petticoats, her white organdie, her pink ribbons. Was her skin rosy as the dawn also? Her arms, her legs, her arms and legs outspread, one outflung arm clutching a fistful of confetti, slowly being released when François...when François... She moaned, slid off the edge of the bed and into the bundle of striped sheets, moaned and writhed.

Why let her imagination stop there? She wasn't innocent. She had used it with Madeleine and Marcel, because she had been brought up on a farm and girls of eighteen are curious and consumed by thoughts of sex. Be honest. Don't stop. Go ahead, imagine François on top of the English girl, her outflung arm which had slipped under the striped pillow, her hand releasing the fistful of confetti when he, when he...she heard her own voice, ugly, strangled, through the wild sobs, 'You...you...how could you with *her...?*'

'Simone!' It was Madame's voice. Very loud. She must be standing at the foot of the stairs. 'Simone! How much longer are you going to be?'

She opened the door onto the landing. 'Not much longer, Madame,' she called, 'I'm coming...'

Chapter Six

Simone could scarcely remember the days after her discovery of the pink ribbon and the confetti in François' bed. She had passed them in a daze of misery, so much so that Madame had said to her in an unusually gentle voice, 'I don't know what is wrong with you, Simone, but you do not look at all well. Would you like to have a few days off?'

'You can't manage without me,' she said.

The difficulty had been in finding places to weep. It had to be done so that she was dry of tears before she shared the little room each night with Madame Claire.

'It will be very hard, I admit, but I have managed before. There is Marie Tenier, and I think she has a niece...'

Her pride made her refuse. 'No, there is no need, Madame. But...' she hesitated, 'now that the peak of the season is over, if I could have an hour or so off in the afternoon? I think it's the heat which is affecting me. Such a summer!' An *églantine* summer.

'Not at your age. You have never been the same since the *Méchoui*. Tell me, Simone, you aren't involved with anyone...a young man?'

'No, Madame Claire,' she said, 'I'm not involved with anyone.'

'It's not...disappointment? I mean, François? I had hoped...'

'François?' She tried to look blank. 'I don't understand...'

Madame Claire shook her head impatiently. 'To tell you the truth I wish that English family would clear off. They've been unsettling, and François spends far too much time with the daughter. Of course it's her fault. She hangs around him...ah, what's the use? One should never plan for one's children. Let them make their own mistakes. One has to find one's own interests. Remember that. Mine is in my cooking. Oh, don't look so supercilious! There was a time when that would not have satisfied me, but one musn't look back. Yes, you have your afternoons, Simone. Do what you like with them. I forget you are only young. You're so sensible, *ma cocotte.*' She patted Simone's arm in a rare burst of tenderness. 'Such a sweet child, but troubled... Ach, get on with you! You and I haven't time for softness.'

She could now make her own opportunities. The heavy burden of tears had to have release. It was insupportable. She knew where she wanted to go. The ruined mill was impossible because she had been happy there with François, but there was the *chateau d'eau.* He had been taken there as a child by his mother. It was a place of innocence and memories. She would feel close to him there, perhaps even find some vestige of hope.

Most afternoons she drove the few miles out of the village in the *Deux Chevaux* and climbed through the maze of gorse and juniper bushes towards the tall tower which stood against the sky. When she was hidden from the road and lying on the warm grass, the tears came as if she had turned on a tap, endlessly. She wept until her throat and the back of her nose ached. She was swamped in tears. The relief was great, the tight band round her heart lessened. At the end of a week she found she had no tears left. The misery was still there, but its intensity had gone.

Once again she found herself able to chat naturally with Monsieur as she hung out the bed linen in the yard, to have girlish talks with Mademoiselle Barbie about fashions and hair, to joke with François at the bar. She was still subject to flashes of pure hatred of the English girl, but less often. If she would only *go*...she found herself repeating the words like a prayer each night in bed.

Barbie's father seemed to be very happy writing his book. He went to the Gramout library every morning and worked there until lunchtime. He had made friends with the town *archiviste,* and had morning coffees with him in Le Paradis, the cafe near the Mairie. He boasted about it to Simone. 'I'm becoming one of the natives, Mademoiselle...' The family had been accepted by the few English residents, and sometimes they were out for dinner. It looked as if they were settled in the hotel for ever.

One afternoon, when Simone was tidying up after lunch, the English girl appeared at the kitchen door. She never crossed the threshhold, as if she was afraid she might be drawn into the endless activity there. She was fundamentally lazy, Simone began to recognize, affable, charming, without any real direction and dependent upon other people to amuse her. 'Is there any place around where we could swim, Simone?' she asked. 'I don't mean the *Piscine*. François wants to take me there, but I hate it. Those screaming children, and you have to put your clothes in a string bag and wear a metal disc on your wrist like a cow in the market!'

Simone laughed, agreeing that Madame at the *Piscine* was a dragon. She had gimlet eyes and blew her whistle at the slightest provocation. 'Hasn't François ever taken you to the ruined mill? There's the river.' She could ask that now without wincing.

'Once, not now.' She smiled richly, secretly. Why should they look for privacy there when she could creep into his bed any night she wanted to? It was much more comfortable. And creep back to her own room without her parents knowing.

Madame Claire seemed to have accepted the situation albeit with a tightening of lips when she saw him dreaming at the bar. Or at least their friendship. 'Wake up, François! There's work to do!' she would say as she passed. Only once, when he wanted Patrice Tenier to take his place in the bar had she lost her temper. 'Can you imagine!' she stormed at Simone, 'that son of mine wished to take Mademoiselle Sinclair to Le Roy for dinner! The nerve of it! "Your place is in the Hotel Delouche," I told him, "not snooping about Le Roy with her. *Il va falloir lui montrer qui commande ici!*" ' She tossed her head.

'Perhaps he wanted to pick up some tips for you,' she said. She hid her bitterness with a joke.

'Tips! It's the other way round! Remember how you said Luc Marmot admired my pâté? Now, *there's* a decent young man. Not a patch on my François, of course, but I'm sure he doesn't worry his mother! He seemed quite struck on you at the *Méchoui*. Is that who you go off to meet in the afternoons?'

'That would be telling,' she countered. Was Madame fishing? She had done her best to disguise her swollen eyes after her bouts of weeping at the *chateau d'eau*. Nor did she tell her that she had met Luc one afternoon in Gramout and he had asked if he could take her out. She had refused, too abruptly. At the time she hadn't been able to trust herself not to weep.

'You might have asked him what they serve for dinner at Le Roy, tactfully, of course.'

'I might, but I didn't.'

'None of your sauce, if you please.'

She smiled. 'You don't need any hints from him. Why don't you write a book of *recettes*. Call it "The White Toque".'

'You've changed, Simone. You didn't

106

have that cynicism when you first came here. No, no, my skill is in my hands, not up here.' She touched her head. 'Jean-Paul's the one for writing, or was. If you could have seen the beautiful estimates he made out for his clients, in the finest copper-plate. And such a reader as well! He got *Le Monde* in the *Maison de la Presse* each morning. Sent from Paris! Now he couldn't hold it steady enough to read it.'

'I've always thought he was clever.'

She raised her chin proudly. 'It's strange, but I always seem to attract men with brains. There was another one...'

'Oh, Madame!' She made round eyes.

'You don't believe me? He was an engineer. Hair as golden as the gorse at the front, eyes like the summer sky...' Her face changed, became vulnerable, and young, but almost immediately she shook her head impatiently. 'Will you listen to me babbling? Get on with your work, Simone! Any excuse with you to stop...'

Now Simone said to Mademoiselle Barbie, 'I have an hour or two off as it happens. Madame Claire allows it. I could take you, if you like. You don't drive?'

'Why should I when there are always people around to drive me. Is the river good there for bathing?'

'I would think so. And there's a weir. It might be possible to stand on a rock under it, like a shower.' She thought of that afternoon when she had lain on the grass listening to its rushing noise and François had kissed her. And kissed her again, later, in the white Peugeot. *'Aigre-doux.'*

'What's bitter-sweet?' She didn't realize she had spoken aloud.

'Memories.'

'You're raving. You're too young to have memories. But that's a super idea of yours, Simone. I'll go and get my bikini. Will you bring some hotel towels?'

'D'accord.' You could see Mademoiselle Barbie's attraction without a doubt. She was like a child when something pleased her, even to the clapping of her hands, the little skip she made.

François was behind the bar when they stopped beside it, Barbie carrying the striped beach bag with their swimsuits and towels. She wore dark glasses and a low-cut sundress showing her brown shoulders and the deep fold between her breasts. A gold locket had slipped into it. Simone saw his eyes following the gold chain. 'We're going swimming,' the English girl said.

'I said I would take you to the *Piscine.*' His eyes were moist with love. 'Is Simone coming?'

'We have our own, thank you very much. No men allowed.' She made a face at him, and turned to Simone, her finger to her lips.

'Where?' He was discomfited.

'We're not telling, are we, Simone? Don't tell him or I'll kill you. Men! They want to know everything. This is *our* secret!' Simone saw his brows draw together under the golden sweep of his hair. She had him wrapped round her little finger. His face cleared, and he smiled his sweet smile.

'D'accord. It's a girls' outing. Take my car, Simone. For two such beauties a decent car is essential, an open car. You will want to show off to the village when you drive through.'

'To cut a dash?' Barbie said, bubbling with laughter. She spoke in English.

'Comment?'

'Isn't he an ignoramus, Simone? His brains are in his...' Her laughter bubbled over. *'Faire de l'effet,* stupid!'

Monsieur Henri, one of the regulars, sitting on a stool nearby, interrupted. Simone had been watching him in the mirror behind François, the curious expression, the eyes moving from one to the other, the bushy blond moustache wobbling, the youthful air although she knew he must be at least fifty. Behind his back in the village he was called 'Weezard Prang'.

Now he turned jauntily to the girls, one hand stroking the moustache. 'Perhaps you have heard, mesdemoiselles, that I learned many English expressions in the war. One comes to mind, overhearing your conversation.' He chuckled and spluttered for a second. *'Pardon.* So apt.' He shook a finger at Simone. 'You must be very careful, mademoiselle, not to prang François' car!' He dissolved with silly laughter.

'Comment, Monsieur?' she said, her face straight. Everybody teased Monsieur Prang.

''Prang'. That's what they say when they have a collision in the sky with the Hun. "Weezard prang!" '

'Do they?'

François laughed at her. 'Simone's a good driver, Monsieur Henri. Have a drink before you set off, girls.'

'I'll have a *blanc cassis,'* Barbie said, hoisting herself onto a stool, Monsieur Prang gallantly helping her. One of the straps of her sundress had slipped over her shoulder showing a white strip on the golden brown of the skin. The eyes of the old man and those of François were on her. Simone felt excluded, of no account.

'Simone?' François said.

'Nothing for me. I'll tell Madame Claire we're going.' No one answered or seemed to care when she left them.

François' car was a joy to drive. He called it *La Mouette* because he saw seagulls only when he went to Les Landes on holiday. He had once told Simone that he was fascinated by them. 'Here people get a thrill when they see the golden oriole, but for me the sight of a seagull skimming over the waves is magical.' On the bonnet of the Peugeot he had fixed an emblem, a silver bird with outstretched wings. It had been his pride and joy until Mademoiselle Barbie came along, she thought, driving through the village and on to the high road which ran along the ridge of the *Causse*.

One could imagine it was the sea because of how the land billowed and stretched away from the road towards the horizon. Near at hand it was green and gold with maize, in the middle distance the bleached grey-white of the limestone shone in the sun, but further away it merged into a soft grape-like bloom on the horizon. When she turned into the side road leading down to the mill, it was dark and enclosed in comparison because of the thick wall of foliage on either side.

'My God!' Barbie said as they bumped in and out of the ruts, 'this is shaking me to bits!'

'We'll soon be there.' Simone laughed. 'Don't worry.' She steered the car carefully, fearful of scratching the white paintwork on the tangle of bushes under the trees. There would be rich pickings here in autumn, she thought. I could make jars of *confiture* for Madame—if I'm still here. At home they were always busy bottling fruit, pounding liver for pâté, filling jars of *eau-de-vie* with the huge plums which they had skinned. She imagined the fat green globes, and how Marcel would fish out one and put it in a small glass. He distilled the liqueur in the barn.

She had a wave of homesickness for her girlhood, no Madeleine, no François, just *Maman* and Marcel, for Zoro, the German sheepdog which followed her everywhere, the steamy rancid smell in the byre, the darkness of the hen house pierced by the occupants' bright little eyes, all the sights and sounds of the farm, even for the rabbits in their hutches unaware of the fate which awaited them.

'What a dreadful road,' the girl said again. 'I don't remember it being so bad when François...'

'You were too bewitched to notice.' Simone glanced at her, met her eyes.

'Perhaps *he* was. You're not jealous, are you?' Simone steered deliberately for a deep rut and saw the girl's breasts bounce under the tight bodice. Lucky her. She looked dispassionately at her almost straight front.

'What a hope! Don't you have country like this in England?'

'Like this! Not likely. This is *sauvage! Mon Dieu!* Sussex where we live is well-tended. We have lovely smooth lawns in front of the houses, and we cut the grass outside our fence as well. We're so tidy!'

Simone thought of the farmyard at home, how one needed to wear rubber boots to fetch the eggs or feed the rabbits, how the scullery outside was a clutter of boots always, caked with mud. 'Can you wear smart shoes when you go outside?' she asked. 'With heels?'

'Of course. The pavements are smooth, and to walk to the shops is no problem. Sometimes I cycle. I'd like to learn to drive sometime. Actually, father's put me off it. He won't teach me because he's afraid I'd want the car all the time, and he's never allowed Mother, far less me, to learn. He's a chauvinistic old pig.'

'Is that bad?'

The girl let out a hoot of laughter. 'Bad! she says. Well, isn't your father the same?'

'I wouldn't know. He was killed by being caught in a threshing machine in a neighbour's farm. Caught in it and mangled.' She wanted to shock this complacent English girl. 'In nineteen hundred and forty-six. I was two, my brother four. It has made my mother bitter, naturally. He fought in the war without a scratch and lost his life needlessly so soon after. That is what hurts her so much.'

'Poor thing!' She seemed touched, then she brightened. 'Perhaps she'll get married again and you'll get a new Daddy. Change is a good thing, they say.'

'No, she won't. She nurses her bitterness.'

'Why didn't you stay at home and help her?'

'My brother Marcel is getting married. There wasn't room for me.' She said, girl to girl, 'I was glad to clear out, especially as Madeleine is having a baby.'

'And they aren't married?'

'No.'

'Oh.' The girl fell silent. Was she shocked? Simone broke the silence.

'You speak French very well, Mademoiselle.'

'Oh, call me Barbie, for goodness sake.'

'Thank you.'

'My brother died in France.'

'Yes, you told me. That was sad.'

'He was Mummy's favourite. He had tuberculosis when he was young. That's why we moved to Nîmes. I think Daddy had a friend there who rented him a house. Do you know it?'

'No, I've never been on holiday. Is it at the seaside?'

'No, the Rhône Valley. I even went to school there. I much preferred Nîmes to this dump, actually. Very *chic*. But you've seen my father. He's always got some bee in his bonnet.'

'A bee in his bonnet? That is bad?'

'Not for him. It started in Nîmes when he visited this cave called La Baume Latrone. He's fascinated by caves. As I am with sweet little François!' She laughed. 'Don't pretend you haven't noticed. We're dippy about each other. I'd *swoon* for that gold forelock of his... Well, anything to escape the awful boredom of this place. How do you stand it?'

'I haven't any time to think about it. I'm lucky to be out at all. Madame Claire has only just begun to give me afternoons off.'

'The stingy old bag!'

Perhaps it was a compliment in English. They had reached the ruined mill, and Simone drove the car carefully onto the grassy plateau beside the pool. 'This'll do,' she said.

'Isn't it spooky somehow!' The girl looked around. 'I didn't notice before but then I was otherwise engaged.' She laughed as she pulled down her short skirt which had wrinkled over her hips. 'Do you think we should really swim over and stand under the weir?'

'I'm not so sure.' Simone had got out too and together they walked over the grass. 'The ledge is quite narrow. No, I think we'd better just swim in the pool.'

Barbie was peering over the edge of the steep bank. 'You're right. And it's miles down, not to mention all those prickly bushes which would tear our legs to bits.' Simone, looking down too, could see the pink of the rose cups amongst the dark green. 'My *églantine* girl,' François had called her...

'I tell you what. Let's get our things and walk along the path till we find an easier place to get in and then we can swim back to the pool. That way we might even manage to stand under the weir as well.'

'Super!' They turned and walked towards the car, but before they reached it Barbie put her hand to her mouth. 'Silly me! I've forgotten the bag!'

'You have *what?*'

'Forgotten the bloody bag. I put it down while we were chatting to François—when I got up on the stool beside that old duffer, remember—and left it there.'

'Mon Dieu!' She had to laugh. 'Well, that's that. No swimming.'

'What do you mean "that's that"? We can surely swim without our bikinis. You said no one ever comes here.'

'There might be fishermen. There are trout...'

'That's just an excuse!' Her eyes were wicked. 'Are you afraid to swim without anything on?'

'No, of course not. But you never know...'

'Don't be chicken. Come on. We'll do what you said, walk along till we find a place. Oh, what fun! Wait till I tell François!'

In the narrow tree and rock-fringed path running by the river, Simone's thoughts were full of him. The little *Causse* blue butterflies were vibrating on the stones, the heat caressed her bare legs. She shouldn't have come here. It was too painful. 'It was François who told me about this place,' she said. 'He brought me here once.'

'Are you gone on him?' She felt the girl's curious eyes on her. 'What's that in French?'

'*Fou.* Of course I'm not.'

'Don't deny it. It's in your eyes.'

'Rubbish! Do all English girls talk such rubbish? If your father is obsessed by caves, you're obsessed by...that sort of thing.'

'Sex? What else is there? Look, there's a gap in the trees. And the bank isn't

117

steep.' She had stopped. 'We could quite easily go in here.' She went nearer and peered through the branches. 'Super! Just the thing.'

'Yes, it looks quite easy.' Simone had followed Barbie. 'Well, why not?' Why was she reluctant?

She knew why when she saw in one swift glance as they undressed, Barbie's voluptuousness compared with her own scrawniness, her small breasts compared with the round ripeness of hers. Ever since she had grown up her greatest wish had been to go into the shop and ask for a *soutien gorge* two sizes larger than she needed.

She rolled up her clothes and tucked them against a tree, then quickly slid into the water. She gasped at its coldness but soon she was revelling in the smooth, silky coolness. Liquid magic, she thought, it smoothes all pain away... 'Come on in,' she called, 'it's lovely!'

In another second the girl was splashing and flailing with her arms beside her. 'Freezing! At first! Isn't it deep? Isn't it marvellous? Isn't it *silky!* And see how easy it is.' They had begun swimming side by side. 'We're *sailing* downstream. The current is carrying us. Oh, it's bliss, utter, utter bliss!'

It was bliss, the sheerest bliss, to swim

downstream, to feel the river taking them along like two paper boats which had been launched from the bank. The sun was hot on Simone's head and on her shoulders. How white they were compared with the golden roundness of Barbie's, but she had been able to sunbathe during the whole of the summer, whereas Madame Claire decreed a sober half-sleeved cotton dress and white apron.

'*C'est bon?*' she said nevertheless, full of joy at the pure sensation of the water against her skin. The girl's ponytail was floating like an eel on her brown back.

'*C'est bon.*' She turned her head, smiling at Simone. 'So easy! I didn't realize you were such a good swimmer.'

'Nor you!' She smiled back. 'It's the current. It won't be so easy going back.'

'Oh, that'll be child's play. We'll take our time. What a scream! If François could only see us! Would he be shocked, do you think?'

'I don't know. What do *you* think?'

She giggled. 'He'd be thrilled. He likes naked women.'

A shaft of pure hatred shot through Simone, making her miss her stroke. Her head went under, she gulped down some water. It had a river taste, green, weedy...I could kill her, she thought, with my bare hands, strangle that lovely neck which

119

François must have kissed...

'I bet he's seen a few of the village girls in the altogether. That Marie-Thérèse, for instance. I should think she would do anything for the son of the owner of the Hotel Delouche, eh?'

'She's going out with Christian Grinaud.'

'The baker? He's a quiet soul. Not like François. He's a sucker for women. I intend to teach him a thing or two while I'm here, some things the village girls have never heard of.' She spat a strand of black hair out of her mouth. 'He's really rather sweet, though. Just asking for it.'

The joy of the cool water on her skin, the feeling of well-being, had gone. She, Simone, was of no account, a stupid girl from a village like Marie-Thérèse. 'I intend to teach him a thing or two while I'm here...' Barbie's words ate into her like acid into bronze.

Didn't the magazines say they were *déchainées*, those English girls? How they had morals, well, like rabbits, or alley cats. Conquests. That was all they were interested in. Tot up the score! 'The Swinging Sixties', one article had been headed. She looked at the golden face of this Barbie, the thick lashes clotted by the river water, the white, white teeth in her partly-open mouth whose lips had a permanent redness, and hated her, deeply and fundamentally, right to the core of her.

They reached the pool. They swam about it, frolicking like puppies, holding on to the protruding branches while they rested, and for a few minutes the bitter resentment left her. If it hadn't been for François she could have got on well with this girl; she was easy to be with, easily amused. They investigated the weir, but when they drew near it the force of the water scared them.

'What do you think, Simone?' Barbie said, her laughing face running with water from the spray. 'Should we risk it?'

'I don't think so.' She was the one in charge. 'I think we should go back now. Unless you want to try to climb out here and walk back for your clothes?'

She was laughing, hanging on to a branch, her head thrown back. 'Can you see us walking along the path without a stitch on? The faces of your mythical fishermen if we met them? They would drop their trout!' The remark struck Simone as ridiculously funny, and she laughed too, uncontrollably. Yes, it was difficult to dislike this girl who had stolen François from her.

'We're going upstream if we swim back.'

'It's nothing compared with Cornwall. You don't know Cornwall, do you? Huge waves. This is *calm* in comparison. Come on, cowardy custard!' She launched herself into the water with a splash.

It might have been calm, but the hidden force of the current was a different matter. Where before they had glided along, now they had to work hard to make any progress at all. And the river seemed to have grown wider. The banks looked very far away suddenly, unattainable...

'Are you all right?' Simone asked after they had swum doggedly for about ten minutes.

'Fine. You just have to work harder, that's all.' She had grown quieter.

They swam steadily for a further ten minutes without speaking, keeping to the centre of the river. When Simone looked at the left bank she thought she saw the same willow she had noticed ten minutes ago. She felt a dragging sensation in her heart as if it were being slowed down too.

'You might...have warned me...about the current.' The girl broke the silence. She sounded sulky, and she was panting. Simone turned to look at her. She was heavier than she was, of course, which would make it more difficult for her. And her breathing was noisy and laboured, her healthy tan had faded to a dingy mud colour. All her vitality had gone. 'I'm not used to swimming in...deserted...places like this.' She was definitely panting. 'I didn't like it when we arrived...' Guilt made Simone speak sharply.

'Don't talk any more than you have to! Take it easily. Whatever you do, don't panic.'

'Who's panicking for God's sake!' She spluttered, suddenly enraged. 'You say the silliest things! I tell you what...I'm going to do. I'm going to...to strike for that bank and have a rest.'

'No, I wouldn't do...' She saw the girl turn and try to swim across the river. The current, which seemed to have become stronger, took her like a leaf and floated her back downstream. Simone saw her fighting against it, saw her go under, reappear, flailing. She heard her high-pitched scream.

To hell with her! The thought filled her mind for a second. To bloody hell with her and everything she stands for! Horror at herself made her gasp and swallow water. She went under the surface into a dark greenness, felt deep and utter panic for a moment herself, then surfaced again. Was she taking leave of her senses?

'You're all right!' She shouted at the pitch of her voice. 'Just let yourself go back to the poo...l! She saw the girl thrashing like a landed fish while she tried to face upstream again. 'No, no!' she shouted louder than ever, treading water, 'I said, don't *do* that! Float!' Was the fool deaf? She turned and swam towards her, finding an added strength from somewhere. It was hard going. She heard Barbie's words as she came nearer, in between her screams.

'I know what I'm doing. It's...your fault, you...stupid...French cow!'

The smouldering hate in Simone's breast burst into flames. She didn't have to do this. She could just let her thrash about, let her sink. Who would know? The bitterness was there again. Just when life had been going so well for her this plump English bitch had come along, upsetting everything, fascinating François, bewitching him, when he had been happy with her. It had been such a good relationship, becoming deeper and more tender each day...

'Help!' It was an ear-splitting scream. 'You've got to help me, Simone!' She saw Barbie's head disappearing under the water. When it came up again the black hair was streaked across her face like seaweed, her eyes were rounded with terror.

It was difficult now, almost impossible. The water was dragging at her legs like a heavy wet blanket. What if the girl didn't come up the next time? She saw the scene clearly, how she would herself manage to get to the bank, clamber out and walk back for her clothes. There would be no need to pretend distress when she got back to the hotel, her hair dripping...she saw Madame Claire's shocked face, François with his head in his hands, his father silent, his shaking head, doubly shaking with sorrow.

That was the second time those mad thoughts had filled her mind, wasting time, wasting energy. Supposing she followed them... Should she ever be able to live with herself afterwards, ever look François in the eye, even speak to him? She knew the answer. Energy rushed through her. She stiffened her body, and with renewed strength sent it forward like an arrow through the water, stretching her arms so far ahead that she felt the strain in the muscles at her waist.

She reached Barbie when she was going under yet again, and was appalled at her appearance. The water seemed to have drained away all her beauty which depended so much on vitality. The face looked smaller, shrunken, her colour was bad, her eyes were glazed with terror. She was shivering and moaning like an animal. 'Hang on to me,' Simone said, putting an arm round her waist. *'Calmez-vous.* There is no danger.' She was using her free arm to steer their progress. 'Don't fight the river. It's too strong for you.'

'We'll never get there!' She shrieked suddenly, frighteningly. Simone imagined that the birds rose from the trees in protest. It grated sickeningly on her nerves.

'If you do that again I'll bang you on the head!' She tried to laugh. 'We're going back to the pool. It's safer. Fix your eyes on the bend. The mill's just coming up. Look, you can see it. We're all right now. Just let yourself go.'

The girl's body was heavy. Her own legs were aching with the weight of it. What if we *both* drown, she thought. That would serve me right for wishing her dead. I would know real panic then... She tried to conquer the lethargy which was creeping over her. 'We don't have...to do a thing. The river...will take us back.' Now there was a suffocating pain in her chest, making it difficult to speak.

'*You* know everything!'

'I'm a French cow, remember?' They glared at each other in hatred. 'Reach forward with your arms. Stretch, go on, stretch! We're nearly there.'

They were coming near the mill pool but again the girl was making no effort to help herself. She was like a stone, pulling Simone deep into the water, under it. A good armful for François, nevertheless. If only my chest didn't hurt so much, I could do more... Her arms ached, her whole body ached. It would be so easy...she closed her eyes.

126

And then, suddenly, it seemed, they were floating quietly in the pool near the weir and the girl had started to move her limbs feebly, taking the strain off Simone.

'Make for the bank!' she shouted, gathering her last ounce of strength, 'I'll guide you, but use your arms! I can't do it all!' With the knowledge that the danger was almost over she had an appalling feeling of futility. Nothing was changed. If she gave up even now, loosened her grip so that they both went under, at least there would be no more pain, no more resentment. Death by drowning could be very pleasant...

Mother would weep but think that it was just another cross she had to bear. They would miss her at the hotel—at least Madame Claire and her husband would—but François' grief would be for his Barbie...she felt something jar against her shoulder, put out a hand and blindly grasped a trailing branch. She clung to it, their two bodies swirling madly for a second before they came to a stop.

'We've made it!' she said. She managed to smile. 'Don't you feel silly now, kicking up all that row?'

'I was scared out of my wits.' Barbie had hold of the branch as well. 'So were you. Admit it.' Her beauty was returning, seeping into her skin, turning it golden again, her eyes were bright.

'Scared? Only for a moment. Scared I was going to let you drown without me. Or with me. I'm going to climb out. Could you hold on to that branch and then I'll haul you up the bank? It's pretty steep.'

'All right. Christ, it was a near shave, though!'

'We're not out yet. Watch where I put my feet, then you can do the same.'

It was easier than she had expected. The difficult part was knowing that the girl was watching her while she clambered. Was she thinking how skinny she was? Well, who cared? She tried to forget her embarrassment while she looked for footholds in the knotted roots, and found the embarrassment speeded her progress. The worst drawback was clumps of nettles which she did her best to avoid. In no time she was on the grass bordering the bank. The warmth of the sun was a benison, helping to subdue her violent shivering. All the same, she had to wait a few minutes before she could kneel and shout down to the girl.

'Now! Are you ready? Push yourself out of the water. Grab that other branch! Good! Put your feet where I did. That's it! You're doing fine. Yes, I know, the nettles sting like mad. Not to worry. It'll heat you up. Only three more steps. Now, give me your hand.' She gave a violent pull and the girl's head appeared beside her own knees as she knelt. She had to grasp her bottom to help her on to the grass. She was slippy, like a wet fish, and she had to make several tries before Barbie threw herself down beside her, panting.

'I...wouldn't like to live through that again.' She blew out her breath.

'Are you all right?' She looked at Barbie, her taut, full breasts, her legs unashamedly apart, her usual position, she thought, a remnant of hatred surfacing.

'Of course I'm all right.' She smiled up at Simone. 'I was only pretending, to give you a fright.' She laughed.

She was an ungracious girl. Although *Maman* was bitter, she had taught Simone to be gracious. 'It costs nothing to be polite,' she always said. It evidently cost too much for this one.

'*Quelle bêtise!*' she was saying now. 'You won't tell them back at the hotel, will you? Especially François. He'd laugh his head off. Let's keep it a secret, shall we, just girls together.'

'If you wish.' It cost nothing to be polite. 'I think we'd better walk back now and get our clothes. A fisherman might...'

'You and your fishermen. OK.' She stood up on her beautiful golden legs with

129

the white band round her middle like a Friesian cow, the golden breasts swelling above the white band. The bush of hair at her crotch was golden, which was strange, considering how dark she was. 'What a scream, wasn't it? Remember, mum's the word.'

Chapter Seven

'The Sinclairs are going,' Madame Claire said to Simone a few days after the episode at the river.

'They're going!' At first she didn't feel anything, only a numbness, and then overwhelming relief, as if she had emerged from darkness into sunlight. 'Why?' For a moment she wondered if it had anything to do with the river, then dismissed it. The English girl didn't seem to bear her any grudge. Once or twice when she had been serving their table Barbie had given her a glancing look of complicity and put her finger to her lips, her eyes dancing.

'*Que voulez-vous?* That's the way with the English. Lords of creation. It's September now. Monsieur has finished his researches. Madame has finished her knitting, Mademoiselle has grown tired of playing around

130

with my François, I hope so.'

'Or maybe it's because of the rain.'

The village had been awash for the last three days, after a spectacular thunderstorm which had kept Simone awake all night. She doubted if she would have slept in any case because of her guilt. Had she really got to the stage that day where she would have let Barbie drown? Become a murderess? She couldn't answer truthfully. It must have been a temporary fit of madness. Thank God she hadn't given into it, however near she had been.

The thunderstorm, as well as clearing the air, cleared her head. She went about her duties in the hotel in a watery prison, while the rain ran down the slope from the hotel and swirled round the War Memorial.

Madame Créon, she of the Parisian Modes, had rolled up her sunblinds and put a few drab brown dresses like withered leaves in her window with a card which said, 'Modes pour L'Automne.' Christian Grinaud had taken in his two tables and chairs and striped umbrellas which he put out each summer in a village imitation of a Salon du Thé. The pétanque players were banished from behind the church by the puddles. They skulked in the café or hung about the bar of the hotel, chatting with François.

Often Barbie was there too, perched on her usual stool. Simone would hear her high-pitched laughter, the deep, throaty, sexy laughter of the men. She stood at the window and watched the children sailing their paper boats down the slope and tried to summon hidden resources of calmness, tried to douse the elation, or at least conceal it—they were going!

'The Sinclairs are going,' she said to François one afternoon. When they were sitting on bar stools having a brief cup of tea. The hotel was quiet.

'I know.' She saw his face in the mirror facing them, pale, the eyes dark-ringed, too little sleep, too much love. Her heart ached for him and yet some devil made her say, 'You'll be sorry to lose Mademoiselle Barbie?'

'What do you mean?' His mouth was a straight line. His eyes met hers in the mirror.

'Just that...she's bright and amusing. I'll miss her too.' She realized she was telling the truth. The girl was likeable. There was no malice in her, just as there was no malice in a straw blown by the wind. 'You have good hair, Simone,' he said, 'thick, with a rich sheen.' His eyes meeting hers in the mirror, were sad, a sadness which had nothing to do with her hair, good or otherwise. It was because the English girl was going away.

They went one morning, with hand-shaking all round and a miserable tip from Monsieur which she would have liked to refuse. Barbie made a swimming movement with her arms, then kissed Simone. 'Mum's the word,' she said, laughing. The day-to-day work of the hotel closed over them as if they had never been there and their rooms lay empty. Everything was the same except that François was pale and silent and went about his work looking neither to left nor to right.

'I thought that would have been the end of the story,' Madame Claire said when they were in their beds one night, 'but he's pining for her.' She was slowly massaging her legs from the knees down to the swollen ankles as if she would massage away the puffiness. 'I thought it would finish when she went away, but she's still here. And he's drinking. Have you noticed? Not eating but drinking.' Simone's heart ached, an additional ache, pity for this man whom she loved but who didn't even see her as they worked together.

He brought trays of glasses into the kitchen. He dried them as she washed. Together they set the tables if none of the black widows were handy at the time (Sophie Rivaud always visited an old school friend in Toulouse in September), they set out the bottles in the bar in front of the mirror with the water lilies painted on it and she tidied the shelves behind the imitation stone front, now finished by the shop-fitters, as well as laying out fresh bowls of olives and nuts for the evening. Madame Claire said in other countries they had what was called 'the cocktail hour', and she hoped to steal a march on Le Roy.

He didn't ask her to go shopping with him in the white Peugeot as he had done before Barbie had arrived. She had the use of the *Deux Chevaux* for anything Madame Claire required in Gramout. She had no need to go to the *chateau d'eau* now. The hurt was too deep for tears. Although Barbie had gone home, she was still there.

She imagined her English perfume still lingered. 'Try some,' she had said to Simone, 'It's Elizabeth Arden.' She saw her sitting on the stool at the bar, heard her laughter, her high English voice, felt again the fierce stab of jealousy when she had found the little heap of confetti under François' striped pillow, conjured up again the image she'd had of her lying spreadeagled on his bed, laughing, inviting, and when that image crucified her, remembered with a kind of joy how she had looked in the river when she had panicked, all her beauty gone.

Madame Claire gave her the whole day off in the middle of October for Madeleine and Marcel's wedding. 'You will want the morning to help your mother, and to get yourself ready to be bridesmaid. Stay overnight if you wish, and take the *Deux Chevaux.*'

'Thank you, Madame,' she said, 'but I'll come back. It may be late, but at least I'll be there to get started on the breakfasts.' The hunters had arrived. Unlike Monsieur Sinclair, they came without their wives. They came with their guns and their rough tweeds and leather boots and with an *idée fixe,* to get up early, have breakfast and get away *pour la chasse.* They liked a good meal in the evening after their pursuit of the wild boar which were hiding deep in the woods as if they sensed their coming.

Once, when Simone had been driving to the Marmot brothers for eggs, a female boar with four babies had run down the field in front of her. The mother stopped, ears pricked, looked at her family as if she were counting them, then lumbered on, squealing softly as she cautioned them to hurry up. 'Be careful of them,' she said under her breath, thinking of those determined men who stalked out of the hotel early every morning.

Madeleine was flustered and fat and

135

tearful. *Maman* had been casting aspersions, determined to spoil the day for them, or perhaps, Simone thought, not even determined, simply unable *not* to spoil the day. 'Your mother says my dress is far too tight,' she whimpered to Simone.

'No, it isn't.' The girl had always been plump. A few extra pounds of baby would hardly be noticeable. 'Leave off the belt and remember to keep your bouquet in front. You'll look lovely.'

'Do you think so, Simone? I'm beginning to wonder if I'll ever be happy here with your mother picking on me all the time. I'm no good in the house. I only like growing things.' *Evidemment,* Simone thought, looking at her swollen stomach.

'She'll calm down when the baby arrives. You'll see. Grandmothers dote on their grandchildren. You and Marcel should make the salon your own room in the evenings. Leave the kitchen to her so that she can relax. She gets tired.'

'That's what Marcel suggested. You're so sensible, Simone. Oh, I wish I had a figure like yours! Your waist is like a lily stalk.'

She was pleased. 'Sometimes I think I'm too thin, but there's so much rushing about at Madame Claire's.'

'I thought you might get hitched up with the son. He's very handsome, isn't he?'

'Yes, very handsome. Let me fix your veil, Madeleine.' She spread the tulle round her shoulders. Madeleine looked remote, virginal almost, her face became Madonna-like. It must be the veil. 'There, you look *super.*' Barbie's word.

'If only Marcel would say that. Sometimes I wonder... *Mon Dieu!* I've burst my tights and they're the only pair I have. *Quel horreur!*'

'They won't be seen. Don't worry.' Poor Madeleine, Simone thought, she would always be in a hassle, never quite sure of herself, and Marcel would give her babies and it was to be hoped he would give her love as well. Sometimes he was too like *Maman.*

The solemn tempo of the wedding changed once the church ceremony was over and the guests had trooped to the barn which Marcel and some of his friends had cleared out for the reception. There were plenty of bales of hay to sit on, and plenty of neighbours to help at the buffet table, which *Maman,* determined not to be accused of niggardliness, had loaded with food from the cellar and additions from the delicatessen where Luc Marmot's mother worked: *confit,* pâté de foie, crayfish, stuffed trout, quails' eggs, roast ham and tongue, and, of course, *gibier* and *gésiers,* flanked with giant · wheels of *tartes des pommes,* bowls of custard, peaches, plums and great foaming jugs of cream. And there were rounds of *Maman's* famous *cabecou*, as well as Camembert and the Causse Bleu which the men liked.

A repast like that needed plenty of drink to wash it down, and there was no shortage of that, the golden Monbazillac and the dark blood red wine of Cahors, as well as the innocuous-looking but potent *eau-de-vie*. It would be dangerous to be spun round in a waltz if one drank too much of *that*.

Around nine o'clock, when everyone had eaten and drunk their fill, the Gramout Five struck up and the guests surged onto the swept floor. It was suddenly a joyful, bucolic wedding, like so many others Simone had attended. The pattern had been set over the years: eat, drink and be merry. Madeleine and Marcel sat on a bale of hay together, bowing and waving to their friends, then when the dance floor was crowded, they gave way to entreaties and joined them. Madeleine was sensitive, of course, of her bulk, although why the secrecy, Simone thought, smiling, when everyone knew she was *enceinte*. Now that Marcel had made an honest woman out of her, she would get plenty of support from the other young farmers' wives, who had probably been in the same position themselves. *Maman* would melt also. What else could she do with a *fait accompli?*

Luc Marmot was suddenly in front of her, tall, smart in his light grey suit with the pink carnation in his button-hole, his fair hair sleek. She had spoken to him from time to time during the day as she had rushed about. He had been Marcel's *garçon d'honneur,* and he had been just as busy. His complexion was pale compared with the outdoor ruddiness of the other young men. 'I've been admiring you all day,' he said. 'You make a lovely bridesmaid.'

'Thank you.' She smiled at him. 'I bought this,' she indicated her green dress, 'in Gramout at the last minute. You know what it's like in hotels.'

'I do.' He understood how the days were filled. 'Would you like to dance?'

'Yes, I would.' She got up and went into his arms. It was a slow waltz. They were able to talk.

'You've got to work in them to realize the work involved.' He looked down from his height. 'Worse than farmers although they'd never believe it.'

She nodded. 'And now when business is slackening off the *chasseurs* arrive.'

'Ah, yes. We don't get much of that in Le Roy. I was visiting my uncles last weekend and I saw a *sanglier* disappearing in the woods there.'

'So did I! Probably in the same place. The one I saw had four babies. Oh, I hope they don't shoot them.'

'You know the *chasseurs*. They'll shoot anything that moves. But we'll hope not. Madame Claire has the adjoining land to my uncles, hasn't she?'

'Yes, she bought it a long time ago with the intention of building on it. Sometimes I think it would be a good idea if François built a house there for his parents and took over the running of the hotel himself. They could do with a rest.'

'That won't be François' decision. Madame Claire is the driving force there. Monsieur is out of the running because of his *Parkinsonisme,* poor man.'

'Yes, that's sad. Sad because he realises his disability. I'm sure he was once very able.'

'In any case,' his tone had changed, 'I hear François' mind has been elsewhere this summer.'

'What do you mean?' She stiffened in his arms.

'The English girl. News gets around. Have I said the wrong thing? They say he's besotted with her.'

'Do they? There are no secrets around here, *bien sur!*' She must calm down. 'Besides they've left now.'

'I shouldn't repeat gossip, I'm sorry.

140

Well, perhaps that's the end of it.'

'If everyone just kept their mouths shut for a change...'

'I don't know why I started on that. I couldn't care less about François Delouche's affairs.'

'Nor could I.' What else were they saying? That she was madly jealous? Had there in fact been a fisherman hidden in the bushes on the river bank who had seen everything that afternoon, how she had let Barbie struggle for quite some time before she went to her aid, and was she going to have to live for ever with this guilt? He must have sensed her disquiet.

'It's funny, Simone, or maybe you'll think *I'm* funny, but I seem to say the wrong thing when I'm with you. I felt the same, that time we met in Gramout. You seemed to...' he laughed, '...cut me off. Or perhaps you just make me nervous.' She looked up and saw his grey, honest eyes. It came as a surprise that he cared about the impression he made on her.

'Nervous!' She laughed. 'But we've known each other for ages!'

'That's just it. You were a great kid. We always had fun when I came to the farm to see Marcel, but lately you've changed. You've become...unapproachable.'

'Maybe it's you who has changed.'

'There's that. Certainly I no longer think

of you as Marcel's kid sister.'

'Everybody has to grow up,' she said. 'And change. And there's my job. I'm pretty busy all day. Perhaps that makes me a bit short-tempered. Well, you know what it's like...' It was only partly true, but his voice was sympathetic.

'It's too hard for a young girl like you. Come and work in Le Roy. You'll have stricter hours of duty, more time off.' He had always been kind, she remembered. Once he had said to Marcel, 'Don't send the kid away. She's all right.' And *Maman* had always liked him coming about the farm which was an accolade in itself. 'I've been made Maître D' now,' he was saying. 'I'm responsible for engaging the staff.'

'You deserve it, Luc. I'll think about it.' But she knew she wouldn't.

'I'm off for a week. Could I pick you up some evening and we could go and eat somewhere? Perhaps to Cahors? We could try the Chateau Mercuès. I know my opposite number there.'

She was impressed. Not even Barbie Sinclair had been to the Chateau Mercuès, impressed but uninterested. It was François she wanted, no one else. 'It's difficult getting off, but I could ring you. Thanks all the same.' She shook her head. 'Evenings are out of the question. There is the serving to do.'

'Simone.' His voice made her look up at him. 'You're putting me off, aren't you?'

'No, it isn't that. I've told you, I'm busy.'

'No one is indispensable. You should know that. Madame Claire managed before you came. But I shan't press you or you'll like me even less than you appear to do.' He smiled without mirth. 'I don't want to seem like an elderly uncle...'

'I've always liked you, but...'

'Let's drop the subject, shall we?' He swung her round. He danced well. She had never even danced with François, far less anything else.

She was disgusted with herself. Life was for living and she was in danger of ruining hers. All she *was* doing was working round the clock and falling into bed each night, exhausted, in the hope that she would sleep.

But there were the nights when over-tiredness kept her awake, when she thought she would die of love of François. She would think longingly of the days before Barbie had arrived, those early morning jaunts with him to Christian Grinaud's bakery, and how at breakfast she had sat and feasted her eyes on that surprising gold wave above his brow, surprising since his hair was so much darker at the back, the smooth brown tint of his skin, his strong fingers as he hacked off a piece of *saucisson* to eat with his newly-baked bread—she could even imagine its hot yeasty smell. Could that time ever come back? Could he forget Barbie? Perhaps if she were patient.

'How are your uncles?' she asked, feeling that the silence had gone on too long.

'Well, you know what they're like.' His face was clear of any resentment. 'Uncle René's pretty well obsessed by that fencing of his. He spends most of the day walking round their land to inspect it.'

'Obsession is poisonous,' she said.

'That's true.' She turned away from his eyes. 'Will you make me a promise, Simone?'

'It depends what it is.' She tried for lightness.

'If you should need anyone to confide in, or want just to speak to me, will you telephone me at Le Roy?'

'What makes you think I will need anyone to confide in?' She forced herself to look at him.

'Instinct. Besides I've known you for a long time. I'll be a stand-in for Marcel. He's going to be very busy for the next few months.' He grinned at her. 'Promise?'

'*D'accord,*' she said, 'Maître D'.'

'And if you want a job at Le Roy...' He pretended to dodge back. 'Don't hit me.'

'As if I would, big brother.' She clowned a little, but there was a thread of comfort in what he had said, if she should ever need his help.

The music changed abruptly to a quick tempo and he whirled her so fast that she felt eighteen again and pretty in her green bridesmaid's dress. And for a time she didn't think of François.

Chapter Eight

Simone drove back to the hotel late that night feeling in a happier frame of mind. The wedding had gone off well. *Maman* had seemed comparatively happy, and had thanked her for her help. 'You are a good girl, Simone. Always have been. I couldn't have done without you. Now take a lesson from Marcel and don't get into trouble yourself. One is quite enough.'

'Yes, *Maman*,' she had said dutifully.

'Do you have to go back to the hotel at this late hour?' she had asked.

'It is necessary. Madame Claire can't manage the breakfasts without me.'

'It strikes me she expects too much of a young girl like you. If you were in Le Roy you would have sensible hours, an easier time. I saw you dancing with Luc Marmot. You don't look out for yourself. Why didn't you ask him if he could get you in there?' It was wiser not to tell her that he had offered her a job.

'I will if it gets too much for me at Madame Claire's, I promise.' A hug without a homily would have been better.

It was restful driving through the quiet country roads with the trees on either side and the moon huge in the sky. Every turn was familiar to her now, where there was a gap in the trees and one glimpsed the quiet fields, the ruined barn on the bend, the pretty *gentilhommière* with the *pigeonier,* the farm where the grandmother sat knitting while she guarded the long-legged sheep all day long.

My land, she thought. All I've ever wanted was to live and die here with someone I love, with François. The moon swung out from behind the trees, huge enough to be unreal. A baby rabbit, sitting petrified in the glare of her head-lights alerted her, and she slowed down and waited until it had scampered away to safety in the ditch.

Poor *sangliers,* she thought, cowering in the thickets, thinking of tomorrow's onslaught. We are all victims. Those are serious thoughts for an eighteen-year-old, she told herself, sighing. There was nothing like unrequited love to age one, there was a certain sad satisfaction in it...

If she was sensible enough to recognize that, she should leave the Hotel Delouche. But she knew she wouldn't.

The fact that Madame Claire depended on her was more than an excuse. She had grown fond of her. But her real reason for staying on, she admitted to herself, was her obsession for François. Any sensible girl would know when to stop bashing her head against a brick wall and would take the opportunity to move on to Le Roy and away from a man who didn't even see her most of the time.

Luc had seen through her subterfuge when she had refused his invitation to go to the Chateau Mercués with him. But he was also kind. 'I'll be a stand-in for Marcel,' he had said. The thought of the grey honest eyes bent on her was comforting, no more.

She let herself quietly into the hotel, walking through the dark *salle-à-manger*, through the kitchen with its shining new stove and into the small bedroom which she still shared with Madame Claire. When the hunters went she could go upstairs, Madame had promised. She had looked at her watch before she locked the car. One-thirty. Everyone would be asleep, or was François, lying awake thinking of

Mademoiselle Barbie? François, always François...

She began undressing without putting on the light. She had changed out of her bridesmaid's dress and left it in her room at the farm. There were only her jeans and a tee shirt to slip off, to wriggle out of her pants, to ease off her sandals. Madame Claire's voice broke the silence.

'Put on the light, Simone. I'm not asleep.'

'Oh, have I wakened you?' She was apologetic.

'No. Put it on.'

The light was startling in its brightness. It illuminated Madame Claire's face. She was generally pale, but tonight she looked haggard. Her dark eyes were smudged underneath, as if she had been crying, which was atypical, to say the least.

'Aren't you feeling well, Madame?' she asked her. 'You stay in bed tomorrow morning and rest. I don't feel a bit tired...' She waved a hand, stopping her.

'It was a good wedding?'

'Yes, everything went well. Madeleine looked lovely, and they gave them a good send-off. Is it your legs?'

'No, it's my heart.' She put her hand on her chest with an almost comical gesture, but there was no doubt about it, she had been weeping. Her eyelids were swollen.

148

'A letter came this afternoon to François. From England.' Now it was *her* heart. A fearful premonition. She sat down on the edge of the bed, preparing herself.

'Yes?' The word didn't make any sound. 'Yes?' she said again.

'He kept away from me. I could see there was something wrong. His face was like a winter moon behind the bar in its whiteness. He avoided my eyes. When the *chasseurs* had gone to bed—you know how early they go off, bloodthirsty...' she said a rude word, surprising Simone, 'I sat down at a table and called, "François!" Like that. Loudly. "François, come here at once!" ' Why was she taking so long?

'Yes?' she said again.

'He was washing glasses. He came reluctantly. I've seen the same look on his face as a small boy when he had been stealing apples from Sophie Rivaud's orchard, when his father had to give him a good hiding. Jean-Paul hated doing that but I insisted. Discipline is everything, I said. But this was far worse than stealing apples...'

'The letter was from...Mademoiselle Barbie?'

'No, not from her. From her father. She is pregnant. By François.'

'No.' Her world tumbled about her. Bitter blackness.

'Yes. Well, of course, I wasn't born yesterday. I suspected they were having an affair, or something, but I told myself not to be suspicious. My François wouldn't...' She gave a short laugh. 'Why should I think that? Well, he had. God knows how often.'

'Did you see the letter?' There was ice in her heart.

'Yes, I made him show it to me, translate it. She taught him English as well.' Again the short, bitter laugh. 'I think he left out the worst bits but even so, such abuse! "How could you be so stupid?" I asked him. I wasn't storming at him—that was the odd thing—I was quite quiet. When I'm really hurt that's how I am. "I loved her," he said. "I want to marry Barbie." '

'Monsieur Sinclair was demanding that?'

'It was difficult to tell amongst the abuse. The only thing that was clear was that he wanted her out of the house before the neighbours talked...'

'Mon Dieu! What about the mother?' She found her voice.

'I asked him that but he said she didn't count.'

'I see.' Simone got slowly into bed like an invalid and lay flat on it, her hands behind her head. That way she didn't have to meet Madame Claire's eyes. It wasn't over after all. It was only beginning. She moved her legs and they were like lead, like her heart. This deadness was worse than any pain which had gone before. 'So there will be a wedding?' she said, looking at the cracked ceiling. Madame hadn't thought to include her own room in the *réparations*.

'Yes, he wrote tonight and went out and posted it in the main PTT in Gramout. He also telephoned to their house but I saw him put down the receiver quickly as if it was burning his ear.'

'Monsieur?'

'Probably. You know I never liked the situation, Simone—she wasn't for him—but I must admit my sympathies are with the girl having a father like that.'

'Yes.' Her heart was swollen, aching. If only she could massage the pain away as Madame tried to do with her poor feet. It was true what she had said when the Sinclairs went back to England—Barbie had never really left.

'You don't say much, Simone.'

'What is there to say? She'll accept François, and we'll have the wedding here. All the villagers will come just as they did in our village today. It is a pattern.' She summoned up her courage and turned towards her. 'Tonight I was offered a job in Le Roy, by Luc Marmot. He is Maître D' there now. Once the wedding is over, I think I'll take it.' There was no reply. She repeated. 'I think I'll take it, Madame.'

She sighed. Her huge breasts rose and fell. 'I don't blame you. I'll miss you, Simone. You've been like a daughter to me. But I understand.' Her voice was almost gentle. 'If I'd had a daughter I should have liked her to be like you. But it was a little boy with a golden *mèche*, golden as the Oriole...' her voice faded. She looked away.

'Still, you were happy, you and Monsieur.'

'Yes, oh, yes. He has a large heart, and a forgiving one.' Why did they only have one child, Simone wondered.

'Does he know about...Mademoiselle Barbie?'

'I told him, naturally. He is my husband. He nodded, amongst all his other nods, poor soul. He is quiet, always quiet. "So," he said. That was all.'

Simone's heart filled. She found herself suddenly out of bed and bending over Madame Claire, putting her arms round her. 'I'm so sorry. I shan't rush away. I'll give you plenty of time to find someone else. It'll all turn out all right, you'll see. They'll be happy, and it will be just like Madeleine and Marcel, a nine days' wonder.'

'You have a generous spirit, Simone. Well, we'll see.' She patted her shoulder.

152

'Get back to bed and get your sleep. Breakfast time will be here before we know it.'

She woke at five o'clock, surprised she had slept at all. Fatigue had won over her misery.

A week later François drove to the station in Gramout and returned with Barbie. She was a changed girl. Simone was setting the tables when they came through the curtained door.

'There's Simone,' François said. She went forward to greet her.

'*Bonjour,* Barbie.' They kissed. '*Ca va bien?*'

'*Très bien, merci.*' She didn't look it. Her skin was a dirty white where the rose-brown had faded, her hair hung limp, and she wore an unbecoming skirt and jumper, both far too tight.

'Can I get you anything? You must be tired.' François had dashed to the bar where some men were calling for him.

'Tea would be fine,' she said, sitting down at a table. 'Where's the old bag?'

'Old bag?'

'His mother. François' mother.'

'Oh. She had to go to the Mairie. She'll be back soon.' Madame Claire had told Simone that she must ask the mayor how one set about the arrangements to have an

153

English girl marry in the village. François was too lax, always had to be pushed.

'Sit down,' Barbie said when Simone brought the tea. 'Get another cup and join me.'

'I shouldn't...'

'Don't be stupid. Aren't we friends? Remember that day at the river? What fun it was! God,' she said, looking around, 'I never thought I'd be back in *this* dump!'

'It can be very pleasant here in autumn. It's cooler for walking although you have to watch where you go because of the *chasseurs.*'

'Don't pretend you don't know why I've come back. They must have told you. His mother thinks the world of you.' She stirred her tea, lifted the cup and took a sip. 'Ah, that's good. I'm pregnant. Isn't it the bloody end?'

'Yes, I know.' She bent her head.

'I wouldn't have come but my father practically threw me out. Mother didn't say a word. She only ever had one child, my dead brother. Those jerseys she eternally knits are for him, although she says they are for the orphans. They're going to tell our friends that I have chosen to stay indefinitely in France, François can go ahead and arrange the wedding but they won't attend. Parents! You can have them! So here I am, *me voici,* in the Hotel

154

Delouche. Isn't life a scream?' Her voice was shrill.

'It'll turn out all right, Mademoiselle. You'll see.'

'I'm Barbie, remember?' Her smile was wistful.

'Barbie,' Simone said. She wondered how she could comfort this girl. 'I've just been at my brother's wedding. His fiancée was *enceinte*. I told you, remember? Once you're married people forget and the baby is welcomed by everyone. Delouche is a name respected in the village. And you'll make François happy.' It cost her a lot to say that.

'Look at him. Does he look happy?' They turned towards the bar. François was busy serving drinks. He had a glass by his side which he raised to his lips from time to time. He was pale, and for the first time she noticed how the clean line of his chin was smudged, heavy. He was not a picture of a happy man.

'*Bonjour*, Mademoiselle Barbie.' It was Madame Claire, puffing a little in her good black dress with the black straw hat which she wore for any visits to officialdom. 'Welcome to Hotel Delouche,' she said grandly, kissing the girl on both cheeks. 'You had a good journey?'

'*Pas mal.*'

'I'll go and get another cup,' Simone

said, getting up quickly.

'*Merci*, Simone. I could do with it.'

When she returned Madame waved her back to her seat. Her face was grey. 'I want you to listen to this, Simone. I can't believe my ears.'

'I'd rather...'

'Sit down, please! Now, say again what you said, Mademoiselle.'

The girl was sullen. 'Why bring Simone into it?'

'She is practically one of the family. I depend on her.'

'I'm well aware of that. All right, I'll say it again, but don't attempt to change my mind, nor bully me the way you bully François. I've told him. He knows. I'll stay here because I have nowhere else to go, but I'm not marrying your son. I told him in the car.' No wonder he's pale, Simone thought.

'I've fixed it in the Mairie,' Madame Claire said, 'the date and everything. You'll change your mind. You can have two rooms upstairs which is more than I ever gave myself, and the flat roof over the outhouses will be a splendid place for the baby to play in. We'll have railings put round it, wrought-iron ones. And later on we can arrange things, perhaps build you a house on our land. Did I tell you I owned land? I have great hopes for this hotel. François and I are building it up. One day it will have three stars in the Michelin, you'll see. Anyone who is married to François Delouche should be proud...'

'I'm not marrying him,' Barbie said. 'Could you help me up with my cases, Simone? I see François is still busy,' she looked over at him, 'knocking them back.'

'Of course.' She got up. 'Don't carry anything. I can manage.' She saw Madame Claire's face and could have wished herself anywhere but standing between the two of them. 'I'll be back in a few minutes,' she said.

Going up the stairs towards François' room Barbie began to giggle. 'Did you see her face? She can't believe that anyone would turn down her precious son. But I don't want to be married and live here for the rest of my life. I don't want this baby, come to that, but that's the luck of the draw. What do you say, Simone?'

'Parents...I don't know.' She was too confused. 'It was a blow, a terrible blow for Madame. I'll go down.'

When she went into the kitchen Monsieur was sitting at the table chopping a pile of *haricots verts*. 'Have you heard the latest, Simone?' he said.

'You mean about Mademoiselle Barbie and François?'

'What else?' His hand shook violently as he chopped. He would cut off his thumb one day.

'It'll turn out all right.' It was all she could think of to say.

'Like mother, like son, eh?' She looked at his bent head, the scalp showing through the thin hair. He must be rambling.

She was glad of the immediacy of all the tasks which had to be done before dinner. Madame had appeared with her large white apron over her black dress, a white toque on her head which she had won in a cookery competition many years ago. Her eyes were reddened but she held her head high. *'Allons-y,'* she said, brandishing a wooden spoon as she went towards the stove, 'There are hungry hunters waiting.' There would be no tears in public. The Hotel Delouche came first.

Chapter Nine

Simone watched daily from the sidelines as François tried to persuade Barbie to change her mind. The girl sat on a bar stool while he harangued her if there were no customers around, pleaded with her, cajoled her. Sometimes she would hear Barbie's clear English voice, *'Non, non, François! Ça suffit!'*

Once she saw him take her by the arm when she was sitting reading some of the English magazines she bought in the *Maison de la Presse,* and pull her through the curtained door to where his white Peugeot stood at the foot of the steps. When they returned an hour or two later she went running up to their room, her face red and tearful. François, equally silent, went behind the bar, poured himself a glass of wine and stared into the room unseeingly, his face set and miserable.

Another time, when Simone was having a bath late at night, she heard them arguing in their room. As she passed their door in her towelling robe François came rushing out, not seeing her, and went running downstairs. 'Tell the old she-devil it's final, positively final!' She heard Barbie's choked voice. The loud sobs which followed made her put her hand out to the doorknob, then withdraw it. It was not her affair. A moment later she heard the noise of François' car starting up in the quiet square and roar out of the village.

It went on for a fortnight, rows, scenes, weeping. Fortunately the hunters were so absorbed in the chase that they didn't seem to notice. It was difficult to recognize Barbie in the sullen girl with the slack figure and dull eyes.

'She must be stupid to be so stubborn,' Madame Claire said, lifting her eyes to the ceiling. 'Who in God's name would want to turn down my François when she is carrying his child?'

It became a parrot cry. 'You can't put me out. I'm here because of François, because I have nowhere else to go. I'll even help in the hotel if I have to, but I'm not marrying him! *C'est tout!*'

'God forbid!' Madame had said, referring to the thought of Barbie helping in the hotel.

They tried reason. No longer was the affair a secret. Simone heard it all.

'But Barbie I *love* you,' she heard François say one quiet afternoon when Barbie was sitting on her usual perch at the bar. 'And there's my standing in the village to think of. I can't have you staying here, unmarried and pregnant, and everybody laughing at me.'

'You should have thought about that before you implored me to come to your room every night!' She no longer cared who overheard.

François looked across at Simone where she was clearing the tables, raised his shoulders at her as if she were an accomplice. 'The English! Impossible to understand them!'

Everyone grew tired of it once the novelty had worn off. Madame Claire said sadly to Simone, 'She's wrong for him, there's no doubt about it, wrong in every way. But I know true love when I see it. My poor François! We'll have to leave her alone...'

With the pressure off, Barbie began to bloom again, to take little walks in the village with her thickening waist and long swinging hair, smiling and chatting to people in the shops. Madame was the first one to accept defeat. 'That's it, François. If she doesn't want to marry you, she doesn't want to. We must accept the tribulations which the good Lord sends. I am pleased at least she has stopped crying. It was spoiling her looks.'

'But *Maman*...' This was round the supper table. Barbie had decided to have dinner in bed and Simone had carried it up to her. The girl had caught her hand as she put down the tray.

'You're on my side, aren't you, Simone?' Her raised face was lovable, like a child's.

Simone had bitten her lip. 'I'm sitting in the middle, Barbie, but, yes, I agree that no one should be forced to do something they don't want to.' I am in the same boat, she thought. I'm trying to force myself to go to Le Roy but it's not what *I* want...

'It is necessary to be diplomatic,' Madame was saying. 'Though how I can expect that from you, God only knows, after the fool you have made of yourself. Let her settle down. She is *enceinte*. She should not be harassed when she is carrying a baby.'

The hunters went away and the hotel settled down for the winter. It became quite cosy with Madame Claire, Monsieur, Simone, Barbie and François, a cosy little family. Simone, when Luc telephoned her, decided she had no real reason to refuse his invitation, and allowed herself—she didn't take much persuasion—to be taken for dinner at the Chateau Mercuès.

She was curious to see how it compared with the Hotel Delouche. Of course there was no comparison. It ran on oiled wheels, the Orient Express compared with *un correspondance*. The food was opulent and unsurprising. Life would be dull in such a place. She preferred Madame's flights of culinary fancy, she preferred the fake stone of the Delouche bar because François was behind it. But she had to admit that Luc was at home in the Chateau Mercuès with his quiet good looks and suavity.

He kissed her in his car when they were parked outside L'Hôtel Delouche, and told her he intended to increase the staff at Christmas. People drove from Paris to spend it in Le Roy because they liked the ambience of a hotel in *un pays sauvage,* with its regional cuisine, especially wild boar.

'Will you come then?' he asked her. She said she would and he kissed her again. He was gentle and she would have liked him to have been *déchainé,* and instead of smooth fair hair to have had a gleaming *mèche.* And to have had some of François' brashness and unpredictability.

In November Monsieur caught a cold which developed into pneumonia, and when he was removed to the hospital at Gramout Madame was distraught. 'I don't give him enough attention,' she wept, 'with all this upset with François and the English girl'—she still found it difficult to call her 'Barbie'—'I have ignored him. One forgets his mind isn't damaged, only his nervous reflexes.'

Simone drove her every day to the hospital and sat in the waiting room while she was at his bedside. She was surprised at the extent of Madame's distress. He was very ill, certainly, but no one had said he was going to die. 'If he gets better I'll be different. I have wronged him enough.' It was an odd thing to say.

Monsieur was allowed home in the

middle of December, shaking more than ever, thinner than ever, but cured of his pneumonia. It was impossible for Simone to desert them. She was doing most of the cooking, and had even learned a few of Madame's less farouche touches. She could break eggs into the soup with the necessary abandon, and she made special dishes for Barbie who was feeling her pregnancy now and was querulous. She was obliged to telephone Luc and say she could not come to work at Le Roy at Christmas after all, because of Monsieur's illness.

On Christmas day Madeleine produced twins and Simone began to feel she was living in the local hospital. Marcel was a gibbering wreck while they waited. The transformation when the nurse put the two tiny infants into his arms was miraculous. 'Isn't she wonderful, my Madeleine?' he said, with the tears running down his face. Simone wondered if *Maman* would be equally transported.

Barbie began to stay in her bed quite a lot as she became heavier. The baby wasn't due until the end of March, but already her ankles were swollen and she had put on a lot of weight. François, too, strangely enough, became bloated, as if he were *enceinte* as well, but Simone still couldn't look at him without love overwhelming her.

Everything had gone wrong since the *Méchoui,* she thought, and her discovery of the tiny heap of confetti under François' pillow. That had been the turning point. Once, after the Christmas festivities were over and she was sweeping the *salle-à-manger* after a party, on impulse she took some of the confetti from the shovel and put it in an empty matchbox. She tucked it behind the flour jar on the shelf. It would be there as a memory, along with her dreams of ever going to the *Méchoui* with François.

She felt a fearful drop in her spirits in the dark days of January and February when they closed the shutters at four o'clock in the afternoon and closed out the world. It was as if they were hibernating with the animals, François behind his bar with the newspapers, a glass at his side, Madame and Monsieur huddled at the kitchen stove, Barbie often in bed.

She knew now what she should do. She should leave and go to work in Le Roy where the Gramout people dropped in for evening drinks, ate in the dining-room with its soft carpets and swagged curtains, danced each Saturday at the dinner dances. She could only blame herself if she remained here, a girl of nineteen now, incarcerated with two unhappy people and an old man and his wife who had aged years in the last few months.

At the beginning of March François' former energy seemed to be born again, like a woman preparing for her *accouchement*. He had the joiners in to make banquettes, had new carpets laid, and central heating installed. It was difficult to decide whether it was in an effort to forget his worries, or to impress Barbie so that she should change her mind and marry him before the baby came.

Once when he and Simone were in the kitchen alone he became talkative. She was at the sink, he was lounging against the dresser with a glass in his hand. His speech, she thought, was slightly slurred. 'You've been a tower of strength to us, Simone, I'll say that, a tower of strength.' Strangely enough she thought of the tall lonely water tower where she had wept out her grief. 'What makes a young girl like you stay with us, I wonder? We aren't fit company.'

'I'll be leaving soon,' she said. 'Your father seems all right and the baby will soon be here. There's a job waiting for me at Le Roy.'

'As well as Luc Marmot?' There was bitterness in his voice. 'God knows, I wouldn't blame you for going. He's got everything, and so have you. All the life seems to have gone out of *Maman,* all the

166

fun out of Barbie.' He took a gulp from his glass. 'When I think of that summer we had...' She turned and saw his dreaming face, a Pucci angel with his gilded forelock, except that his face was too worn for an angel.

'*Un été des églantines,*' she said, feeling the bitterness as freshly as ever. It had been transient, like the *Causse* butterflies. One couldn't go back, and in any case it had meant nothing to him. Not once Barbie had appeared.

'I'll never forget it, nor that *Méchoui.*' He drank deeply from his glass. 'And the confetti. Confetti everywhere.' He laughed, spluttering, 'Do you know what Barbie called it when it got into her hair? Coloured nits!' He laughed again, then suddenly sobered, almost as if he hadn't been drinking. 'She enchanted me. Always will. But I'll tell you this, Simone. You are the only one I could ever tell.' His eyes were sunken. 'She can't bear the sight of me now.'

'No, François. All women are like that when there's a baby coming...'

'I'm right. I know the way she looks at me. How she turns from me...'

The ache in her heart was overwhelming. It made her want to take him in her arms, to say, 'I've always loved you, always will...' But what good was that? It was

Barbie he wanted, not her.

'Madeleine couldn't put up with herself at all,' she said. 'But just wait. You'll both be so happy!' She went on talking, mindlessly, anything to subdue the ache. 'You should see Marcel! He *dotes* on the twins. But the surprise is my mother! She is a changed woman. Her bitterness about my father's death has gone, she talks nonsense talk to Geneviève and Gervase. I scarcely recognize her. Your mother will be the same.'

'Do you think so?' He looked dazed. And she saw he had emptied his glass while she had been speaking.

'Of course I do!' She had to go on. 'I wouldn't be surprised if Barbie changes her mind and will want to give the baby your name...' He stopped her, waving his hand.

'You're...an oracle, Simone.' She saw his eyes were glazed, his cheeks flushed. 'A bloody oracle. I should have stuck with you...oh, yes, you were everything any sensible man would want. But I'm... not...sensible. Not sensible.' His face seemed to collapse. 'But you understand. You're the wise little owl. I can't help myself. Barbie...' he shook his head, 'Barbie is in my blood.' He seemed to fall towards her. She was in his arms, held closely against him.

'François!' She struggled, taken by

surprise. His breath reeked of wine.

'You don't mind, Simone?' His voice was in her ear. 'It's...for comfort only. Old friends. Barbie...won't let me near her...' She felt his body now, hard and thrusting through her dress and a fierce thrill leapt through hers followed by a searing self-disgust. She wrenched herself away from him.

'God, François, what a nerve you have! Don't come crawling to me after all that's happened. You're drunk!' She was beside herself with frustration and anger.

He released her, staggered to the kitchen table and sat down, his head in his hands. 'What was I thinking of?' He moved his head between his hands. 'Mad, mad! I must have gone out of my mind for a second.'

'You're drunk! You're disgusting!'

He looked up at her, and she saw the tears in his eyes. 'Could you forget it, please? I'm...ashamed.'

'I'll try.' Her body was like ice where it had been fire a moment ago. She took a deep breath, made herself speak calmly. 'I'd get up to bed if I were you. You'll feel better in the morning.' She watched him go unsteadily out of the kitchen, feeling as if she had died inside. His back view was pitiful.

They had put Monsieur into one of the

bedrooms upstairs, and Madame ascended them painfully each evening to be beside him, as if it were the stony road to the Cross, Simone thought, watching her. Her offer to help had been spurned. At least it gave her the little room to herself now, room to weep. She thought she had wept her last tears at the *chateau d'eau*. Now they were as bitter as gall. She wept for the love which refused to die, and for the sadness of life.

Barbie's baby arrived at the end of March, a boy, and with the spring Monsieur felt well enough to be out and about again, at least as far as the yard. When Simone hung out the bed linen there were now two occupants, little Bernard in his baby carriage, and Jean-Paul in his chair very close to the baby.

He adored the child. So did *Maman*, and François. The dark winter days were forgotten, the gloom and despondency which had pervaded the hotel were banished, they were transported with delight and love. The only one who was unenthusiastic was Barbie, slim again, hair glossily black, full of a sparkling, febrile kind of gaiety.

She was openly loving with François, sitting flirting with him and the men who came into the bar, and she began her walks about the village again, sometimes pushing the baby carriage, but not often. She was a cuckoo mother, Simone thought. Now, having produced the baby, she didn't mind who took care of it. Madame took her place, and Simone, and Sophie Rivaud, Marie Tenier, and her niece, Leonie, who came each day to help, and to wash the diapers. Bernard cooed and gurgled indiscriminately, but his grin seemed to be widest for his grandfather.

Guests were beginning to trickle back again. Soon the hotel would be busy, and Simone realized that she would find it difficult to leave if she waited much longer. She hadn't seen Luc recently. Perhaps he would no longer want her at Le Roy. On a day in early April, when she was sitting on the porch at home plucking a fowl—it was her afternoon off—she looked up and saw him getting out of his car in the farm yard.

'Here's Luc,' she said to her mother who was bending over the cot with the two infants.

He came up the steps. 'What a nice domestic scene! *Bonjour*, Madame.' He kissed Simone's mother, then Simone. 'A typical little farmer's wife as well as all the rest?' His smile was warm. He didn't seem to bear her any grudge.

'Simone has always been good at

171

preparing fowls for the pot,' her mother said. 'What do you think of my two little darlings, Luc?' Simone had still not grown accustomed to her new softness of expression.

'I go from one doting grandmother to another,' Simone said, smiling at him. 'Something happens to them when a new baby arrives.'

'And it's doubled here.' He had got up to look at the two infants, packed like apples in a box. *Parfait.* I'm no expert, Madame, but one looks like Madeleine and the other like Marcel.'

'That's what I think!' She beamed on him.

He went back and sat down with the air of a man who had said the right thing. 'I came to see Marcel about a business proposition actually.'

'He's gone to Gramout,' Simone said.

'Quel dommage! I was hearing Madeleine has induced him to grow vegetables?'

'Yes, half an acre of them on the high field.' Madame Bouvier nodded. 'It's south facing up there and sheltered by the wood. It's a strange thing, you know. She is absolutely no good in the house, that girl, but she has green fingers. She's done wonders with my little plot behind the house. They've both gone to buy seeds today.'

'Do you think they would consider supplying Le Roy?'

'They wouldn't turn it down.'

'We have more and more vegetarians as guests now, and we want to give them plenty of variety. If he could deliver fresh vegetables to us each morning, it would be splendid. We only have the market ones twice a week. In Paris where I trained it was a joy going out early each morning with the chef to Les Halles.'

'Did you like Paris?' Simone asked.

'Yes. I want to go back there some time. I used to think I might settle down here, but now I'm not so sure.' He gave her a straight glance, and, confused, she bent her head to the chicken, her usually expert fingers fumbling with the string she was looping round its legs.

'Tobacco sales are falling slowly,' she said. 'I think Madeleine was very wise to think of an alternative, don't you, *Maman?*'

'Yes, I give you that. My daughter-in-law has proved herself to be quite an asset.' Simone's eyes met Luc's and she saw the smile in them. He had a sense of humour.

'Trust Marcel to choose well,' she said, laughing.

They laughed at each other when Madame Bouvier had excused herself and gone to prepare the meal. 'It's marvellous what a baby will do,' he said, 'or in this case, two.'

'It's the same at the hotel. Barbie's the only one who is unaffected.'

'The English girl? Well, her worries are over now.'

'What do you mean?'

'She's assured a home for the child. Now she is free.'

'Free for what?'

'To do what she wants.'

'François still hopes she'll marry him.' She looked at him, made curious by his remark.

'She's not been brought up in a little French village. I've lived in Paris. Things are different elsewhere. People are more liberal in their thinking, women want their own lives, don't wish to be pale shadows of men. Mademoiselle Sinclair comes from England. It's the same there. I've read of it, flower power, they call it, protests against the Bomb...' he broke off. 'I seem to have strayed away from the point.'

'It's interesting. And you seem to have definite views of Barbie.'

'Sorry. It isn't my affair. You call her Barbie?'

'Why not?'

'You must be one of the new women.' He grinned at her. 'No, I haven't. I only saw her once, but I've seen many like her. Why should one mistake close all doors for her? That could be what she is thinking. It depends how much she loves François.'

'Wouldn't she marry him then?' She shrugged. 'All I know is that he loves *her*. Nothing will change that.'

He was sitting opposite her, and he bent forward and took her hands. 'Let's leave the subject of Mademoiselle Barbie and the Delouches, Simone.' His eyes were serious, full of meaning. 'You can't change things. That's how François is.' She turned away, feeling the old ache start up again. 'He'll cling to her to the end whatever she does to him. I know, believe me, I know.' She didn't want to meet his eyes. 'She's captured him, it's a thing of the spirit, not only of the body.' She thought of the evening in the kitchen when he would have made love to her, as second-best, and felt ashamed that she had been stirred. But wasn't it true of her also? That she would never grow out of her love for François?

'You're right,' she said, 'you can't change things.' The ache had spread throughout her body, a profound, unalterable sadness.

'But you can accept. You can grow out of acceptance into maturity.' He shook her hands gently. 'Look at me, Simone.

I won't talk any more like a guru.' When she did he was smiling. I never noticed before that he had a sweet smile, she thought. 'You know the job is waiting for you at Le Roy. I would like to offer you more, but I know what you would say.'

'What would I say?' she said, smiling at him.

'All right. I'll test you. Marry me.' He was calm.

'Marry you?' Of course she had known but had refused to face it. 'But you're my big brother!' She spoke lightly, 'You said it yourself.'

'Big brothers can love. I love you. I have ever since you were a little girl playing with chickens instead of trussing them...' He turned her hands, palms upwards, in his.

'I should have washed them...' She tried to withdraw them.

'Never mind your hands.' His clasp was firm. 'Think about what I've said, will you? It's time for you to think hard. My love, I can assure you, is constant.' She looked into his eyes and saw the constancy.

'I'm sorry, Luc...' She couldn't speak. He waited, and she felt in the silence his immense patience. He would wait. He was constant. She didn't deserve that.

'All right,' he said. His voice was level. 'Leave the loving for the time being. But take my advice. Get away from the Delouches. You cannot help in their problems.'

'I'm fond of Madame Claire...' She saw his smile and felt ashamed. He lifted her hands and kissed them. 'Yes,' he said, 'they do smell of chicken.'

They laughed together, and she almost loved him.

Luc's gentleness decided her. She couldn't marry him, of course, but she could admire his good sense. Before she changed her mind again she told Madame Claire that she had made up her mind to go to Le Roy now that affairs here seemed to be sorting themselves out. 'I'll miss you, Madame,' she said, 'but I think it is best.'

'It had to come. I knew it.' She sat down heavily at the kitchen table as if bowled over. Simone saw the pale face, the eyes which had become darker. She bent down and put an arm round the woman's shoulders. 'I'm sorry, Madame, really sorry. I've been meaning to go for a long time. You understand?'

'Yes, I understand.' She searched her face. 'I understand far more than you think. You're doing the right thing.'

'I'll miss Monsieur, and the baby, and Barbie, François...all of you.'

'It's time to live your own life. Past time.' She turned and embraced Simone and then pushed her away.

'We'll miss *you*. We haven't deserved you half the time. Now, get on with your work or you'll have me crying too.'

'Who's crying?' she said, wiping her eyes.

François and his father both said they were *desolés*, but Monsieur said a strange thing. 'I think you'll be back.' He seemed disturbed. His head nearly flew off his thin neck and he smiled apologetically, as if he knew how ridiculous he must appear when he wanted to be sensible.

François said at the table that night, 'We'll never forget you, Simone,' and she saw his hands were trembling as he filled his glass with wine. The bottle was always at his side.

Barbie was honest, if selfish. 'Oh, how could you desert me, Simone? I'll never forgive you. I rely on you in this loony bin. Now I have no one.'

'You have François.'

'But he hasn't me, and that really gets him where it hurts. He's always saying he can't show his face in the village, but I'm damned if I'm giving into him. I need support at the moment, for me and the brat, but I don't see myself ending my days in this one-horse place. I'll get out of it by hook or by crook.' Her lovely mouth had become a straight line.

Madame Claire gave her a gold watch the day she left. 'You're the daughter I never had, Simone, and she would have had a gold watch. Don't stay away. Come and see us. And good luck. You deserve it.'

Monsieur took her hand in his own trembling one and kissed it in a most gallant manner. François looked embarrassed, which he had done ever since the episode in the kitchen. His kiss was formal. 'You're right to clear out, Simone,' and then, surprising her, 'Do you know how I think of you?'

'No?'

'As part of my youth. There you were, when I came home from Toulouse, like springtime in your freshness. Life looked good, an hotel to run, *Maman* and Papa, and you. And then Barbie came...'

'You can be young with her. And the baby. She'll change her mind. You'll see.'

'Do you think so?' She saw the heavy line of his jaw as he turned away from her eyes, and her heart twisted in the old pain. She didn't want to remember him like that.

Chapter Ten

1967...

François was driving to the Marmot brothers' farm to buy the weekly supply of eggs. Barbie had refused to go but little Bernard was sitting beside him. She was invariably happy to get rid of the child. She enjoyed being in the hotel when there were English people staying, and now in May the older couples who no longer had young children had begun to trickle back. She could sit chatting and reminiscing with them on the porch all morning, and she complained that Bernard kept interrupting. 'Stop chattering,' she would say.

'Comment?' He steadfastly refused to speak English. His friends at school were French, and Papee and Mamee were French. He loved Papee, his grandfather, particularly, and in sympathy when he was talking to him, he nodded his head in the same way.

It was a strange thing to François that although Barbie appeared not to miss her parents, she was avid for information about England. He himself had sent stilted little notes to them enclosing pictures of Bernard ever since his birth, but she steadfastly refused to add any messages herself or help him in his task. He had been forced to ask Yvette Levrault, the village schoolteacher to help him.

'You weren't there when they told me to leave the house and go to you,' Barbie said. 'You didn't hear what he said to me. The filth! And her standing silently beside him wringing her hands! Some mother! No one can forget that sort of thing. They'll have to make the first move.' François wondered sometimes if it was to spite them that she refused to marry him.

'We will see the hens walk on the table where we go, Papa?' Bernard said. He turned his little round head with the black fringe towards François. The love he still felt for Barbie seemed to be transferred to Bernard and it flooded into his eyes so that for a moment they were misted as he saw his innocent face.

'*J'espère bien.* But don't talk about it when you are there. It is not *comme il faut* for hens to walk on tables.'

'They are naughty, the hens?'

'No, simply untrained.'

'Could we not have untrained hens on our tables? To amuse the guests?'

'No, they might...' he nudged Bernard's

181

arm, man to man, 'you know what hens do in the dirt.'

Bernard put his hand over his mouth, squealing with delight. 'Oh, yes. Oh, what would people say!'

'They would leave and go to Le Roy, the *chic* hotel in Gramout.'

'Isn't our hotel *chic?*'

'I'm trying to make it so. Haven't you seen how I buy beautiful pictures for the walls, and neat cotton dresses for Madame Tenier and Léonie, even Sophie Rivaud, only she won't wear one, how I polish the glasses at the bar till they are crystal blue? "We are within striking distance of the Route Nationale," ' he was quoting from the brochure he had had printed, 'And we do all the catering for the village and beyond. No one can lay on a wedding dinner like François Delouche, they say. Remember that one of Mademoiselle Marie-Thérèse Brabant's and Christian Grinaud's when you were three years of age and wore the uniform of a *tambour-major?*'

'*D'accord*, Papa.' Bernard began nodding his head rapidly, and then, remembering he was not with his Papee, stopped.

What a fuss *Maman* had made when he installed the neon lighting in the dining-room. 'It is harsh, horrible! Now you will have us looking like blue-faced baboons and staring at each other with empty eye sockets!' She had ranted and raged.

Once after a September storm the current had failed and she had put candles in wine bottles and placed them on the red and white checked covers which were Barbie's idea. She preferred the Provençal decor. 'Now, that is pretty. More *intime*. See how the girls are beautiful now and old Pierre at ninety looks handsome.'

This was an old widower who dined each evening at the hotel and generally sat with Madame Carrione, their *pensionnaire*, hardly less aged. Barbie had said to François, 'I'm bored. I'm going to sit beside that old fool and tease him.' She had walked over to their table, her hips swinging.

'You like me in candlelight?' he heard her say, and saw her leaning towards the old man who was very deaf. Her beautiful bosom was swelling over the top of her sundress like two ripe peaches. He had groaned under his breath as he watched. He saw old Pierre's rheumy eyes light up and Madame Carrione draw the front of her dress higher over her own scraggy bosom. 'How can she do it?' he had thought, burning with desire. He would have liked to have taken her then and there which no doubt would have added to old Pierre's vicarious pleasure...Bernard

183

was speaking again.

'I like weddings, and the summer fête.'

'The *Méchoui,* it is called. Why?'

'I can gather the confetti. I found a matchbox filled with it tucked behind the flour jar in the kitchen, and now that is what I do. Collect it. See!' He produced a match-box from his pocket, slid it open and when François looked down he saw the tiny green rubber figure of a naked woman lying in the confetti bed.

'Where did you get that?' he said harshly, transferring his eyes to the road, 'the woman...?'

'Monsieur Pierre gave it to me. I put new confetti in it for her bed. See, this is what he tells me to do.'

François glanced down again. The tiny figure was moulded round a spindle. Bernard was revolving it with his finger, causing the rubber woman to move, to undulate, slowly, seductively. It was lifelike in the extreme. 'Isn't it pretty? He attached his car key to it when he used to drive, but he gave it to me because they are playing *pétanque* behind the church and he said I was a nuisance and...'

'Shut the box at once!' François said, the anger rising in his throat and almost choking him. His scalp prickled and he rubbed his hand over the top of his head, feeling the baldness meeting his palm. 'It is not *comme il faut. Tu es grossier!'*

'Like the hens who walk on the table at the farm?'

'*C'est ça.* Look out of the window. See if you can see any rabbits and then you can tell Monsieur Maurice when we arrive.'

Barbie, my Barbie, he thought...that night when she had come to his room after the *Méchoui*...she had undressed and thrown herself flat on the bed, naked, laughing, her arms outstretched...the magic of it. There had been a girl at Toulouse, a typist, but she had been a poor tired thing with a sniffle who complained always that he was hurting her...

Not Barbie. 'Come on!' she had whispered, arms outflung on the bed, 'Give it to me, give it to me, good!' Her eyes had flashed, her lips had been half-open, the tip of her tongue showed. Days afterwards he had been dislodging specks of confetti from the waistband of his trousers, his pockets, inside his socks, picking up specks from his bed.

He remembered how he had torn them off while she had lain there, how he had tumbled over his trousers in his hurry to fling himself on top of her. She would have been surprised how often he had thrown himself on that bed and wept after she had gone back to England with her parents.

'*Un lapin!*' the boy cried, '*un petit lapin!*'

'Good!' he said.

'I have decided. I shall not tell Monsieur Marmot. I should not be able to sleep if he shot the poor little *lapin*.'

'Good boy.' He put his arm round his son. 'Papa's good, kind boy.' His heart flooded with love again. Was there ever such a child, so high-spirited, so wise, and with such a kind heart? Surely it should have made any girl anxious to marry him, to become part of a respected family in the village? But, no, she was adamant. 'Nothing will change my mind,' she had told him.

He could not understand her, felt he would never understand her. She teased and tantalized him in bed, sometimes excessively loving, sometimes cool, telling him to *foutre le camp*. He could not believe such words could come from such beautiful lips, like that *putain* who hung around the Gramout market on Saturdays.

There was inconsistency about her which perplexed him. Sometimes she sat at the window of the *salle-à-manger* staring into the square, not seeing, he was sure, the children marching sedately from school in their overalls, breaking into a run when Yvette was out of sight.

Sometimes she would hug Bernard excessively, and he would see tears in her eyes, other times scold him and tell

186

him to go and play and not bother her. Usually he went to Papee. The child knew where he was with him. He would get his stool and sit beside him in the yard, and they would have long conversations, or rather Bernard talked and Papee listened. Their heads would nod together, like two wise old men.

François even spoke to Yvette Levrault about it with whom he had been at school. 'Don't worry, François,' she said. 'It is a rapport they have. I had three children in my class once, the Dubusiers, who all walked with wry necks like their father who sustained an injury at work. It is empathy.' He had not known the word but he had accepted her explanation. Papee would not live for ever, and at least Bernard was giving him joy while he did.

Maman was a different matter. She certainly loved the boy and boasted about his prowess to the black widows and anyone who would listen, but sometimes he got the rough edge of her tongue. She was still ashamed, he knew, because Barbie refused to marry him. It was an insult to the Delouche family, lowered their standing in the village.

'And why does she sit staring out of the window?' she asked, 'when she could be helping in the kitchen? *Mon Dieu,* how I miss Simone Bouvoir! Le Roy got a good girl when they got her! I hear she and Luc Marmot are engaged. His mother says there is nothing to stop them being married except Simone's reluctance. That's the modern girl for you. Too independent by half!' Her vehemence made him wonder if she believed what she was saying. 'By God, he'll get a good wife in Simone when she comes to her senses! It's a pity someone else hadn't snapped her up first...'

He knew she would have liked him to marry Simone. She had made no secret of it in the early days. Well, of course, he had liked her then, had begun to more than like her. She was so pretty and capable, so well-liked by everyone, almost too much of everything. Was that the fault? But in any case Barbie had put every other girl out of his mind for ever. He would never change.

This constant shame. Why *wouldn't* she marry him? He would have liked more children, but she was taking precautions now, and even insisted on him doing the same as a double precaution. 'I got caught once,' she said, 'but never again. Some day...' Her beautiful eyes would become unfocused, would see beyond him as if he had ceased to exist. Nothing demeaned a man more. It would drive anyone to drink.

They were welcomed by both brothers who were sitting at the table with a bottle of wine between them, a half-eaten loaf and some *cabécou*. A hen stalked daintily amongst the crumbs, its head going up and down like an automaton, its beady eye gleaming avariciously.

'*Bonjour,*' they both said, getting up. Maurice waved his hand expansively, frightening the hen which flew off the table. 'Will you join us in our simple meal?'

'No, thank you,' François said hastily, 'we have eaten.'

'A boudoir biscuit for *le petit,*' René said, smiling his fearful smile. Bernard had always been enchanted by it.

'*Merci, Monsieur.* Papa,' he said, turning to François, 'when I grow up shall I have shining teeth like Monsieur René?'

'Perhaps.' François rolled his eyes apologetically towards the man, 'Children...'

'*N'importe.*' René had found somewhere in the muddle on the table a plastic bag of boudoir biscuits, and he laid them out one by one in a row on the dirty surface. '*Serve-toi,*' he said to Bernard.

'René! A plate for the little monsieur!' Maurice had jumped up and taken one from a pile on the dresser, put the biscuits on it and lifted Bernard onto a chair.

'See,' René said, 'nothing I do pleases my brother. He nags and nags at me all day. Sometimes I think I will run away, hide up in the *causse*. I knew some good places when I was in the *Résistance*...'

'A glass of Monbazillac, François?' Maurice said, interrupting him.

'If it is not too much trouble...'

'I like children,' René said. 'So innocent. So honest.' His eyes rested on Bernard who was making short work of the plate of boudoir biscuits. 'It is only the Huns I do not like. So far I haven't managed to trap any, only an occasional rabbit which gets caught...'

'We are not telling about the baby rabbit we saw in the bottom field,' Bernard said in his clear childish voice. 'It is a secret.' He blew out crumbs of boudoir biscuit as he spoke. 'I do not mind the Huns but baby rabbits are different. I do not mind the *sangliers* the hunters shoot because they are big. Are the Huns big, Monsieur René?'

'Big and fat and full of bad blood.' He gleamed.

'Not good to eat?'

'Pah!' René grimaced, his teeth flashing. 'That makes me sick!' He went through an elaborate pantomime, spitting and hawking, 'Pah! Pah! Pah!'

Bernard burst into gales of laughter.

190

'Pah! Pah! Pah!' he shouted, showering crumbs over the table. The hen jumped back up again and began pecking at them to his delight. Barbie would have a fit, François thought.

'Have you used up all your barbed wire now, René?' he asked.

'All that I need. If you wish I will show you where I have my cache. It is in the quarry between your terrain and ours.'

'Perhaps I could have a look on the way down. I came for eggs, Maurice.' He downed his Monbazillac. It was a shame to hurry it. Its warm liquid goldness should be sipped and savoured.

'Five dozen?'

'If you can spare them. *Maman* uses a lot.'

'Ah!' René said. 'What a cook Claire Delouche was in the old days!' He kissed his hands. 'Her *Îles Flottantes*, her rabbit casserole! And what a woman she was when she was young!' He drew a curved shape in the air with his hands, making smacking noises with his lips.

'René!' Maurice said.

'Oh, I know more than you do, Maurice! I saw her near the *chateau d'eau*. And she was not alone, oh, dear no! Nor was she with her husband-to-be, Monsieur Sobersides, the *menuisier*. When he was sawing his wood she was keeping time

191

in a manner *tout à fait different!*' He was convulsed with laughter.

'René!' Maurice got up, shaking his head at François. *'Que voulez-vous?* Come with me, François.'

'Bernard?' François beckoned the boy. 'Say thank you nicely to Monsieur René for the boudoir biscuits.'

'Merci, Monsieur,' he said, wriggling off his chair.

'De rien. But I am coming with you to show you my cache. You and I will travel in the back seat.'

'No, René.' Maurice spoke as if to a child. 'François is in a hurry. Don't detain him.'

'But it is *en route,* and the little one wants me with him. He likes my jokes.'

'I like his teeth,' Bernard said earnestly.

'It's all right,' François spoke reassuringly to the brother, 'we will be happy to give him a lift to the cache. But I'm afraid you will have to walk back, René.' He turned to him. 'I am pressed for time.'

'That is no problem. I tramp over the terrain most of the day to keep watch. We may hear the golden oriole too. I think it flies from the woods round the water tower. Once I thought I saw its flash of gold there, but when I got nearer...' he chuckled suddenly and put his hand over his mouth. *'Je m'excuse.* It wasn't the oriole. I tell you, François, nothing escapes me.' He exploded into his hand. How did Maurice stand this every day, François thought.

'But will the baby rabbit escape you?' Bernard asked anxiously.

'Of course, *mon petit*. It is not the rabbits I am after. It is the Huns. Come.' He held out his hand and Bernard took it, smiling up at the man. The answering pewter smile made François wince, but not his son. Such a charming, trusting little lad, *mignon*, everybody loved him. Why wouldn't Barbie agree to becoming his legal mother? Anyone else would be glad to.

They stood at the lip of the ravine looking down at the steel rolls of netting which had the same sheen as René's teeth. 'A good cache, is it not?' René asked.

'Splendid,' François said. 'No one could possibly find them there.'

'I've surrounded all the terrain with the wire but who knows, in time I may need more.'

'And there's our land,' François said, pointing to the other side. 'I'd like to build my mother and father a house there. They are getting old.'

'Ah, yes.' For once the man was sensible. 'That's the tragedy. One gets

old. Sometimes I have to fan my hatred...'
He gleamed at François. 'I tell you what.
You build a house for them there and
I will make them guardians of my steel
netting.'

'Done!' François said, laughing, and as
farmers did at the market, he slapped
René's hand with his. 'We'll come to
some arrangement in a year or so.'

'Do it before they die. Remorse is bad
to live with. It eats into your soul.'

'Yes, you're right.' Was he an idiot or
a *savant*...or both? 'Well, we must get
on, René. *Maman* will be waiting for
the eggs.'

The man didn't reply as if he had lost
interest in the conversation. He inclined
his head, held up a finger. 'Did you hear
something move?'

François listened. 'Perhaps a bird in the
thickets?'

'I'll have to find out. A golden oriole...
That might be it...must find out.' He
strode away without saying goodbye.

In the car driving towards the hotel
François said to the boy, 'Do you like
Monsieur René?'

'The smiling one?'

'Yes, the smiling one.'

He considered, head on one side. 'Yes,
I like him. But I cannot understand one
thing.'

'What is that?'

'He smiles all the time, Papa, and yet he is sad.'

He put his arm round his son and held him against his side as he drove. 'Yes, he is sad, because he has an obsession.'

'What is that thing?'

'It's...' How could he explain, or should he? But when he turned towards Bernard he was asleep, cuddled against him, one hand under his cheek. He looked like Barbie.

Chapter Eleven

A week or so later François lifted the telephone when it rang at the bar. The voice was familiar.

'Ici Simone. Is that François?'

'Yes, it is.' He was pleased she hadn't forgotten them altogether. *'Ca va,* Simone? It's a long time since we saw you.'

'Yes, but you knew where I was. I thought you and Barbie might have been at Le Roy for dinner one evening.'

'I think Barbie would like it, but I'm tied here as you know. Patrice Tenier used to stand in for me, but he isn't so keen now.'

'I have a day off and I thought I might drop in this afternoon to see you all. I would love to see Bernard. He must be quite a little boy now.'

'He's had his fourth birthday. We would all love to see you. Why not come for lunch? *Maman* would lay on something special.' He laughed and she laughed with him, reminding him of the carefree days when he had first returned from Toulouse.

'No, thank you. I'll be at the farm for that. Marcel and Madeleine have just had a new baby, that's four children now, and they're building *Maman* a bungalow on the road to the village.' He felt a twinge of guilt.

'I have the same idea. Well, we'll get all your news when we see you.' There were a few men at the bar listening with interest to the conversation. 'I have to go now. *Au 'voir,* Simone. *À tout à l'heure.'*

His mother was delighted at the proposed visit, as was Barbie. 'Ages since I've seen Simone! It will be a change to speak to someone different. All I hear from the girls around here is boring stuff about where to go for the cheapest knickers in the market. And Marie-Thérèse Grinaud is the most boring of the lot. Babies, babies, babies! '

'You are pleased that Simone is coming, Papa?' he asked, to stop her. The old man's hands seemed agitated. He smiled and nodded vigorously.

'It will be like old times.'

Simone had changed without a doubt. She was composed, self-confident, but still with the air of neatness and efficiency which was part of her nature. Her clothes and hair were fashionable, her skirt short, showing her slim legs, her hair professionally cut.

Barbie greeted her enthusiastically, flinging her arms round her in an English way. 'Lovely to see you, Simone! Why did you stay away so long? And how smart you look! Oh, you *are* lucky to be near the shops. I can only get to Gramout when François chooses to drive me.' She said he wasn't a good teacher, that he made her nervous, but she had refused his offer of professional lessons at a driving school.

Maman was the first to notice after the greetings were over. 'A beautiful ring, Simone. He is a lucky man, Luc Marmot.'

'I'm lucky too.' She smiled as she showed his mother her ring, expensive-looking, certainly, with a huge blue stone surrounded by diamonds. That was the way things ought to be done, a proper engagement ring, a wedding with all one's friends, Monsieur and Madame Delouche...he noticed for the first time, or perhaps it had become deeper, the cleft on the side of her mouth. It gave her great charm. 'He's worn me down at last.' She was shy. 'He's going to work in the Crillon in Paris for three months, and he says he was afraid I wouldn't be there when he got back.'

'I'm not surprised, looking as you do,' Madame Claire said. 'Fetch a bottle of champagne, François, and we'll drink Simone's health. There's a crate of Veuve clicquot in the cellar. Bring a bottle. No, two.'

'May I have some?' Bernard said, who had been listening shyly to the conversation.

'Yes, *mon petit,* a tiny sip from my glass.' His grandmother hugged him.

'And boudoir biscuits? Monsieur René gives me boudoir biscuits when I go with Papa.'

Simone laughed. 'And was there a hen walking on the table, Bernard?'

'Yes, it ate my crumbs. I would have liked one here for the guests, but Papa says it is not *comme il faut.*'

'I told you not to take him there,' Barbie said to François.

'Oh, they're happy in their own way, the brothers.' Simone laughed at her. 'But Luc's mother despairs of them.'

'I don't like Bernard going into that smelly kitchen, far less eating their biscuits.' Barbie changed the subject. 'Do you

intend to have a white wedding, Simone?'
Why should she show any interest in
that, François thought, she who could
have the best white wedding in the
district?

'I haven't given it a thought. I'll visit
Luc in Paris when the work slackens off
at Le Roy and we might talk about it.'
It was she who now changed the subject.
'How are you, Monsieur Delouche?' He
didn't reply at once and she went and sat
down beside him. How fragile he looks,
François thought, watching them together,
as if he was seeing with her eyes. And the
shaking was getting worse. He had raised
his trembling head to Simone.

Très bien, Simone, très bien, merci.

'You remember me, eh?'

'Naturally. I remember when you used
to hang out the bed linen in the yard and
we had our little talks. Simone was always
polite, always had time for me.' He spoke
to the others.

She had kept her arm round him.
'And you were always so busy with the
vegetables. Do you still prepare them for
the kitchen?'

'From time to time. Sometimes...' he
raised his hands and looked at them. They
were trembling noticeably. 'Sometimes it is
difficult.'

'You will be interested to know that

Marcel, my brother, grows all the vegetables for Le Roy.' Simone included the others. 'And Madeleine employs two village women to prepare them and put them in plastic bags. It is a thriving business.'

'So your mother is reconciled to Madeleine?' Madame Claire asked.

'Oh, yes, there's a complete change there! She may not be a housekeeper to *Maman's* standards, but she has proved herself to be an excellent businesswoman and a devoted mother. *Maman* dotes on the children. There are the twins, Geneviève and Gervase, little Luc who is barely two, and now the new baby, Marguerite. Ah, she is mignonne!' Her face lit up. She would make a good mother too. If only Barbie...you bore even yourself, he thought, Barbie, Barbie...he got up and went to fetch the champagne.

When he came back Bernard was sitting on Simone's knee while she talked with Barbie. His mother had gone to the kitchen—probably to fetch some *amuse-gueule*—and his father was sitting with his eyes closed. He looked content.

'You actually bought this dress in Paris!' Barbie was saying, her eyes round with envy.

'Yes, I went there with Luc when he started his new job. To hold his hand!' She laughed. 'Oh, it is fascinating, Paris!

200

We went up the Eiffel Tower, and on a *bateau mouche* for lunch, and I bought this in Galeries Lafayette.'

'I know it.' Barbie was dismissive. 'In the old days we always stopped off in Paris when we were on our way down south.'

'Do you hear from your parents?'

The girl shrugged. 'Not directly. François is a stickler for propriety, aren't you, *mon ange?*' She blew a kiss at him. 'He writes periodically with the help of that frump in the school, and sends pictures of Bernard. If they want to see us they can come here.'

'I have another Papee and Mamee far away,' Bernard told Simone. He was leaning against her, half-asleep. August was an oppressive month, François thought, as he poured the wine. One became lethargic in the afternoons, and he often would have liked Barbie to come up to bed with him, not to make love necessarily, but to be *in* love, to lie naked and cool in bed and talk. But, no, she sat at the window staring out at nothing, or played her Beatles records interminably. Bernard could sing them all. He had a good ear. 'Please, Please me...' He danced as he sang. 'Help!' He was a comical little soul. 'See,' she would say, 'you can speak English perfectly well when you like.'

His mother came back with a plate of

marzipan fondants which he had bought for her in Gramout. They were her favourites. She must have kept them for an occasion such as this. She sat down, her breathing quickening with the effort, her bosoms sagging heavily, it seemed, under the cotton dress, her face pale. Why was he so clear-sighted today, he wondered, as he distributed the wine.

'We all wish you every happiness, Simone, you and Luc.' Madame Claire raised her glass. 'Come on, Papa. Hold up your glass to Simone.'

'Yes, we do,' François said, 'every happiness. We think of you as one of the family.'

His father's hand was steady for once. 'One of the family, Simone.' He raised his glass. 'That's what you should be.'

'But she belongs to her Luc now,' Barbie said. 'This is flat, François,' she had taken a sip, 'you took too long in pouring it.' She burst into laughter, 'Oh, Simone, do you remember that time I nearly drowned in the river at the ruined mill?'

'You never told us about that.' François looked at her. When she laughed she was beautiful, her eyes flashed, her whole face was illuminated.

'It was a girls' secret.' Simone looked ashamed. 'You would never have forgiven me, François, if she had been...in any danger.' He tried to think what his life would be like without Barbie. It was impossible. Perhaps easier, but the gap would never be filled. Love flooded into him. He spoke softly.

'I can't imagine life without my Barbie.' The champagne was making him senti-mental. He thought he saw sadness, like a film, pass over Simone's eyes. Not for him, certainly. She would never forgive him for that evening when he had been drunk. 'God, François, you disgust me!' she had said...

'François is half-seas-over,' Barbie laughed. 'Of course, he tipples all day, Simone. Did you know that? A little nip here, a little nip there, "Have one on me, Pascal", "Christian", "Christophe..." '

Simone looked down. 'I think Bernard is asleep.'

'It's the heat,' his grandmother said. Yes, she was pale, an unhealthy paleness, and there were dark rings under her eyes. 'I do not like August. The kitchen is too hot and my legs swell up like balloons. Remember how I used to massage them at nights, Simone, in our little room?' She sighed. 'I can only manage the dinners now if I have a rest in the afternoon.'

'Go upstairs with Papa, *Maman,*' François said. He felt tender and caring towards his parents. One didn't appreciate them enough. 'We'll sit here and talk and then I'll bring you a cup of tea at five. You like your tea, don't you?' Barbie had instigated the tea.

'It refreshes me, *bien sûr.*' She got up slowly. 'Are you coming, old man?' She too spoke tenderly. 'Time to rest.'

'Is it, Claire?' His head was still for a second, and François saw what a fine face he had, the straight nose, the well-set eyes with the thick brows, the look of sweetness about the mouth. He helped them to the foot of the stairs and waited until he heard the door close before he went back to the girls.

'You said on the telephone that your brother had built a house for your mother?' He replenished Simone's glass, then Barbie's. 'I intend to do the same for my parents.'

'You said so. I see a change in them,' she said. 'They are frailer. Yes, you should do that, François. Your mother has been at it long enough.' She turned to Barbie. 'Do you like cooking?'

She shrugged. 'My own kind. I wouldn't go near the kitchen when *she's* in charge. She has some weird ideas. I would have a more conventional regional menu, not whatever came into my head at the moment. I'd use a lot of the stuff you get in tins, *pâté de foie, confit, gésiers, canard,*

204

and so on. And I'd keep a lot of pre-cooked food in the freezer. That way you can have a varied menu. More impressive. People like to know what they're getting.'

'But nothing would be fresh,' François said, looking at Simone to see if she agreed with him.

'Barbie has a point. You can certainly save yourself some labour. Luc is very clever about what is available nowadays. When he comes back from the Crillon he hopes to give our chef some new ideas—if he comes back,' she said, smiling. 'I think he would like to become a manager in Paris, even own an hotel there.'

'You have a lot going for you,' Barbie said. 'Another spot, François.' She held out her glass. 'The next thing he'll be going to London.'

'Yes, he has spoken about that too.'

'I don't miss my parents,' Barbie said. She was speaking carefully, and François saw her cheeks were flushed. 'Why should I when they flung me out? But I miss London. It's all happening there, Carnaby Street where everybody goes now, Mary Quant—her clothes are fabulous—the Pill, and Pop!' She laughed. 'Discos, too. Fancy being buried here with all that going on! Have you heard of Mick Jagger?'

'No?' Simone looked puzzled.

'He sends me! I have some Beatles

records, but none of his. He's really wild. Promise me if you go to London you'll bring me back some of his records. They haven't even *heard* of Jagger in Gramout.'

'I'll take you to London, Barbie,' François said. He had never seen her look so beautiful with her flushed cheeks. And yet there was a wistfulness about her...perhaps it was the talk about Paris and London which had caused it. 'I'll fix up someone to look after the bar and we'll go to London and hear the Beatles and the Jagger and the Pop. She has the Pop records, you know,' he said to Simone.

'I'd like to hear them sometime, Barbie.'

'Why not now?' She got up quickly, staggered a little and clutched the back of the chair. 'Little Barbie is drunk. Whoops!'

'Not on a few glasses of champagne!' Simone laughed.

'It's the heat,' François said. He felt hazy himself, as if the three of them, and the sleeping child, were in a capsule, divorced from the world. Even the village sounds had stopped as if everyone was resting like Papa and *Maman* and they were the only people alive. He heard the tick of the clock above the bar...

The curtained door shook and burst open. A young man stood there with shoulder length hair and wearing an open-necked shirt in brilliant colours over shorts. He banged down his knapsack on the nearest table, looked around and saw them. *'Bonjour,'* he said, 'Where's the boss?'

'The boss?' François repeated.

'Le voici.' Barbie pointed to him. She laughed. 'The boss.'

'Ah!' the young man said. 'Have you a room by any chance, monsieur?' His French was laboured.

'Yes, we have.' Barbie spoke for François. 'As it happens.' She was smiling. Her eyes were brilliant. 'You're English. Where do you come from?'

'London. Are you?'

'Oh, yes, I'm English.' She smiled again, slowly.

'You speak damned good French. Where do *you* come from?'

'Sussex, originally. You're travelling around?' She looked at the knapsack. 'Silly question.' She laughed. Laughter was in her eyes, it played around her half-open mouth, and for some reason, François thought, she suddenly seemed very English as if the man's presence had emphasised it. He felt this intuitively, since he was only able to pick up the drift of what they were saying.

'Yes,' the man said, 'bumming around, if you prefer it. Looking at frescoes.' He got that. *Les fresques.* 'I believe you have

207

some fine ones in the church here.'

'Do we, François?'

'Yes.' He spoke in French to her. 'I remember when I was at school our teacher took us there and gave us a lecture.' He dragged the word from his memory. 'Romanesque.'

'Romanesque, eh?' The man seemed impressed. 'Well, I'm glad you can put me up. God, I'm exhausted. Could you give me a beer, please? Shall I come to the bar?'

'*Un bière*, François,' Barbie said as if he were a fool. 'Bring it over here. We're just having a tipple ourselves to celebrate Simone's engagement.' François saw Simone look from one to the other when she heard her name. Barbie had lifted one of the champagne bottles. 'I'm afraid this is a dead man.'

'I'd rather have the beer. Not to worry.' He nodded to Simone.

'My friend, Mademoiselle Simone Bouvier,' Barbie said.

'Hi!'

'Now it's your turn.' Barbie laughed at him.

'Ah, yes! Steve Rawlins.' He came over and sat down beside them. 'Pleased to meet you. Thanks, pal.' François had brought the beer and set it down in front of him. *Maman* always said the

English thought they ruled the roost. 'How much?'

'It's on the house,' Barbie said. 'From both of us.' He saw the man's quick puzzled look.

'You're...?'

'I'm Barbie Sinclair,' she said, her head thrown back, looking through half-closed eyes, smiling.

'So you're on holiday too?'

'No, I live here.'

The man took a sip of his beer, raised the glass to François, 'That's cool, man, real cool. Thanks.' His teeth were white in his brown face. He wore round steel spectacles which magnified his very blue eyes, his very English blue eyes. 'Right, you live here,' he said to Barbie. 'I'll buy that.'

She seemed to find something very amusing in what he said. Her eyes were sparkling. 'How did you find this place?'

'A chap in a bar at Brive told me about it. He said the food was out of this world.'

'You can say that again,' Barbie said, bursting into laughter. 'Yes, I would go along with that, yes, sir!' François gave up trying to understand them. He watched Barbie as she spoke, her animation, how she waved her hands, put her head on one side provocatively as she listened,

209

smiling. What did this man have which so enchanted her? Well, of course, he came from London. He had at least heard that. He looked at Simone and met her eyes. What was she thinking of it? He raised his eyebrows. She bent her head to Bernard. He thought he saw her smiling.

The chatter must have disturbed him. He woke up and whimpered in Simone's arms, rubbing his eyes, looked around and saw François. 'Papa!' He held out his arms and François took him on his knee. He sometimes reverted to babyhood when he had been asleep. He loved him most of all then, the childlike trust, the little warm body cradled in his arms.

'Don't you want to go to *Maman?*' The child shook his head, snuggled against him.

'You keep him,' Barbie said, 'I'm busy.'

'I get it,' the man said, as if he had won a prize,'You're Monsieur and Madame Delouche! I saw the name above the door.'

'So you can read, Steve?' She laughed at him. 'But you've got it wrong. I told you, I'm Barbie *Sinclair,* Mademoiselle, if you prefer it, and this is,' she nodded at François, 'Monsieur Delouche. *Now* do you get it?'

'The penny's dropped.' He said something in English very quickly and they both burst into laughter. It must be a good joke although François couldn't understand a word. Neither did Simone, he knew, by her polite look of incomprehension.

'A situation situation,' the Englishman said.

Simone rose, politely smiling. 'If you will excuse me I'm going to have a walk round the village and visit Marie-Thérèse and Christian, if they're in. And perhaps Sophie Rivaud. I'll be back to say goodbye to your mother and father, François, when they are downstairs again.'

'I would come with you, but I have to mind the bar.' The feeling inside him wasn't new. God knows it wasn't the first time, especially with the English, but this was worse. It twisted his guts. He sat outside the conversation going on between Barbie and this Steve Rawlins, feeling superfluous.

'Faire pi-pi, Papa,' Bernard said.

He got up. At least that gave him something to do.

Chapter Twelve

The guests began to tail off as August ended, but Monsieur Rawlins showed no signs of going. It was as if the situation when Barbie's parents had hung on for so long was being repeated. Its familiarity gnawed at him, made him constantly apprehensive.

From the bar he watched Rawlins and Barbie giggling together at a table in the corner when she had brought him his coffee. She generally fetched a cup for herself and sat down with him. François would hear strange words which were meaningless to him, 'Woburn', 'psychedelic', 'Epstein', 'flower children', 'Sergeant Pepper', 'Rolling Stones'—that one he did know, as well as 'Viet Cong'. He read the papers too when he got time.

The sight of Barbie laughing, her head thrown back, her long mane of black hair swinging, tore at his heart, drove him to near distraction. Once she looked over and met his look. She waved, animated, eyes sparkling. 'We're talking about *les flippers,* François.'

'You should install a few machines here,' Steve Rawlins said. He was always friendly, give him his due. 'People would come rolling in.'

'Oh, no,' Barbie said, 'it would not be *comme il faut,*' and then they were laughing again. He shook his head and bent to rinse some glasses, trying to appear unconcerned.

They began going for walks together, at first in the afternoon. When he remonstrated with her, she told him, 'I am interested in the frescoes. Perhaps someone like you cannot understand that.'

'Why, then, didn't you go to see them before Monsieur Rawlins came?' he asked her, and one night, when she came in very late, 'Could you see the frescoes in the dark?'

'Don't shout at me,' she said. 'Remember you are not my husband.'

'Whose fault is that?' He was tormented by her. He felt she was going to send him off his head with jealousy. 'Haven't I pleaded with you, begged with you? Why don't you marry me? It's irregular, this situation, people take advantage of it.'

'Which people?'

'Monsieur Rawlins, for instance. They think you are free to do as you wish.'

'Don't you see,' she said. 'I am! That's why I won't marry you. The only thing that's left to me since I came to live here with you, dependent on you and that old she-devil in the kitchen for every crust I eat, is to keep at least a shred of my independence! I have my morals too, you know. It's bad to be pushed into a marriage!'

And once, when they were in bed and she had turned away from him when he tried to fondle her, 'Look, François,' she said in a quiet voice, 'I'm not the heartless bitch you think I am. I'm trying to be honest. We don't suit each other. Our minds are different. That's more important than bodies. I know that now. You'll come round to my way of thinking in the end.'

He was in torment. He thought of telling Steve Rawlins to go, but the expenses of the hotel were heavy, and it would ruin their reputation in any case if he turned anyone out.

He spoke to *Maman*, trying to be casual about it. 'I'm beginning to think this man, Rawlins, is a repetition of Barbie's father. Remember how he stayed on and on?'

'At least this one is more pleasant,' she said. 'He speaks to me, and to Papa. He tries to be friendly. He looks strange, but I think underneath he is not so bad. You are jealous of him, aren't you?'

He nodded miserably. 'Barbie would say I had no right to be jealous. But he pays far too much attention to her. I don't like it.'

'It's Barbie who pays far too much attention to *him*. She's deep, that girl. I know her through and through now. She's lazy, but she gets her own way in the end, by waiting.'

He tried diplomacy. '*Maman* says Monsieur Rawlins is *gentil*,' he said.

He could see she was pleased. 'Your mother sees behind his get-up. It's only

214

a facade. He's from a good family, but like many of his age in England just now, he has to try out the hippy style just to see how it feels. If he had been a real weirdo he would have gone to Katmandu and been into drugs instead of coming to France to study church frescoes.'

'Are his parents wealthy?'

'Comfortable. His father is a partner in a legal firm. Steve will be taken into it when he has had his year abroad. That's how it's done. His parents aren't like mine. They're liberal. They trust him and give him a bit of rope, and so he'll play fair with them.'

Bernard, after being shy for a week or so began to make advances to the Englishman in his childlike way. He brought him his toys and shyly proffered them. Once from his post at the bar François saw him showing Rawlins the matchbox, indicating to him that he should open it. He watched the man's face, the embarrassed smile, the slight drawing together of his brows as if it were not quite *comme il faut*. But a child, *mon Dieu!* Where was the harm? Surely there were very few people who could resist Bernard with his black curls, his great eyes, his innocence?

He noticed that Steve Rawlins never lifted Bernard on his knee as most people did. Once François saw him wave dismissively at the boy and saw how he walked away, head down, discomfited. He felt as if it had been he who had been rebuffed.

'Your friend doesn't seem to like children,' he said to Barbie.

'What are you talking about?' Her eyes flashed.

'Monsieur Rawlins and Bernard. He hasn't any time for him. Most guests find him *mignon,* play with him, lift him on their knees.'

'He's a spoiled brat. In England the children of hoteliers are never seen. Steve's an only son. He hasn't known any young children. But he'd like his own eventually. That's a very different matter. His parents would dote on *Steve's* son, but not anybody else's.'

'He has told you that?' The gnawing apprehension was there again. He poured himself a glass of wine and gulped it. I'm drinking too much, he thought, I'm getting bloated and fat. Unattractive. No wonder she has no time for me. But the only way he could get through each day was to take the edge off reality with drink.

September came, and with it the first of the hunters, avid for wild boar. It seemed like a good excuse. He spoke to Monsieur Rawlins when he was having a drink at the bar before dinner. 'I'm afraid we shall have to ask you to vacate your room pretty soon, Monsieur. We have a regular *clientèle* who come each year for the hunting, and as you know, we are limited for space. I have plans to enlarge the accommodation upstairs, but what with one thing and another I haven't got round to it yet. Next year, perhaps. The bedrooms will all be *en suite*, of course. It is the coming thing.'

'You're telling me to go?'

'In a day or so if you would be so kind.'

The man looked at him. Behind the round, wire-framed spectacles François saw the lawyer he would become, the steeliness of the gaze. Barbie was right. He was only having a year of freedom before he settled down and followed in his father's footsteps.

No doubt his mother would suggest he should have his hair cut short, and he would be fitted out in the striped trousers, the black jacket and the bowler hat which all Englishmen wore in London. He was the sort of man who would do what his mother suggested. Didn't all men when it came right down to the nub of things?

The letter was waiting for him one morning when he went down late for breakfast. He had drunk too much the night before with the *pétanque* crowd.

Maman was in the kitchen rattling pans in a bad-tempered way.

'I'm in a fix this morning, François. Leonie Ternier hasn't turned up to do the breakfasts, and as for you and Barbie—well, you're both a dead loss. You stagger down with a face like a cod on a slab and she's still in bed. One drinks too much and the other sleeps too much. Thank God the hunters haven't arrived yet!'

'I thought Barbie was down.' He poured himself some coffee from the pot on the stove. He felt like death.

'I haven't seen her. Little Bernard is running about unwashed in his pyjamas. He's in the yard with Papa. Needless to say, he'll be late for school. *Mon Dieu!* Some hotel this! When I think how it ran like clockwork when Simone was here.'

'I'll set the tables.' The coffee was churning sourly in his stomach.

The letter was lying on the bar counter addressed to him. He knew Barbie's copperplate. She said it was the only thing she had been taught at school. He tore it open, not understanding. Had she written it before she went to bed last night, or...the gnawing was at his guts again, the apprehension becoming comprehension, becoming reality, not to be borne.

'Dear François, I am going away with

Steve. He says he will marry me in England. He is my kind, you are not, nor ever have been, nor your close little village nor your she-devil of a mother. Steve is the one I've been waiting for, *mon liberateur!* (The words were underlined, blackly.) 'Deep down, in time you will be glad I have cleared out. I have told Steve everything and he understands. We all have to have our fling, he says. He's had his. But he wants me alone, with nothing of the past, no encumbrances, a clean start. That's how his parents want me too. This part of my life here must disappear completely. He's willing to forget and so am I. This includes Bernard, I realize, but I have never really thought of him as my child. He's French through and through, in the way he looks at you, in his speech, everything about him has been conditioned by this village and the people in it. He'll forget me in no time. So will you.'

'Your once-loving Barbie.'

He stared at the letter, hardly believing it, and for the first time in the last year or two, didn't put out his hand to the bottle beside him. There was no panacea on this earth which would modify the blow, nor help him to bear it.

He went into the yard and saw Bernard in his pyjamas sitting on the ground beside his grandfather. They were chatting amicably together. The sun shone on their faces, the up-raised innocent one, the thin grey face of his father, the quiet closed smile as he listened. *'Bien sur,'* he heard him say, one man to another.

'Bernard!' he said sharply, 'you will be late for school! Come, Papa will dress you.' He spoke sharply because he didn't want his son to say, 'Where's *Maman?*' That would have released the tears. It would have been like floodgates opening.

'A tout a l'heure, Papee,' the boy said, throwing his arms round the old man's skinny neck.

'Work hard, *mon petit.'* François turned away from his father's nodding head above the boy's, the shrewd gaze directed at him.

The tears came that night when he was in the bed which was too wide for him now. 'Heartless, heartless bitch!' *Maman* had said, 'you are well rid of her.' And then, when she had seen his face, she had taken him in her arms, a rare occurrence. 'Oh, I know heartache, son, I know heartache...' He had stumbled upstairs as if he were drunk.

Chapter Thirteen

It was a nine days' wonder, of course, in the village.

'When is Mademoiselle Barbie coming back?' the *pétanque* crowd would ask as the days lengthened into weeks. 'I thought you said she had just gone for a holiday, François?'

'I'm not so sure. She will have plenty of people to visit in England, I expect.'

'Why did she wait so long before she went back there?' He could see their knowing smiles, their covert winks at each other.

Christian Grinaud came straight to the point when he went for the *tourtes* one morning. 'It's four weeks now. Has she walked out on you? I'm an old friend. You can tell me.'

He nodded, almost relieved to give up the subterfuge. 'It was that Englishman who came to the hotel. She went off with him.'

'I thought as much. Well, count yourself lucky. I married Marie-Thérèse when I got her pregnant, and I've landed myself with a frigid nagger for the rest of my life. It makes one a philosopher. I tell myself, "Well, Christian, you have your little business and the smell of yeast in your nose is as good as the smell of a woman and you have *pétanque* in the evening. And the children. They are a great joy." You still have Bernard.'

'Yes, she didn't want him. Can you understand that, Christian? A woman who would go off and leave her child?'

'She'll have more to offer the Englishman. She'll think of Bernard eventually as her French mistake.'

He stopped pretending. When they asked him in the village shops when Mademoiselle Barbie would be back he said shortly, 'She's gone for good.'

It had the desired effect. The women were immediately on his side. They took Bernard to play with their children, included him in outings they made, to the *fêtes* in the surrounding villages, to the *cirque* at Cahors. Marie Tenier bought him a tee shirt with 'I Love John Lennon' printed on it. Bernard looked bemused but had the time of his life.

'*Maman* isn't coming back,' he told his son, 'She's gone to England to live.'

'That is her real home, England?'

'Yes.

'And should I have liked it there?'

'I doubt it. They speak a different

language. And it would have been difficult for you to settle down in a new school.'

'Mademoiselle Levrault has made me the boy Jesus in the Nativity Play. I couldn't leave.'

'No, that's right. But you still have me, and Papee and Mamee.'

'But no *Maman.*' His bottom lip stuck out, his eyes filled, and François, his heart aching doubly, for his own loss and for his son's, gathered him to him. Part of my body, he thought, caressing the little round head pressed against his chest. It hadn't meant anything to Barbie. They were both her 'French mistakes'.

'Shall I have a new *Maman* sometime?' Bernard's voice was muffled.

'Perhaps.' It was a strange idea which had never occurred to him. There was only one Barbie.

Maman quietened down after the expected tirades and accepted the situation. 'It is a nine days' wonder,' she said, 'and this is the tenth. We are still running a hotel and there are the hunters to be looked after. And when they go we'll get busy on those new bedrooms upstairs. Next year, son, we shall be able to put up our prices. Look ahead. That's what I've had to do. Look ahead and do not think of Barbie.'

'Yes,' he said. But she was in his blood.

223

'Everyone has their problems, but remember you are a hotelier. Present a smiling face and for God's sake, keep off the wine. It is not a solution.'

His father said surprisingly. 'She was *vivante*. I liked watching her about the place. Some of the lightness has gone.' Of course, Papa was merely an onlooker because of his affliction, but he was right. She had taken away some of the life of the hotel, a radiance, as if the shades were permanently down. Sometimes he thought he heard her full-throated laugh when he came downstairs, and imagined he would see her sitting on a bar stool teasing and laughing with the *pétanque* crowd.

She had the common touch. It had crossed the barrier between the two cultures. No one had ever said they didn't like Barbie, however much they disapproved of her morals.

But by the end of October she was no longer a topic of discussion. The village settled down to its autumnal activities, the men hunting for game every hour God sent them, the women cooking it and preserving it, bottling the fruit of the gardens and hedgerows like people possessed, the children practising for the Nativity Play and giving their mothers plenty of extra sewing to do. The waters had closed over Barbie's head, as they had nearly closed over it, in the river by the ruined mill.

On a late October afternoon when the pale sun slanted over the yard, François found his father's body huddled and stiff in the foetal position on the cement. He had gone there to sit after lunch to warm his old bones, as he put it, while *Maman* rested her legs in the small room off the kitchen which she had once shared with Simone.

He got down on his knees and turned over the inert body. The eyes were open, there was a slight smile round the mouth as if at the time of his death he had been enjoying the last rays of the sun. The shaking head was still at last.

He wept on his knees, choking sobs of unadulterated grief and regret that he had been alone when he died, then he dashed his hand across his eyes and went to tell *Maman*.

He had to help her up from the narrow bed. She wanted to meet her grief on her feet. She had grown even stouter in the last year, an unhealthy corpulence, and her legs were mountainous. She had demonstrated to him once how she could press her thumbs into the oedematous flesh and make deep holes in it.

'Where is he?' She was dry-eyed.

'In the yard. I came running to tell you.

I'll get the doctor right away...'

'Help me to him. I am surprised at you leaving him lying there.' She was still dry-eyed in the yard when she got down painfully on her knees to kiss his brow. 'A good man,' she said, 'I didn't deserve him.' And looking up, 'We'll carry him to my bed in the little room.'

'You can't manage to do that, *Maman!*' He was horrified.

'He's skin and bone, as light as a feather. Take his feet. I'll take his head.'

They carried him, still in that foetal position and laid him on his side in the narrow bed and she lay down beside him. 'Go away, François,' she said. 'I want to be alone with him.' She was still tearless. Her face was shockingly pale, her eyes deeply sunk in its paleness.

He went. On his way across the *salle-à-manger* to telephone the doctor, a woman stopped him, one of the black widows. 'François, you promised to come and help me to shift my *armoire*. Where have you been?' They could speak to him like that because they had known him since he was a child.

'My father has just died,' he said. 'I am sorry but I am unable to come, Madame Crozier.'

Her look of astonishment, sorrow and yet scarcely-concealed gratification in her

226

snapping black eyes that she was the first to know, assured him that the whole village would soon be buzzing with the news of his father's death. In our village, he thought, there is no need of a *Presse* such as they have in Gramout.

Maman was in the kitchen the next day, but her vitality seemed to have gone with her husband's death. She sat at the table twisting her hands, her eyes unfocused, and replied in a polite voice to the village people who came to pay their respects. 'Thank you. Yes, a great blow. One is never prepared...' They would have preferred her to have been weeping extravagantly. They did not know this polite woman with the distant look.

Had there been any guests in the hotel it would have been a disaster from the culinary point of view, but fortunately they were left with only old Madame Carrione, the *pensionnaire*, who, seemingly invisible at the height of the season, emerged like a weevil from wood when the guests had gone.

Marie Tenier took over the cooking, but told François that it would only be for a day or so as Patrice objected to her being out of the house now that he had retired as roadman, and Sophie Rivaud helped François with the washing up, tottering from sink to cupboard on her spindly black-stockinged shanks. Marie's niece, Léonie, still came in each morning to make the beds, but announced that she was being married at Christmas and would not be available after that. It seemed to François that his world was tumbling about his ears.

Christian Grinaud said that Marie-Thérèse would ask about the village for a replacement for Léonie. 'With her tongue clacking like a bell all round the place, there should not be any difficulty,' he assured François. 'Don't despair. Think how lucky you are that all your problems have happened when the hotel is empty.' Luck was a matter of degree, François thought, but took heart.

When his father's body had been taken away to the *Dépôt Mortuaire*, his mother took to the narrow bed again, still tearless, still with the incessant twisting of her hands, as if her husband had bequeathed to her some of his involuntary movements. In between his many duties, François tried to spend as much time as he could with her.

'Marie is cooking adequately, *Maman*. Do not worry.

'Pigswill.' She dismissed Marie in a word, and immediately, 'I wasn't fair to your father, François.' Her eyes, smudged and dark, met his, 'Now I am haunted by the thought.'

He tried to cheer her, 'He was happy in his own way, helping you with the hotel. We all knew he was ill.'

'I was responsible for that.' He was worried by the intensity in her eyes.

'No, no, *Maman*. You heard the doctor. It was a heart attack, he said. It is grief which makes you talk like that. I know. I blame myself constantly for Barbie going away. I didn't pay her enough attention, and I kept on asking her to marry me...'

'That was different. She didn't want you.' She could be cruel. 'Jean-Paul wanted *me*.'

He sighed, and took her hands between his. 'I tell you what,' he said, 'after the funeral I'll take you to our land and you can choose the spot for your bungalow. That would please Papa. When I get the staff sorted out for the new season I want you to be living there in style with nothing else to do but rest your legs and potter about in your new garden.'

'It's overrun with rabbits, that *terrain*. Nothing will grow.'

'Then we'll get Monsieur René to put some barbed wire across your side of the ravine. He has plenty left.'

'That idiot! I don't know how Maurice stands him. Perhaps you could ask Monsieur Cavel to draw out a design for the bungalow all the same?' She looked happier. It would give her something to look forward to, instead of looking back.

I am slowly becoming a philosopher, he told himself that night in his lonely bedroom. I am learning to live with life, although at what a cost. He was in the habit of examining his bald patch in the large mirror Barbie had insisted on. It was still dusty with her powder. Léonie might take to spectacles now that she had captured her man. The bald patch seemed to have grown larger as his quiff at the front grew sparser. When he had more time he would do something about it. Nevertheless, looking at his heavy chin and shadowed eyes, he certainly was not the man Barbie had fallen in love with. He pressed his hands to his cheeks, sighed heavily. And with Marie's execrable cooking, no one could blame him for drinking instead.

But he kept himself sober for the day of Papa's funeral. He had bought a new black suit for Bernard with a white collar and a black bow tie, and made sure his own was in good order and his shoes well-brushed. The school and the shops of the village were closed in sympathy, blinds drawn, and he noticed that Yvette Levrault had stationed the pupils in a respectful line in front of the War Memorial when the cortège passed by. Bernard gripped his hand tighter than ever when they walked past his *copains*.

He, like *Maman,* had withdrawn into himself when he was told by Sophie Rivaud and Marie Tenier that his Papee had gone to Heaven. 'Didn't he like it here?' he asked. There was a look of hurt disappointment in his eyes, as if he had found himself wanting. François, as he rushed about, would see him sitting quietly in the corner of the yard where he had so often sat with his grandfather. Sometimes he saw him turning the matchbox with the rubber figure over and over in his hands, and the sight of it could pierce his heart, the pain of his loss as fresh as ever. 'Barbie...' he would say under his breath, 'Barbie...' but there was no hope. She had gone. *'Vivante,'* his father had said of her. 'I liked watching her about the place. Some of the lightness has gone.' Now there was only death.

The church could never be said to be packed since it was ten times too big for the population of the village, but the war comrades of his father were there, resplendent in their medals pinned on their hairy, pepper-and-salt suits, all the black widows—they at least were not put to any expense to buy the appropriate mourning—Madame Creon in one of her own Parisian Modes, possibly a left-over from the Fourteen-Eighteen War judging by its style. Christian Grinaud, and Marie-Thérèse looking like a black spinning top— she had no waist now; Monsieur Cavel, the architect with his wife and unmarried daughters who looked as if they had been dressed by Madame Créon; and Monsieur Sachet, the postmaster, whose features fell naturally into the suitably melancholic expression required at funerals.

The priest's address was lost in analogies, 'A good craftsman who has laid down his tools', 'a man who has carved out a niche for himself in the affections of the village', 'suffered and triumphed on Time's Anvil', and so on, and so on. He saw Maurice Marmot there with his brother, both dressed in rusty black tweed which looked as if it had been carved out of lichened bark. He noticed René, incongruously wearing a late rose in his buttonhole, head aloft most of the time as he admired the frescoes. That mad steel smile was still on his face. How did Maurice support him?

Amongst the many people who offered their sympathies after the service were Simone and Luc. They must be quite the smartest couple there, he thought, soberly but fashionably dressed in black, neat, composed, admirably suited to each other. Luc shook him warmly by the hand.

'My deepest condolences, François. Your father was greatly loved. A sad loss.'

Simone kissed him, her eyes moist. 'He was always so kind to me when I worked in the hotel. I shall never forget him.'

'Thank you.' His throat was thick because of their sincerity.

'Your mother was unable to come?' she asked him.

'Unfortunately. She has been ordered to keep to her bed until the swelling in her legs goes down. The doctor worries about her heart. She is taking my father's death badly. She doesn't weep, but...in a way I'd rather she would.'

'Her grief is too deep. The tears will come. It must be difficult for you, François. Who is doing the cooking?'

'Madame Tenier, but she threatens every day to leave...however, we don't have any guests just now so it could be a lot worse.' He shrugged. 'You won't have the same problems at Le Roy, Luc?'

'Every hotel has its problems.' He looked at Simone. 'Neither of us is there now. I've taken a job as manager of a hotel in Paris, and Simone,' he smiled at her, 'is going to join me there at Christmas as my wife.'

'Congratulations.' He tried to summon up some enthusiasm, 'You couldn't get a better one, Luc. I wish you both every happiness...' If you had agreed,

Barbie... He drew in his breath, squared his shoulders, 'So where are you now, Simone?' he turned to her.

'At home with *Maman* in her new house while I prepare my trousseau. That's what Luc wanted.'

'Ah, yes.' Was there no end to regrets? 'I didn't get round to building a house for my parents before Papa died. Barbie left me, you know.' He steadied his voice.

'Yes, we heard.' Her eyes were full of sympathy. 'I'm so sorry, Perhaps it was for the best.'

'I hope so. Well, if you'll excuse me...the priest will want me...' He saw the cortège had gathered at the church door. This was the part he dreaded. He had decided that Bernard was too young to stand at the graveside. 'Where is Bernard?' He looked around. 'I seem to have lost him.'

'I saw him with the other schoolchildren,' Simone said. 'Yvette Levrault had him by the hand.' She had understood.

'It would be too disturbing for someone of his age.' He was suddenly able to say what he thought. 'I think sometimes we do not realize how long childhood impressions last. I remember clearly my grandfather's funeral.'

'I agree, François,' Luc said. He was warmed by their sympathy and understanding. 'Simone was taken to the cemetery when her father was buried. She has told me she has never forgotten it.'

'It's true.' She nodded. *'Maman's* weeping...I used to have nightmares. You go on yourself. Bernard will be all right. We'll see to him.'

'Thank you...' His eyes filled. *'Je m'excuse.'* He left them hurriedly.

The cemetery was on the hill beside the old *chateau,* and the cortège wound slowly along the village street, slackening even more when it turned to climb the steep road towards it. A few neighbours had gathered at their doors, eyes cast down, and he saw the younger members of the *pétanque* crowd in a respectful huddle in front of the cafe. There was a cluster of half-empty wine glasses on the tables behind them, and he thought, Guy Mathieu never misses a chance to steal my business. He was surprised at such a thought at a time like this. He bowed his head.

The golden light of a perfect St Martin's Day fell on the stone fronts of the houses, making the pavement ink-black in comparison, and giving a transient, dreamlike quality to the familiar street. Was this real, this silence, this lack of voices and noise of cars, the column of black figures walking behind the slow-moving hearse? Was Papee lying there in his grave-clothes, his thinning hair neatly brushed over his scalp, his hands folded, or would he find him sitting quietly in the yard when he went back to the hotel, the shaking head raised to him with that closed smile of his, that secret smile? What was he doing in this line of people with bowed heads, in a thick black suit which made him itch, in unaccustomed narrow black shoes which pinched his feet? He took out a handkerchief from his pocket to mop his brow and its whiteness blinded him for a moment.

When they paused at the cemetery gates at the top of the hill, he turned and saw the *chateau d'eau* in the distance rearing up beside their own land. *Maman's* bungalow would be built there, and with the thought reality returned, bringing with it a lightening of mood. Nothing could bring Papee back, but Simone, by telling him of her mother's house, had given him the necessary impetus. He would arrange with Monsieur Cavel to have plans drawn up right away. *Maman* needed a rest now, and if he found it impossible to manage the hotel without her, he would sell it and care for her until she died. It would fetch a good price once the three new *en suite* bedrooms were ready for occupancy...

'Come away, François,' Father Furent was saying, putting his arm round his shoulders, 'It's time to lower your father to his final rest, his day's work done, his busy hands folded at last...' He went obediently.

That evening, when he had tucked Bernard in—he had surprised him by falling asleep immediately—and said goodnight to *Maman*, he went back to the bar to clear up and collect the glasses. The black widows had greatly assisted the clearance by filling their baskets with the leftovers from the *repas funèbre*. He was sweeping the floor of the *salle-à-manger* when the telephone rang. He went back to the bar to answer it.

'*Ici* Simone.' He knew her clear voice. 'How are you, François?'

'*Assez bien, merci.*'

'A sad day for you, but now it's behind you. How is your mother?'

'She's in bed. It's...it's as if she had lost her will to live.'

'She'll get it back. I know her. She always rises again. And Bernard?'

'Fast asleep, mercifully. It's been a sad day for him too. He adored Papee.'

'Poor child. François, I've been thinking. Luc goes back to Paris tomorrow and I'm with Mother as I told you. Would you like me to come to the hotel for a week or two until Madame Claire is on her feet again?'

'Luc...he wouldn't like it.'

'It's partly his suggestion.'

'You're both too kind. I don't deserve it.' Their generosity swamped him. 'But you must be far too busy getting ready for your wedding.'

'Oh, I hardly get any peace around here for that! Madeleine and Marcel's brood are running in and out all day. I was thinking of Bernard too. He and I were always good friends, and I know how much he'll miss your father. If I could be of any help..'

'There is no need, thank you.'

'Be honest.'

'What can I say?' The words rushed to his lips before he could stop them. 'Simone...I feel so lonely. If you were here it would make all the difference...no, it's too much.'

'It's what I would like to do. First thing tomorrow, then. I am very fond of Madame Claire, François, and if I could just be there...she was like a mother to me, don't forget,' he thought she might be smiling, 'when I was immature.'

'She will be overcome by your kindness. As I am.' He spoke formally. He must show resolution at a time like this.

'Wait till you taste my cooking! You might be overcome in a different way.' He found he was laughing with her.

Chapter Fourteen

It was almost like a return to the halcyon days over four years ago when he had come home from Toulouse and found *Maman* and Papa waiting to greet him, and a smiling shy young girl in the background, Simone. She was not shy now, although she still had the same sweetness.

She organized the kitchen in no time, said to Marie Tenier how sorry she was that she must go, but, of course her first duty was to her husband, and took charge of the cooking herself. The dishes she prepared, while lacking *Maman's* flair, were delicious. *Maman* began to eat a little, was able to get up in the afternoons, and sit in the kitchen where she took over Jean-Paul's task of preparing the vegetables, while chatting with Simone, the faithful Sophie Rivaud, or Léonie Tenier, who was still coming in to tidy the bedrooms.

Bernard was perhaps the chief beneficiary of Simone's presence. She saw that he bathed at night, that his clothes were clean for school, got him up and dressed in plenty of time to eat a good breakfast:

chilled orange juice, freshly squeezed, hot *croissants* from Christian Grinaud with thick creamy butter and apricot conserve, and a foaming bowl of hot chocolate. He thrived on her care and discipline.

Her influence spread round the whole hotel. Where Barbie had been unpredictable with her alternating gaiety and sullenness, Simone was constant, calm, efficient and cheerful.

'She's a wonder,' *Maman* said to him. 'Any hotel she and Luc Marmot run in Paris or anywhere else will be a success. It cannot fail.'

As it came near Christmas she drove *Maman* on her first outing to Gramout to see the shops lit up. Her legs were too painful to allow her to walk about, but Bernard, who was, of course, with them, bought decorations for the *salle-à-manger* and toys for his *copains* at school, as well as a present of a box of handkerchiefs for his teacher, Yvette Levrault. He was busy rehearsing for the Nativity Play each afternoon, and Simone bought him a pair of leather sandals which he agreed were just what the boy Jesus might have worn.

She began cooking and freezing *confit d'oie*, game casseroles and pies for Léonie's wedding two days before Christmas. The reception was to be held in the hotel. It was strange, he said to Simone, that one

240

always said 'Léonie Tenier's wedding' as if there was no one else involved. Perhaps it was because she was marrying a shepherd from one of the Causse villages, and he might as well be a Hottentot as far as their village was concerned, although only twelve miles separated them. She had met him at a *fête champêtre* in the summer. 'Serves her right for straying like a lost sheep from home,' he said. He found himself relaxed enough to joke with Simone.

'It's so good of you to do all this extra preparation,' he said once when he was in the kitchen alone with her. 'You have enough to do without preparing for someone else's wedding. What about your own?' He suddenly remembered. 'Simone! Luc said you were going to Paris at Christmas as his wife! You should be at home getting ready. You were only coming for a week or so. It's six now.'

She was stirring a pot at the stove and she kept her back to him. 'It's been postponed.'

He went over and stood beside her so that he would see her face. 'What do you mean, it's postponed? You are making me feel very guilty.'

'There's no need.' She was calm, her self-composure intact. 'I made up my mind. I couldn't leave Madame Claire

241

till I saw her on her feet again. And there was Bernard. And you. I owe you all a lot. You gave me a start. I don't say Luc was pleased,' she lifted her head to smile at him, 'but he understood. He has a kind heart. Besides he has run into difficulties with the chef in the hotel where he is working and he has decided to buy one of his own. He can wait.' He felt uneasy.

'I still feel...responsible.'

'You musn't feel that. It was my own decision.'

'You're good at making up your mind.' He looked at her calm face. 'I wish I were so positive.'

'I've had to do it. Life's a matter of decisions. And being sure. I could have stayed with my mother and not come to work here, but I didn't. I could have turned down Luc's offer to work at Le Roy long ago, but I didn't. I chose to come here instead of sitting at home sewing my trousseau. I chose to postpone my wedding.'

'You make it all sound so easy. I have so many regrets.'

'Don't think *I* haven't.' He saw a Simone he didn't know for a moment. The sweetness had gone. 'Yours are about Barbie?'

'Yes. If I had told her I understood

her reluctance to get married instead of worrying about what other people thought, she might have changed her mind. I don't know...'

'I don't think she would.'

'Why do you say that?'

'She had made up her mind to go. She was good at...waiting.'

'You mean until Steve Rawlins came along?'

She shrugged. 'Have you heard from her?'

'No. I know in my heart I never shall.' She looked at him with dark eyes as if she understood, and grieved for him.

'Does Bernard miss her?' she asked.

'Not now. Perhaps at first. He would like to be like the other children, to have a *Maman*, but it doesn't worry him too much. He lives for the moment. He loved Papee, but he's still got *Maman* and me. And now you. I've noticed how he runs to you often when he comes out of school. *Maman* has never made a great fuss of him and he's rather wary of her. Maybe when I have her bungalow built he will visit her and then he'll feel very important. I shall give him a bicycle soon, a bicycle for Christmas. I have an idea! Why don't you and I slip off to Cahors and buy it this afternoon?'

'Is there time?' Her eyes brightened.

243

'Three hours would do it. Nothing happens until five.'

'You would have to hide it.'

'I'll put it in a cupboard in our...' he stumbled over the word, '...in my bedroom.'

'I'll have to tell your mother I'll be out.'

'Yes, of course. Just say you are going shopping. You might help me to choose something for her as well.'

He felt excited, youthful again. While she was with his mother he went into the hairdressing salon and rubbed some unguent on his hair and back-combed his *mèche* so that it looked thicker. It gleamed gold in the bright light. No, he thought, looking critically at himself in the mirror, I haven't greatly changed in spite of all the vicissitudes of the last few years. Some might say I am still quite good-looking...Barbie had called him her 'young bull'...ah, Barbie! He felt his loins tighten as he thought of her.

Where was she now? Wherever she was, Monsieur Rawlins would be enjoying her, fondling her breasts, running his hands down her sides...he swore, turning away from the sight of the fat slug of a man he was looking at.

The afternoon at Cahors was entirely pleasurable. In summer it had a southern air, the word 'midi' had meaning, and now, even in December, it was difficult to believe it was winter. The dank air—it lay in the valley of the Lot—still retained some of the summer's heat.

There was a festive air in the streets with their hurrying shoppers laden with parcels, and after they had parked the car they walked along the Boulevard Gambetta, stopping now and then to look at the gaily-dressed shop windows. Simone had loosened her coat. 'It is always warmer here.'

'And noisier. Can you imagine those lorries rattling through the village day in and day out *en route* for Spain! It would drive one crazy.'

'Why don't we go down one of the side streets to the Badernes? I love markets, and we might see a bicycle shop. I know a good café near St Etiènne if we want a rest.'

'I didn't realize you knew Cahors so well?'

'Oh, yes. Luc has a friend who works in the Chateau Mercuès. We came sometimes on our half-day.'

He saw them as she spoke, a smartly-dressed couple dining at the Chateau then strolling across the Pont Valentré in the moonlight, so well-organized, so right. He should have laid on outings like that for Barbie, let her see he was a man of substance who had a lot to offer if she married him. It was still strange Simone had postponed her marriage, even allowing for her feeling of loyalty to *Maman*...

'I still feel very guilty about you being with us,' he said.

'You mustn't. Luc and I discussed it. It gives him a little more time to look around for an hotel. He has been saving up for a long time.' He looked at her small pale face, a healthy pallor, unlike *Maman's,* the thick straight hair which fell diagonally across her brow, the large eyes, the thin nose, everything *comme il faut.* She was, as she had told him, good at making decisions. He must believe her.

They strolled through the market looking at the stalls, but Simone said they should buy his mother's present at one of the reputable shops in Rue Joffre. 'There are some good lingerie shops there. Would that appeal to her?' He thought it might. He had no knowledge of his mother's lingerie beyond the vast, tent-like bloomers which he sometimes saw on the clothes line in the yard. Simone was saying that on second thoughts it would be better to buy the bicycle near the car park as it would be awkward carrying it amongst the crowds. '*D'accord,*' he said.

He marvelled at her competence and

foresight. He had seen a beauty with shining handlebars and a neat rear basket just as they had turned into the Boulevard Gambetta and would have bought it right away. 'Do you think of everything?' He smiled at her.

In the lingerie shop she suggested a fleecy nightgown for his mother since she felt the cold so much, and he asked her to choose it. 'Get her a *peignoir* as well,' he said with a careless wave of his hand. 'I can't remember her ever having one.'

Simone laughed. 'When I was sharing a room with her she invariably wore an old coat.'

Her taste was unerring. She examined the *peignoir* thoroughly to make sure that the material was good, and asked the assistant if it were washable and if the stitching was firm. She chose it in a warm pink bound with satin ribbon of the same shade. 'What would I have done without you?' he said, impressed, 'Now I insist on you choosing something for yourself.'

'Oh, no, François,' she lost her composure a little, 'you mustn't.'

'It's a thank you as well as a Christmas present.' And to the assistant, 'Will you please show the young lady some...*combinaisons?*' The word came to him, but he wasn't sure if it was right. Barbie had had matching sets of panties and slips in various colours. She rarely wore two of the same colour at the same time.

She chose one in well-cut white satin, quite plain, untrimmed with lace and only a hint of embroidery. Barbie had liked black with froths of lace. He remembered a pair of black panties she wore with a pink heart appliqued above her crotch. 'My naughty panties,' she had called them. She had danced and wiggled her pelvis in front of him so that the shell-pink heart moved tantalizingly...

They had a drink at one of the cafés in the Boulevard. They were protected by the glass screens since it was winter, which reduced the noise of the juggernauts to a muffled roar. There was a sense of intimacy, of being cut off from the world. He had the black wine of Cahors and she had coffee. 'If I hadn't to be back to open the bar,' he said, 'I would have taken you to dinner at the Chateau Mercuès.'

'Then you would have regretted buying the presents!' She laughed. 'Have you any idea how much it costs?' Was she inferring that Luc Marmot could afford it but he couldn't? He had another glass of Cahors wine because the thought angered him, but she refused more coffee. 'I feel terrible about you buying me such a beautiful gift,' she said.

'Don't. It will do for your trousseau.' Perhaps it had been unwise. 'As long as Luc won't mind.'

'No, he isn't like that. He isn't...small-minded. Well, thank you, François.' She smiled at him. 'I'm enjoying this day so much. It takes me back to when we used to go in your Peugeot to do the shopping. Not as far as this, certainly, but I was...very happy.'

'So was I. And then...' He remembered Barbie coming into the hotel that day with her parents and the impression she had made on him right away, her lusciousness, her beauty. He had wanted her from the beginning. He wanted her now. And yet up until that time he had been feeling a growing tenderness towards this neat, pretty girl sitting across from him with her neat bobbed hair like a cap, her immaculate make-up, her big eyes, her smart cloth coat. But never passion...

He didn't remember Barbie ever having possessed a coat, merely an assortment of jackets and anoraks which lay as often on chairs as hung in her wardrobe. He had kissed this girl in the coat with the neat fur collar that time he had driven her to the ruined mill, kissed her and wanted to do more, but not strongly enough. Before Barbie..

'You look sad,' Simone said.

He shook his head. 'Do I? I try not to be. There are a lot of good things ahead, I tell myself. I'll be involved with the repairs to the hotel immediately after Christmas, and I'll arrange for the builders to start on *Maman's* bungalow. And there's Bernard.' He felt his eyes mist up, looked at his empty glass. He should know the effect by this time. 'He's a joy to me, that little lad. You like him too, don't you, Simone?' He had seen him sitting on her knee when he was tired, snuggling into her breast, had watched them coming in from school where she had waited for him, hand in hand.

'I love him,' she said. She laughed. 'He asked me the other day if I was going to be his new *Maman!* I can tell you that since I am going to marry Luc.'

'Lucky chap.'

'It's I who am lucky. I find it difficult...to take the plunge.'

'Most girls are dying to get married.'

'Perhaps we were both...waiting.' She was looking down at her hands. He thought he saw her shoulders lift in a sigh, then she looked up, giving him a half-smile. What a sympathetic, sweet girl she was. 'I expect Barbie is married now,' she said, 'to Monsieur Rawlins.'

The words were like a chisel going through his heart. 'Yes, I expect so. Yes,' he said again, 'it wasn't marriage she was against, it was being married to me.'

'It still hurts?' Her eyes seemed to have grown bigger and darker.

'What do you think?' He signalled to the waiter. He suddenly felt claustrophobic in this glass cage. 'We'd better get going.'

'*D'accord.*' She gathered up her bag and gloves. 'You should try and forget, François. Think of marrying someone else. When your mother goes to her new bungalow you will be lonely. You need a wife to help you to run the hotel, perhaps a brother or sister for Bernard. It would be right for you.'

'No one would be right for me...after Barbie.'

'That you have to learn to live with, like everyone else,' she said, getting up. He saw her face was set and stern, unlike her. Was it because he had drunk two glasses of wine?

'Don't worry,' he said, 'I'll drive carefully. We'll be back in forty minutes.'

'Have you forgotten what we came for?' she said, 'Bernard's bicycle?'

He laughed. 'I need someone like you to run my life.'

Chapter Fifteen

She had been busy for the past few days preparing food for Léonie Tenier's wedding party, making sure that Sophie Rivaud had the tablecloths starched and white. She had bought centre-pieces of silver leaves and cupids for each table and red table napkins since it was so near Christmas. The cake had been made a month ago by Christian Grinaud to allow it to mature, and now it had been iced by his expert hand.

She was so well ahead with the preparations, the tables set in the afternoon, that she was able to drive Madame Claire and Bernard to the church for the wedding ceremony. François would try to look in later, but he had miscalculated the amount of champagne he would need and would have to drive to Gramout to buy some more. 'We want to let this Causse shepherd of Léonie's see how we do things down here,' he said.

She thought he looked much better than he had done when she had first come to help out after his father's funeral. He was trimmer, his eyes were clear, he was drinking less, he was more like the François she had known as a young girl.

Last week, driving along the dark Route Nationale Twenty from Cahors, she had asked herself why she still loved him. Luc spelled security; François was an uncertain factor, sometimes unsure and dependent, sometimes boastful like a small boy, too given to self-reproach, and yet with an attraction for her which was renewed when she was near him. How to define it? Certainly not by itemizing his faults or his virtues. It had been there since the first time she saw him getting out of his white Peugeot and going into the arms of his parents, a true simplicity.

There was no explaining love. He, unlike her, had never learned from experience. She would have to bolster him up, constantly reassure him, and yet this sweetness and appeal for her was irresistible and unexplainable. As his love was for Barbie. He was lovable whereas Luc was too quietly self-confident to be lovable. With him there were no surprises. Luc would take care of her, but she would have to take care of François. She told herself she must leave.

She sat in the church with Madame Claire on one side and Bernard on the other and watched Léonie coming down the aisle with her father, saw her come to stand beside her shepherd and look shyly up at him with a woman's trusting look of love, a commitment which said, 'I give myself into your keeping.'

You should be walking down the aisle, she thought. Marcel would give you away, and Geneviève and Gervase would attend you. Luc would be standing waiting at the altar, not awkward-looking like this man from the hills in his lumpy suit, but tall, slim and well-dressed with that acquired suavity, that ease of manner because of his job, those quick, graceful movements. His country breeding had been submerged long ago.

Paris would suit him, would suit both of them. They were hardworking and adaptable, chameleon-like in their ability to fit into any situation. Was it that they were too alike, too unexciting together? Was there something in *her* character, still unexplored, which did not want such a safe prospect?

'Her dress has turned out better than I thought,' Madame Claire whispered. 'Madame Créon ordered it for her. God only knows where *she* got it from...the Ark?'

'It's charming, all the same.' The girl was too fat for the tight waist and bouffant skirt, but the dress was unimportant. She could not forget that look of trusting love she had exchanged with her shepherd.

She didn't wait for the nuptial mass. Christian and Marie-Thérèse would bring Madame Claire back to the hotel with them, but she took Bernard. He was too young to sit for that length of time.

'You were very good in church,' she told him.

'*Merci bien*, Simone. Why didn't he have his shepherd's crook, Léonie's monsieur?'

'He only uses it when he is out looking after his sheep, but you could ask him later. He needs it to hook round their necks.'

'Or lean on it and look far away, like in the holy pictures?'

'*C'est ça*. This is the first wedding party you have attended, is it not?'

'Yes. They envy Pascal and I at school because we both will attend. Especially as I go back with him to sleep in his house. I am glad Léonie is getting married. It gives me a good time. Pascal tells me there are bunk beds in his room and I may climb up the ladder to the top one since I am the guest. When Barbie was here she never arranged such a thing with one of my *copains*.'

'Well, you were too young. You are five now. When you get back you can help me by laying out the little tulle bags of dragées at each place, and there will be one for you.'

François was in the *salle-à-manger* when they got in. 'Didn't you go to the wedding?' she asked him.

'Yes, I looked in. I saw the service from the back.' His eyes had a bitterness in them. 'I came away...too much to do.'

'Well, we're here to help, aren't we, Bernard? Doesn't he look smart in his suit?'

'It is strange, Papa,' the boy said, 'it is my funeral suit for Papee and now my wedding suit for Léonie and her shepherd.'

'It is a versatile suit,' François said, hugging him and laughing over his head at Simone. He looked young and vulnerable, like his son. I love him, she thought. Quite simply, I love him still.

The crowd flooded in like the Lot under the Pont Valentré where the weir is; the whole village, it seemed, led by the triumphant Léonie and a shy-looking husband who was probably more used to sheep.

She organized them to their tables, placing Monsieur and Madame Yves Fromat under a flowered arch which she had made and fixed to the wall behind them. Leonie in her new marital state looked beautiful, even with her coronet awry and her bursting cheeks and bosom. All brides looked beautiful, she thought, as she hurried to the kitchen where a bevy of black widows were assembled around Madame Claire at the table with her feet on a stool, but still in charge.

'*Au travail, Mesdames,*' Simone said, smiling, 'You all know which tables you are responsible for. Just ask Madame Claire if you are in doubt. She has the list. Are you sure you don't want to join the wedding party?' she asked her.

'No, it is too soon after Jean-Paul, and once I am wedged in, it would be difficult to slip away if my legs began to throb.' She generally retired early to her room off the kitchen. She could no longer climb the stairs. Simone had been allocated to an upstairs bedroom at the end of the corridor, 'Our sharing days are over,' Madame had said, influenced perhaps by the fact that there were no guest requiring accommodation.

The noise and laughter in the *salle-à-manger* were deafening after the enforced silence in the church. Some of the widows threw their part in Simone's work plan to the winds and joined the party, and Simone was forced to fly between the kitchen and the tables, occasionally crossing François' path who was attending to their liquid consumption which was formidable.

In between she drove Bernard and Pascal to the Saval household. She had promised Pascal's mother that she would deliver them by nine o'clock at the latest. She also managed to find time to take upstairs a selection of the wedding dishes to Madame Carrione who had elected to stay in her room.

She sat down with François for a few moments to listen to the speeches. He put a glass of champagne in front of her.

'I bet you haven't eaten,' she said.

'Have you?'

'I've been sampling the dishes all evening.' She thought by his flushed cheeks he had been sampling the wine.

Monsieur Yves Fromat surprised everyone by being able to speak at all. Here they regarded themselves as cosmopolitan because they lived five miles from Gramout. He was eloquent and even witty, and Simone revised her opinion of shepherds in general. Perhaps the time he spent tending his sheep, or simply leaning on his crook, had been put to good use. The Causse, empty under its vast sky, could well make philosophers of those who worked on it.

She remembered an afternoon she had spent there last summer with Luc, and how they had wandered over the short grass pierced by the limestone, and how he had held her hand to guard against her stumbling in a hidden *aven*, those mysterious holes which were supposed to lead to underground caves. She remembered the silence of that arid country except for the high trill of a lark hovering in the blueness above them. The air had been sweet with thyme, and the tiny blue butterflies had clung to the rocks as they had done at the ruined mill.

'Don't let us wait any longer, Simone,' he had said suddenly, 'Marry me.' He had stopped and took her in his arms. His face was tense and she became afraid, not of him, but of having to agree.

'I'll think about it,' she said in a teasing voice, and knew she had struck a wrong note. 'Let's find a nice place and we'll sit down.' She tried to make amends. 'It's too hot for walking.'

They had lain down on the springy turf and she had closed her eyes against the sun, and as it warmed her thinly-clad body she had felt a pleasant kind of lethargy. Why was she struggling against the obvious? Luc loved her. François didn't. Luc would care for her. They would have a good life together.

She turned to him and was taken closely in his arms. Between them it was as if they had trapped the heat of the sun. She could feel his heart beating strongly and she moved restlessly, even closer. She wanted to feel his passion, to be overcome by it. He groaned and his voice had changed, was harsh and trembling. 'Why should we wait, Simone?' This wasn't Luc, her suave Luc, this was an unknown man...she sat up suddenly and pushed him away.

'I thought...' He had sat up beside her. 'You seemed eager. I've waited a long time.' She turned to him and saw his grim face, mask-like in its hurt. If he had raped her she would have welcomed it to assuage her guilt.

'Christmas,' she had said, 'we'll be married at Christmas.' And she had broken that promise, made worse by his agreement. He was proud...

She turned and looked at François. 'You look thoughtful,' he said. His forelock gleamed, his eyes were smiling at her. It's impossible, she said to herself, the whole situation. I should be in Luc's arms just now, I should never have come here.

'*They* look happy,' she said, nodding at the newly-married couple. She had seen a look of love pass between them and had felt a stab of envy.

'Yes, everyone should be married,' he said. 'Léonie!' He raised his glass to her. 'You look lovely!'

'To you, Léonie,' she said, raising her glass. 'And to you, Monsieur Fromat.' He bowed, smiling, looking, she thought, with his long face and his close thatch of curls, like one of his own Causse sheep.

260

It was midnight when the last guests had trailed away, laughing and singing, and half-past twelve when François came into the kitchen. He had taken home the remaining black widows and one or two of the village worthies who had temporarily lost the power of their legs. 'Black coffee, Simone.' He drank a lot of black coffee. 'Has *Maman* gone to bed?'

'Yes, a long time ago. Talk quietly in case we disturb her.' He nodded.

'Is there much to do?'

'No, the bulk of the washing-up is done. I hope you recompensed the widows. They were a great help.'

'I always do, though I believe they would come for nothing just to be in the thick of things.'

'I've brought the glasses from the bar. If you dry them I'll wash.'

She had been tired before he came in but now she was wideawake. It was the effect of his presence, as always, she thought, and because their conversation in hushed tones created a sense of intimacy. She said softly, 'When we have finished we'll drink our coffee in the *salle-à-manger* so as not to disturb your mother.'

'*D'accord.*' He seemed like her, untired. His eyes were clear. She tried not to look at him.

They sat facing each other at a table in the empty room, and once again, when she had poured the coffee she was afraid to meet his eyes. The hotel was silent. Madame Claire would be asleep. Madame Carrione also, Bernard was with his friend. They were alone, the only two people awake. Do not, she warned herself, get carried away by this man. Remember that last time when Barbie was pregnant and you told him he disgusted you...

'Monsieur Fromat excelled himself,' she said.

'Perhaps he didn't.' His eyes compelled her. They were full, bright, alert.

'What do you mean?'

'We don't know him. That may be what he is like.' He shook his head, smiling at himself, 'What's come over me? I've never felt my mind so clear, as if I could see *behind* people's faces. Perhaps I'm over-tired. What I mean is...people are sometimes quite different from one's ideas about them.'

'One's preconceived ideas?'

'*Mon Dieu!* You have swallowed the dictionary!'

'No,' she laughed. 'I read a lot, believe it or not. The word just came to me. I know what you mean. We make snap judgements. Take your mother, for instance. I always thought of her as capable, practical, unsentimental...but she's different now. As if your father's death had changed her. It's more than a bereavement. It's a deep kind of regret, remorse...that must be the worst thing to feel...'

'You speak as if you had felt it too.'

'Oh, not through bereavement, but, in other ways...' she hurried on, 'And there's another thing I've just thought of about your mother...that original kind of cooking of hers, so spontaneous, abandoned, even...' she laughed, 'that was another side of her which had to be expressed, some kind of frustration...' She blew out her breath. 'Where am I getting all this? My mind seems sharp, crystal-clear. Over-tiredness, as you said. I'll probably drop off in front of your eyes any minute.'

'We're both the same tonight. As if we were on a different plane, together. Excited...' He looked at her, and his gaze seemed to be full of tenderness, 'You're right about *Maman*, though. She's an enigma when you think of it. She was a beauty in her day. Everyone says so. Look at me!' He ran his hand over his hair, grinned. 'Why would she marry a man so much older?'

'She loved him?'

'I suppose so. It doesn't...fit.' He put his

hand on a bottle standing on the table, said abruptly, 'I'm going to have some wine. Would you like some?'

'Not for me. I've drunk a fair amount of champagne tonight, hence the speechifying.' She gave him a straight look. 'So have you.'

'*C'est vrai.*' He got up, went to the bar and came back with a glass. 'You are thinking I shouldn't?' he said as he filled it.

'I am not thinking anything of the kind. That's your preconceived idea of me!' She laughed and said, coquettishly for her, 'Tell me truthfully, François, how do you see me?'

'Mmmh.' He looked at her, glass in hand. 'A girl who knows her own mind.'

She shook her head. 'Go on.'

'Competent, clever...' She raised her eyebrows, 'Very pretty.'

'That's better.'

'You were greatly admired tonight. You have become...*chic.* That dress, and your hair. How wise you are not to have it screwed up like the black widows. *Le tout ensemble.* You made the others look like a collection of Madame Créon's Paris Modes.' She laughed with him, satisfied.

'Dress isn't important.' He didn't know she was wearing the white satin slip he had bought her in Cahors. Her dress had slid

264

richly over it. She met his eyes. He reached out and took her hands.

'What do you think of me, Simone?'

'Very pretty.' She laughed.

'Come on. This is truth night. Say!'

'Lovable...unsure...' She tried to draw her hands away.

'Go on.' His clasp was firm.

'Easily influenced...charming, an asset to any hotel...lovable...' She looked away.

'When you say "easily influenced" you are thinking of Barbie, aren't you?'

'No,' she said, lying. 'I liked Barbie. We got on well together.' She remembered the incident in the river when she had nearly let her drown.

He let go of her hands suddenly, lifted his glass. 'She belongs to the past. I've been giving it a lot of thought recently. If only I had followed my instincts when I found you here when I came back from Toulouse...'

'What were those?'

'To love you.' His voice was low. 'To marry you. It would have been right for me, for *Maman* and Papa, for the hotel...' Their eyes met, and his were swimming, moist. This man will be the death of me, she thought. It's too late.

'Well, it's over,' she said, 'or it didn't happen that way. Barbie came along and she was the only one for you. You said so yourself. I could see it. Everyone could see it.' She got up. 'I am suddenly tired, François. I must go to bed.'

'I'll come up with you.' He rose. 'You put out the lights in the kitchen. I'll see to them here.'

They went up the dark stairs together and at the top she pressed the *minuterie*. The corridor, illuminated, stretched in front of them. On the left was François' room, on the right, Madame Carrione's. There was a tray outside its door with used plates on it and a note held down by an empty glass. She bent down and retrieved it, read it aloud, softly.

'*Chère Simone. Merci pour mon repas. Délicieux.*'

'She's a sweet old soul,' she said softly, 'What age is she?'

'Close on ninety, I think. Been here for years.' The *minuterie* expired. They were in the dark.

'I'll creep along to my room,' she said. She was standing too close to him. Their shoulders brushed and then she felt his arms round her. 'Don't François,' she said, 'it's stupid.'

'I'm lonely. I want you.' His voice was in her ear.

'Now you are *fou.*' And so was she. Her arms were going round his neck, she felt his body, the soft belly because of too

266

much wine drinking. The hardness under the belly. *'Fou,'* she said again. They had been through all this before.

They were in his room and on the bed. She didn't remember him opening the door. 'My God, François,' she said weakly, 'what are you doing?' He had stood up and was undressing hurriedly, throwing his trousers and shirt on the chair, then his pants and socks. He kicked off his shoes.

'Going to bed.' He was naked. 'You can go to yours if you want to.'

'Fou,' she said again as he threw himself on top of her. 'Yes, I will...' But the surge of feeling going through her was uncontrollable, her body was in the grip of it, making her arch towards him, then fall back on the bed, breathing quickly. This should have been for Luc, she thought, hearing her heart thump in her ears.

'Shall I undress you?' He was now kneeling beside her. She moved her head on the pillow.

'Go away,' she said.

The dress slid smoothly over the satin slip. He knew his way about women, she thought with a touch of sanity as she felt his hands on her. She too was naked except for the satin slip, the straps pushed down so that her breasts were bare. Was it more seductive that way? Had Barbie done the same thing to make him feel good, in this same bed?

And then it didn't matter, bad, good, *fou*, it just *was*, entirely natural, entirely as it should have been years ago and she might now be Madame François Delouche being undressed and made love to by her husband after a wedding party. One of her arms was outflung, the hand raising the pillow. She curled her fingers, thinking how long ago she had found the tiny heap of confetti there and how much she had suffered...

But the suffering which had been a pain was now a pleasure-pain since it was the first time, although it should have been with Luc. Nevertheless it felt right and wonderful and she had never felt like this in her whole life, pure sensation, dark rivers of delight surging through her body, retreating when it was too much to be borne, surging again even more strongly and threatening to overwhelm her. Could she bear it any longer, should she bear it any longer. 'Ah, no,' she was begging now, 'please, please.' And then he was lying on her breast, breathing heavily like someone who had been rescued, dripping from the river.

'François,' she said, 'François...' and realized by his now soft, steady breathing that he had fallen asleep. She tugged his forelock and he moaned softly, 'Barbie...'

She rolled from under him and lay flat on the pillow. He moved close to her, and mole-like, she felt his mouth nibbling against her cheek, his free hand over her body. 'Barbie...' he said again, 'my Barbie...' The tenderness in his voice broke her heart.

Chapter Sixteen

It was Christmas Eve. François was busy all morning with his customers and she was as busy in the kitchen preparing the turkeys for the oven. The *Bûches de Noël* had arrived from Christian Grinaud, and Madame Claire was sitting at the table peeling chestnuts to make the stuffing for the birds.

'You look tired, Simone,' she said. Her black eyes pierced. They didn't miss a thing.

'It was quite an evening. I thought they'd never go away.'

'I feel we are imposing on you. Won't they miss you at home?'

'I'll look in tomorrow. It's a children's Christmas there now with the little ones.'

'Your mother will be hoping you and

Luc have a family some time too.'

'Yes...'

'Is he coming home for Christmas?'

'I'm afraid not. He is too busy with his new hotel. You know all about that, Madame Claire, the trials and tribulations.'

She nodded. 'Sometimes I ask myself if it is worth it. Very little private life...François looked heavy-eyed too. What time did you both get to bed?'

She managed not to blush. 'Around two o'clock, I think. Well, that's that. I'll go and set the tables now.'

François was behind the bar. *'Bonjour,'* she said. What did one say to a man with whom you had so recently made love?

'Bonjour. Come here, Simone.' He was boyish, charming.

'You know I'm busy. Do you feel angry with me?'

'No.' She sat down on a stool facing him. 'No, not angry.' It was deeper than that. Humiliation.

'You wanted it too?'

'It happened. But there's Luc...' She hadn't been thinking of him. 'I feel terrible.'

'Do you love him?'

She hesitated. 'I...care for him. He loves me. He's never looked at another girl. I trust him completely...' Chagrin

270

overwhelmed her, 'You called me Barbie last night!'

'*Flute alors!* Did I?' He looked ashamed. 'In my sleep...what can I say?'

'It doesn't matter. Not now. But it made me realize you loved her first, still love her.' He shook his head as she spoke.

'Being with you last night made up my mind for me. You were so sweet, Simone. You...*obliterated* Barbie for me. I'm sorry I said her name. It must have...sort of floated up in my mind when I was asleep...' He was ingenuous, and lovable. He leant forward and took her hands, 'I know there's Luc, and it's a terrible thing to ask you, but, please, don't rush into anything with him if you aren't sure...'

'You could scarcely call it rushing. I've known him most of my life. And we've been going out together for five years now.'

'Doesn't that *prove* you aren't sure? I see now I made a mistake too, with...with Barbie,' she saw his eyes waver for a second, 'that it should have been you and me, living here together, working together, married. Couldn't we...wipe out the past, start again?'

'You can't do that, François. And there's Bernard.'

'She didn't want him. He loves you, he would be happy with you. And *Maman* always wanted you rather than Barbie.

271

It would make everyone so happy.' He raised her hands and kissed them, 'Simone, please. Think it over. If I had any doubts, last night convinced me, as it must you. We could be so happy together. Please, please marry me...'

'François!' Simone started, withdrew her hands quickly and turned. His mother was standing at the door of the kitchen, her black eyes blazing. 'Haven't you heard the telephone? It's been ringing for five minutes!'

'Merde!' He struck the side of his head and looked comically at Simone before he went running out of the bar.

Simone screwed up her courage and walked towards Madame Claire. 'I'm sorry...' She ran the last few steps. François' mother had collapsed rather than sat down on a chair at the table nearest to her. Her hand was pressed to her side. 'Oh, Madame!' she said reaching her and bending over to see her face. 'Were you dizzy? You should always take your stick...'

'It's not my stick, stupid girl.' She looked up, her face ashen, 'it's my heart!' She was breathing heavily, 'Not helped by that fool of a boy putting off time...with you...' she groaned, her head dropped.

'Oh, dear!' She was distraught. 'Shall I get the doctor?'

'There's no need. It isn't...the first

time. Run to my room and bring me the pills...you know...in the drawer...'

She knew which drawer, the one at her bedside. She was back in an instant, opened the box and gave Madame Claire a pill with shaking fingers which she placed under her tongue. Simone noticed that there was a blue tinge round her mouth. She ran again to the bar for water, brought it, and watched her anxiously while she took a sip, then another. The blue tinge had disappeared, although she was still deathly pale.

'I'll help you back when you feel strong enough, Madame,' she said. 'Once you're in bed I'll phone for the doctor.'

'Can't you take a telling? I said, "No!" There's nothing he can do except warn me against upsets...which seems impossible around here.' She gave Simone a look.

'François was just...'

'...passing his time? Well, you know your own affairs best. Help me up. The turkeys are more important.'

'Oh, Madame! Never mind the turkeys!'

'Never mind the turkeys, she says! Let me tell you, girl, they are more important to me than you and François. You go and put them in the oven and make some coffee. Bring it to my room...'

'Shouldn't you at least let me help you there?'

She shook her head impatiently. 'I know myself. I'll go when I'm ready. Now on you go like a good girl and stop fussing. The turkeys, then the coffee. And bring a cup for yourself.' She half-smiled. 'I'm sorry I shouted at you.'

She saw François holding my hands, she thought, as she lifted the heavy birds into the oven. Now the timing switch. Three-and-a-half hours at least. And possibly she saw François kissing my hands, oh, God! Or was it not so terrible? She stood up. The stuffing and vegetables could be attended to later. Madame liked to do the *farce* herself, and cook it separately. Now, coffee. Fortunately there would be no one in for lunch.

Perhaps seeing us had nothing to do with the attack, she thought, as she ground the beans. More likely she was already feeling ill. She stopped turning the handle. Or had she been awake last night and heard their footsteps going upstairs and stop at François' door? Then, silence? No, she reassured herself. The hotel was old and stone built. It would be impossible to hear at that distance.

Or could Madame Carrione have told her? She stopped again. For an old woman her hearing was acute. But, then, she had looked innocent enough when Simone had taken up her breakfast, the soft buttered bread because her old gums would not let her eat *croissants* now. No, that wasn't possible either. Madame Claire was unable to go upstairs and Madame Carrione hadn't been down this morning...

Nevertheless her hands were trembling as she spooned the ground coffee into the jug and poured boiling water over it. They were still trembling when she knocked at the door of the small room with the tray but she made herself smile as she went in. 'Good!' She was the efficient Simone once more. 'You managed to lie down where you should be. I'm glad you had the sense to do that.'

'Somebody's got to have sense around here.' She looked much better.

'You should have let me send for the doctor. Anyhow, here is fresh coffee, the way you like it.'

'Oh, I'm back to normal. I told you, I know myself.' Her cheeks, always without colour, were no longer ashen, her eyes had regained their usual sharpness, the glazing of pain had gone. 'Or as normal as I'll ever be. Now, pour yourself a cup. You'll need it after all that excitement.'

'*Vous êtes gentille.* Just for a few minutes, then. Bernard will be home soon.'

'Not for another hour and his father can take care of him when he does.' This woman, Simone thought, as she obediently sat with her coffee, with whom she had shared this small room for so long, was making her feel very guilty.

She was sipping, nodding. 'You make excellent coffee, Simone, but then everything you do is excellent. You have a talent for order and efficiency—for attention to detail. Tell me, are you in love with my son?'

Simone put down her cup on the table beside her, drew in her breath. No escape. She looked at François' mother. 'You have known me since I was a young girl, Madame. We are both going to speak frankly. Is that it?'

'That's it.'

'I was impressionable then. I admired François. Yes, I did fall in love with him, but...'

'Barbie came along?'

'Yes. I could see there was no hope so I left. Not immediately, if you remember. Once away I tried to forget him and I told myself I had grown out of loving him. Luc was there in Le Roy. He had always been fond of me, and I thought I loved him. I was sure...'

'Why did you put off your wedding?'

'You know why!' Her anger flashed. 'I offered to help you out here!'

'Yes, you did, and that makes me feel very guilty, but I can't believe it was the only reason. I know you, Simone. You make up your mind and everything has to fall into place around that.' Her black eyes held hers. 'You've always been honest with me because that is the kind of girl you are. I respect that. Was it *only* because you were needed here?'

'You haven't any right...' She shrugged, gave up, 'No, not entirely.'

'Was it because of François? Drink your coffee. It's good.'

She took up the cup obediently, took a sip. *'Now*...I know it was.' She looked down at the cup. 'I thought it was all over. You say I make up my mind and everything falls into place...not with François. He was...first in my heart, just as Barbie was first in his. That's something that stays *here.'* She put her hand on her heart.

'I am sorry for Luc in that case. Where does he stand now?'

'I don't know. It's so difficult. François says he is over Barbie now. I *want* to believe him. I tell myself that Luc will understand. He is ambitious, single-minded. At the moment he is wrapped up in making his new hotel successful...'

'You delude yourself. The hotel will mean nothing to Luc without you at his side. He is counting on that. He has been very lenient with you. *Mon Dieu,* you aren't thinking of deserting him, are you?'

She didn't answer. This woman had no right to pry into her affairs. But it concerned François too. Still, she wasn't *her* mother. She thought of the long time she had spent in this small room with her and how natural it had been. She had confided in her, had been helped through her adolescent years, she had been taught how to cook, how to live, she had taken her own mother's place when she had been absorbed in her own grief. She owed her something. She looked at the woman, resting on her pillows, the slack lines of her body, so long stripped of any grace, but still the black intelligent eyes.

'Your son has asked me to marry him,' she said. 'He needs me too.'

'He has...asked you to...marry him!' She sat up, as if to meet better this information.

'Yes. He intends to put the past behind him. And Barbie. He thinks we could be happy together.'

'So.' Her eyes were fixed on Simone. She put her cup carefully on the side table, leaned back again. 'Thank you, Simone. Now I think I have the necessary strength for what...' she paused, '...I must tell you. Jean-Paul was not the father of François.'

She stared at the woman, stunned. 'You are telling me...that...'

'François is not his son.' It penetrated. The shock was great. She felt the blood drain away from her face, and it seemed, from her heart. But *her* heart was all right.

'It's difficult...to take in.'

'Haven't you ever wondered why he has different colouring? Well, of course, Jean-Paul had lost his dark hair when you came. But, eyes as well...'

'It can happen, I mean, children being a different colouring from their parents...'

'Oh, anything can happen, but he is *not our son.*' She emphasized the words. 'I have wanted to tell you often but hesitated because of your youth, and your virginity.' A subtle smile lifted the corner of her mouth. 'In this little room where we were such good friends together I should have liked to confide in you. I have never told anyone. Only Jean-Paul knew. That is not to say that the villagers may not have guessed. They don't read much but they have an extra sense, like animals.' She laughed without mirth.

'Does he know? François?'

'I never told him because my husband, Jean-Paul, did not wish him to know. That was the only condition he made when he married me.'

'You were pregnant?'

'You're a bright girl. Yes, I was pregnant. I worked in this hotel although it didn't belong to me then. I was a girl like you.

The couple who owned it are now dead. I worked as hard as you, and like you I enjoyed working hard, the satisfaction of it. I had an unhappy home life. My father had left my mother when I was ten. There were plenty of customers, men, who were interested in me, but I was proud. I had always thought there was something special about me, different...and then *he* came.'

'Who?'

'The real father of François. He came the way the Sinclairs came, Monsieur Rawlins came, walked into the hotel and asked if we had a room. He was English too. Do you find it difficult to believe in the coincidence?'

'No, it is more like the past repeating itself. Perhaps,' she smiled, 'there isn't a great variety in situations...'

'*C'est ça*. Still, it is an hotel, and we do get the English. He was different from the Sinclairs in every way, that I can tell you. He was an engineer. He had taken a temporary job in our region because of this peculiar interest of his...so English,' she smiled at Simone, 'he wanted to see the golden oriole and had read it was found in this part of France.'

'The golden oriole?' A memory stabbed at her brain. That strange Marmot brother, René...hadn't he talked about the golden oriole, 'a flash of gold amongst the bushes?'

'He was fair-haired,' Madame Claire said, 'or at least golden at the front, perhaps bleached even more by the sun. François has the same kind of hair—two-coloured.'

'Yes, he has.' A golden wave which fell over his brow. She had touched it, last night. 'What was this temporary job?' she asked, trying to be calm.

'Oh, didn't I say? He had been sent by the *Conseil Municipal* from Gramout to mend the *chateau d'eau*. You know it.'

'Oh, yes, I know it.' Hadn't she gone there to weep, day after day, when she had first known about Barbie and François?

'A guest had complained to the *patron* about the supply of water in the bathroom. You may be sure he was English. Always wanting hot baths.' She shrugged. 'Joseph, did I tell you that was the name of my lover, Joseph Delaware, asked me to go with him when he was investigating it. I got off most afternoons. I was fascinated, bewitched by him, his fair hair, especially where it was fairer at the front, his long limbs, his smile, his strong fingers, most of all by his strange Englishness. I said I would have done anything he asked me. I did. I became pregnant.' She stopped and looked at Simone.

She stammered stupidly, 'You mean with François?'

'Naturally. I have only one child. My mother had been left without a bread-winner, and I was pregnant.'

Simone put her hand on Madame Claire's clasped ones. 'I can understand how you must have felt.'

'*You* thought *your* mother was strict! Mine would have *killed* me if I had told her I was pregnant.' She shrugged. 'Jean-Paul had always shown an interest in me. He had known my father. He was twice my age, sober, respectable, the *patron* employed him for all his joinery work. We became friends. Once when he caught me crying I was so distraught that I confided in him. He asked me to marry him, said he had always loved me. He didn't hesitate.' She looked at Simone. 'I accepted, but I think I broke his heart.'

'Wasn't he happy with you?'

'I could have made him happy, but I pined constantly for my English Joseph as if he had laid a spell on me with his foreign words. It was a sickness on top of the pregnancy. I wanted to die.'

'He went away, this Joseph? He didn't know you were pregnant?'

'I don't know. I'll never know. Once or twice I imagined he was looking at me strangely. On the day I had decided to tell him, I went to serve his *petit déjeuner,* and the *patron* tells me *il est parti.* No goodbyes.' She shook her head. 'You can imagine the blow that was. I can't tell you the distress I felt, how I even thought of ending it all as day followed day, and yet...I still pined. It was like a canker. Poor Jean-Paul. Any man knows if the woman in his arms isn't there, if she is substituting someone else.' Or any woman. 'Barbie...' François had said when he had lain close to her, his free hand moving over her body, 'My Barbie...'

'This is taking too much out of you, Madame.' She saw how her eyes were sunk in her head. 'Lie back and rest.'

'Not yet.' She shook her head. 'I have this picture in my mind. I don't want to blot it out... yet, the best part, the beginning, the heat of those afternoons when I lay with him in the green thickets around the *chateau d'eau.* The sky was like one of our blue china plates on the dresser. There was a distant sound of goat bells. A boy in a red shirt herded them on the other side of the ravine but he never saw us. I'm sure of that. We were in our own private world. Only the young can experience it. Once, when we were lying very still, after...I thought I saw amongst the bushes a crouching figure...but it was only my imagination, fear...'

She remembered the stillness when she had lain there also, but alone, the silence, and yet not a complete silence because of the rustling of the birds in the juniper and wild thorn, or the bigger rustling of an adder in the grass, and there had also been the bells Madame Claire had heard, coming across the ravine in little tinkling rushes of sound...

'Remorse,' Madame Claire was saying, calmly, 'remorse has eaten into me constantly because I caused my husband's death. It is killing me.'

'No, no.' She spoke sternly. 'You're wrong. He was ill.'

'Because of me. One needs love to live. I deprived him of it. I want to tell you this, Simone, I have to tell you this, François will never get Barbie out of his mind. He is too like me in his obsession. Oh, he would jump at the chance of marrying you, just as I did with Jean-Paul, because he knows it would be his salvation. He would become conventional, with a child and a wife, perhaps more than one child. But he *isn't* conventional. Nor will he ever be. He has my obsessional nature—I've seen it since he was little—and, don't forget he is half his father, strange, not to be trusted.'

'No, that's not so!'

'No? Didn't his father walk away and leave me without a word? Don't think I wouldn't want you as a daughter-in-law. Don't think it wouldn't be my dearest wish. When you first came here you were the answer to my prayers! But I tell you, Simone, he would constantly compare you with Barbie because he is still obsessed by her in spite of the fact that she left him, and their son, without a backward glance, when Monsieur Rawlins came along. Just as his father left me.'

'It's in the past. I could be a mother to Bernard.'

'But could François be a husband to you? I say this of my own son, Simone, I do not think so. But you could be a mother to your own son or daughter and Luc's...' they both heard Bernard's voice in the kitchen.

'Simone! Mamee! I'm back from playing, with Pascal.'

'I'll go and give him lunch,' Simone said. She got up. looking down at the woman. She seemed exhausted. 'You don't care, then, if I make your son unhappy?'

She looked up. 'He hasn't the capacity for happiness as you know it, as Luc knows it, nor constancy. It is a question of temperament. Nothing will change him.'

Bernard was sitting at the table. He had the matchbox he played with in his hands, and he was opening it and shutting it in a discontented sort of way. The thought occurred to her. Could it be the same one which she had tucked behind a jar on the kitchen shelf, a long time ago?

'I've always meant to ask you, Bernard,' she said, 'Where did you get your matchbox?'

'I can't remember.' He put it in his pocket. 'If you had seen the toys Pascal has already and still not Christmas! A gun, a double-barrelled shotgun! I've hardly anything. Just this old matchbox.'

'Poor you, I don't believe it. But just wait till you see what your Papa has bought you.'

'François doesn't buy such good things as Pascal's Papa. His gun doesn't fire real pellets, naturally, but he let me hold it and pretend, lying on the ground the way soldiers do. That is the one thing I want from *Père Noël*.'

She tried to deflect him. 'What is in your matchbox?'

'Some old confetti. I found it on a shelf in the kitchen.' The same one, she thought. How strange. 'And a little lady. It is of no account. It is a gun I want, like Pascal's.' Unfortunately he has bought you a bicycle. She still felt stunned, incapable of thinking properly, of paying attention to this son of François, this grandson of a man called Joseph, an Englishman, who had lain in a clearing in the thickets round the *chateau d'eau* with Madame Claire, and then gone away without telling her. Had he done so deliberately, realizing she was pregnant, and could Madame Claire be right when she said François would never forget Barbie? She knew the answer.

Chapter Seventeen

It was a tradition that the Hotel Delouche laid on a Christmas Eve dinner to which many of the villagers came. Madame Créon of Paris Modes (in reality, Mademoiselle Mauprat, an elderly spinster with dyed red hair), Monsieur Sachet, the postmaster, who was known never to smile even in his cups, Christian Grinaud and his wife, Marie Thérèse, Mademoiselle Yvette Levrault, the schoolmistress, Monsieur Boniface, the butcher, better known as Monsieur le Boeuf, the *pétanque* players en masse, and the usual bevy of black widows, or as some called them, the Mesdames Tricochets.

As well as the locals there was a fair sprinkling of people from Gramout who preferred the bucolic festivities of the village to the sophistication of Le Roy.

The ambiance was more *rustique*. Friends spoke to friends across tables, children played about the floor, and the elder ones, trained by Mademoiselle Yvette, sang their Christmas hymns, grouped around the bar.

When they had finished eating, quite a few of the guests trotted off to the church for midnight mass, led by the chattering choir armed with lanterns. The only thing that the scene lacked was a blanket of snow. They still talked of the wonderful fall they'd had twenty years ago.

On Christmas Day, when, by tradition, the hotel was closed, Simone went home. She had been invited, along with Madame Claire and François, to the Grinauds for dinner, but they had accepted her excuses. François looked pleadingly at her but she pretended not to notice.

Her mind was still too disturbed by Madame Claire's revelations about François' real father, and the thought of the night she had spent in François' room. What had possessed her, she would think, and then, as she castigated herself, fierce thrills of remembered desire would course through her body, causing her to close her eyes and tense her shoulders until the feeling had died down. It was so strong, so urgent, that she felt it must be noticeable. She needed to get away to think.

The atmosphere at the farm had completely changed with the advent of the children, her mother barely recognisable as the embittered woman of a few years ago. Now, with her own life seemingly out of control, Simone could better understand how her mother must have felt when her father had died so suddenly and so tragically. She was still only in her forties. The deprivation must have been almost unendurable.

'I was hoping you would come, Simone,' she said as she embraced her. There was a new softness in her features. 'I only wish Luc had been here too. Was he too busy?'

'Yes, *Maman*. I told you he has bought a hotel on the Left Bank. It's been his dream for years.'

'You should be with him instead of stuck over there at Madame Claire's. She has no claim on you.'

'She was kind to me...' when I needed a mother. How could one say that? 'And she lost her husband, remember?'

'At least he died naturally.' It was a momentary return to the bitterness. 'There's no call for gratitude. You worked hard for her. Take my advice. You get off to Paris and get your wedding plans fixed. Luc needs you, needs a wife. See how happy Madeleine and Marcel are.'

It was true enough. Madeleine, mother of four, was as serene as her mother-in-law. 'I can't tell you how I dreaded living with your mother at first,' she confided to Simone. 'But Marcel was wise. He got that house built for her and so she hadn't to put up with my untidy ways for long. The children give her a new identity.' She was no fool, Simone thought. 'Then she can boast about my market garden, which makes up for not being able to boast about my lack of expertise in the kitchen. She has her own place now, doting grandmother as well as supervisor of the packing shed. She boxes the lettuces, grades the tomatoes, and puts the *racines* into plastic bags. She has even had a rubber stamp made, "Legumes Bouvier". Finding one's own niche. That's the way of it.'

'I don't think I've found mine.'

'Oh, you'll come down on the side of sound common sense. Don't worry.' Madeleine had also developed a gift of prophecy. Perhaps it came with maternity. At any rate it was impressive.

They had an early Christmas dinner in the big farm kitchen with an unexpectedly jolly Marcel at the head of the holly-wreathed table, the dogs lying in front of a roaring wood fire, little Marguerite in her cradle, Geneviève and Gervase propped up on cushions on either side of their mother, and Luc on his high chair. It was a picture of domestic bliss. 'Why is not my *copain* here?' he joked when he was pouring the wine, 'Luc's godfather? Has he found the attractions of Paris too hard to resist?' Yet his eyes were shrewd.

'Perhaps.' She laughed. 'He couldn't possibly leave his hotel to come home when he's just bought it.'

'But you might well have left the Delouches to go to *him*. Don't tell me there's another attraction there!'

'Didn't I tell you I had fallen for Monsieur Sachet?'

'That sobersides! *Quel type.* You'd be better with François.' She laughed too loudly, putting up her hand to her face to hide its heightened colour. Did the whole family talk of her behind her back, wonder what was behind her insistence on helping out the Delouches? She hardly knew herself.

She helped Madeleine to put the children to bed, then joined her mother in the kitchen to wash the dishes with an odd sense of alienation. She neither fitted into her mother's new house nor here. It was time for her to find her own niche, as Madeleine had put it. She drove her mother home with eulogies to the children ringing in her ears.

'You're a good girl,' she said when

Simone had seen her in and was saying goodnight. 'Now, do what I tell you and get yourself away from that place. They're only using you, take my word for it. The Delouches have always been, well, odd...' Did she know about François' real father? 'Luc is personable, and ambitious, and you're a lucky girl. He won't wait for ever.'

She was tired when she got back to the hotel. It was in darkness and she crept upstairs, tiptoeing past François' door in case he would hear her. Her heart was beating unsteadily when she got to her own room.

I'm not comfortable with myself, she thought, as she began undressing. Memories of the night they had made love flooded over her, strong urgent memories which revived sensation and made her want to go to him, to be taken into his arms again, to relearn those acts of passion which had so shaken her.

And yet, did she really know him? Her mother had said the Delouches were 'odd'. And hadn't he changed somehow in her estimation because of what his mother had told her? He was no longer familiar, no longer the son of that gentle old man, Jean-Paul. He was not the François she knew. He had an English father who had been 'strange', who had left the girl he had made pregnant without a backward glance. And could it be, she thought, François' own Englishness which had drawn him so strongly to Barbie, an unknown bond shared?

Compared with this new strangeness in him, there was Luc's total familiarity. He was part of her background, with parents whom she had known from infancy, who still had a mother who worked in a delicatessen in Gramout. He had been Marcel's friend since childhood. There was nothing strange there.

And in her case she was a French farmer's daughter with a mother who had been a local girl. Like her parents, she was practical and hard-working, common-sensical, as Madeleine had said. Would not she be going against all her tenets if she chose François rather than Luc?

But, she trembled, that deep dark ecstasy she had known with François, that passion when he had thrown himself on her, that abandon, his need for her...or was she only an instrument, an assuagement of his need for Barbie? Would not she always be second-best as his mother had warned her, when she might be first with Luc? She got into bed and lay flat, stretching her limbs. It had been a long day. Her mind as well as her body was tired. Sleep overcame her.

She wakened suddenly with the sound

of a quiet tapping at her door. She lay listening, tense, her heart thudding against her ribs, then something made her spring out of bed, hesitate for a second, then walk softly towards the door and turn the key in the lock.

'Simone...' Her heart hammered in her ears at the sound of his voice, making her head swim. 'Simone...' She leant against the door, sick with longing. 'Why did you lock me out? Let me in...' His voice was harsh, sibilant.

'No. Go away! I was foolish...' Her hand went slowly towards the key. He had only to plead once more and she would give in, then she would know again that deep, thrilling, heart-hammering darkness, that shaking up of her senses so that she was no longer in charge of herself...she heard his footsteps slowly receding, the soft slip-slap of his slippers. Her sense of disappointment was so keen that she turned flat against the door and wept, choking, bitter sobs, scraping the surface with her finger-nails, bereft.

A long time later she found herself in bed, empty with weeping. She did not know how she had got there. There seemed nothing of her as she drew her hands down each side of her body. She was a shell, merely a carapace, the real Simone was with him again, in his own room, part of him. And yet, when she finally began to feel drowsy and her fingers curled under the pillow, she was that other girl, the one who had clutched the small handful of confetti in *her* ecstasy, who had come first, who would always be first with him, and she knew a small relief that common sense had won. The terrible sense of loss, she recognized, would take a long time to go, if ever.

A letter came from Luc three days later.

'*Mon amour*, The hotel goes like a bomb and already I have a clièntele who appreciate my Perigord cooking. I need you beside me, not only for help but because this is only a half-life without you.

'I have never demanded or commanded, but there comes a time when it is necessary to make up one's mind. I appreciate your feelings of obligation to the Delouche family. I have not permitted myself to read any more into it, but I am not foolish. Decide, Simone, I beg you. I offer you my love which has never faltered. I know we would be happy.

'Paris is a good place to be, would be for the two of us. I have already carved a niche for ourselves in the little streets around the *Place* with their holy books and sculptures, their *objects d'art*. I meet men like myself in the cafe on the corner, shopkeepers and hotel-owners who live around and about the rue du Vieux-Colombier where our hotel is—I call it *our* hotel.

'Did you know that le Père Teilhard lived here? And that he went with l'Abbé Breuil on some of his excursions to *grottes*, to study prehistoric paintings? The thought brings me nearer to my beloved south-west, and to you, to the placid villages, and the high *Causse*.

'We could be married in the church here—it is so beautiful—or at your church if that is what you want. The main thing is, decide, and decide quickly. And remember, I love you.'

Chapter Eighteen

He thought this month, March, was the dreariest he had ever known. The hotel was empty, which was probably a good thing since it was difficult to get help, but at least the clientele gave a feeling of life to the place. Of course, there were the usual drinkers at the bar, and it was easy enough to drink along with them as well as after they had gone and *Maman* was in her little room off the kitchen. She was disgusted with him, he knew that, but what could one do when everything seemed to have gone wrong since Simone had left.

There had been the business of Madame Carrione. That seemed to have started the trail of bad luck. François had taken her tray up one bitter February morning and found her lying in her bed in a pool of blood. Her claw-like fingers had tried to keep him from pulling down the covers. She had moaned softly all the time, in shame at the cancer which had eaten at her for so long.

He had driven *Maman* to visit her at the Gramout hospital where they had taken her, and the two women had clasped hands. '*Merci mille fois, Madame Claire,*' she had said, 'and you too, François. But where is the little Simone who brought me such lovely trays...?' The eagle-like lids had dropped over the eyes which had become milky. She died while they watched her, as quietly as she had lived.

And that fool of a girl, Martine Chapou, whom he had engaged to help, was no good at looking after Bernard. His clothes were always half-washed, half-ironed. When she was reprimanded, she only giggled. He didn't know what he would have done without Yvette and Madame Saval, Pascal's mother, who both realized how difficult it was for him when his mother was partly an invalid, and took Bernard off his hands as often as they could.

Sometimes Bernard would come and sit on a bar stool and lean his elbows on the counter the way the *pétanque* crowd did. 'I become tired of all those ladies looking after me, François (he often called him François now). There is only you and Pascal I can talk to about guns.'

'Why do you want to talk about guns all the time?' He would give him a Cassis and take a glass of red wine himself. 'The same colour, *n'est-ce-pas?*'

'Mademoiselle Yvette tells us of Vietnam. Always there is shooting there.'

'You should not think about things like that,' he said, realizing that he should, 'you are just a little boy.'

'Mademoiselle Yvette says we must be *au courant*. Everyone is *au courant* about Vietnam, even in London. They don't like the shooting there. They shout and make speeches against it, and march.'

He spoke to his mother one evening. He was helping in the kitchen to clear up after dinner. Martine Chapou had gone home after seeing Bernard up to bed. He seemed to like her and her giggling, which seemed strange to François. 'We'll try to get a

298

chef when the season begins, *Maman.'*
He felt light-headed from drinking too
much. All he wanted was to be in bed,
like Bernard.

'How often have I heard that,' she said,
'along with the bungalow you were going
to build me on our land.' She pushed
out her breath impatiently. 'You're ruining
everything with that drinking of yours.'

'It's because I don't feel well.'

'Who does? Get yourself to the doctor.
There's no reason why a young man like
you shouldn't feel well. You have to pull
yourself together, show some drive, work!
Take Simone Bouvier, for instance. There
was a girl who knew how to apply herself,
who was neat and quick, yet had time to
be kind to everyone.'

'And walk out on us.' He felt swift anger
flame through him.

'Could you blame her? She had a suitor
like herself in Luc Marmot, hard-working
and reliable. I hear that hotel they have
in Paris is a great success. Certainly there
is a lot of trouble on the Left Bank
just now..

'What kind of trouble?'

'Don't you read the papers? The students
are protesting against the Americans and
Vietnam. Who wouldn't? And yesterday
there was a mass sit-in at some university or
other. But it all means a busy bar. Madame

Marmot was telling Sophie Rivaud when she was buying some of her *pieds de porc. Delicieux!* She brought me some. Students have to wet their throats to voice their political opinions. Ah, if I were only fit! Hard work. There is nothing like it. One should never allow oneself to sink into self-pity.'

'Stop it! Stop it!' He suddenly realized he had his fist in the air, that he was standing over the chair where she sat with her stick propped against it. 'Forever criticizing, never praising! You don't accept that it has been difficult for me, Barbie walking out on her child...'

'That child is more of a man than you are!'

He looked down on her. Her eyes were steady. He lowered his fist as the anger left him, leaving him feeling only cold and dead inside.

'I'm sorry,' he said. 'I am going to bed.'

Sleep didn't come to him, and in a way he dreaded it because of the nightmares, the terrible feeling of desolation as he wandered unchartered country, lost, forsaken, a darkness of the soul. No doctor could cure this misery.

He tried to steer his mind towards pleasant times, when Simone had been here and the whole hotel had taken on her character of smiling efficiency. How sweet she had been with that thick straight hair round her pointed face, the dark, intelligent eyes, that slight air of primness, or rectitude. One could see what she would be like as an older woman.

How had she ever brought herself to go to bed with him? You didn't give her much alternative, he reminded himself. Still, he must have looked better that night than that man with the bloated face whose reflection he sometimes caught in the mirror with the dull, heavy eyes staring back at him.

But that night he had known she felt that same surging desire by the soft heaviness of her eyes, the pliant body. One had seen the same thing in Barbie. There had been no need for persuasion, just a mutual need. But the sweet vulnerability of Simone was different, and the surprise that she was a virgin. What had that stuffed shirt, Luc Marmot, been thinking about with all the opportunities he must have had? She hadn't had, of course, quite that particular sexual abandon of Barbie...

Ah, she was in another category! No woman he had ever known had had her fire, her wildness. He sank into his pillow to think of her warm softness against him, her black hair in his mouth, her smell. She had not been immaculate like Simone, and yet her female odour had inflamed his senses like nothing else.

She was different in every way, lazy and careless where Simone was brisk and careful. She didn't shave under her arms, she was earthy, she had the damp smell of the dark woods where they hunted the *sangliers*, she was beautiful, sulky like a cat, except that cats were clean by nature. She didn't bathe daily. When her period was over she would revel in 'long soaks' as she called them, she loved scented lotions which she bought in Gramout or Cahors. He drifted into sleep thinking about her.

The next morning he slept late which made Bernard late for school.

'You must give me a note for Mademoiselle Yvette,' he said severely to François. His overall had splashes of paint on it from the day before. 'She says I live nearest the school and yet I'm always late. She is going to come and see you.'

'Yvette is an old friend of mine,' he said, partly annoyed. 'If she does I'll tell her what's what.'

'What *is* what?' Bernard asked. François looked at him. He was always asking questions.

'Come along,' he said. 'I'll ask to see Mademoiselle and tell her that it is my fault. That I slept late and that Martine Chapou didn't turn out for some reason and that your grandmother is complaining about her legs and so on and so on and so on...' Sometimes he felt his head would burst with the thousand irritations which beset him. It had never been like this with Barbie...or Simone.

In spite of the black dog on his back—this was how he thought of the heavy load of depression which was there each morning when he wakened—he busied himself all day about the *salle-à-manger*, filling paraffin stoves, taking dirty sheets to the Gramout laundry. When he was there he went to the delicatessen where Luc Marmot's mother was employed and bought a salmon loaf for dinner that night, as a peace offering.

'How is Luc?' he asked her. She wore her blonde hair high on her head and had a fine bust shaping the white overall she wore which sparkled with cleanliness. What was this secret of really clean linen? Simone had had it, not Barbie, certainly not Martine Chapeau.

'*Très bien merci*, François. The young people crowd into his bar each evening from the rue St Germain, he says. Discussing that business at Nanterre, I expect.' He nodded, not knowing *what* business. 'He and Simone and a waiter are rushed off their feet. But they're shutting up shop for their wedding. You will be receiving an invitation, I am sure.'

'It is difficult for me to get away. The demands of a hotel, as your son well knows...'

'*D'accord.*' She put two cartons, one of macedoine of vegetables and one of cucumber in cream along with the salmon loaf in a neat paper bag with handles. She didn't charge him for the two cartons, he noticed. He couldn't understand the look of pity on her face. Why should she pity him? He was a well-known hotelier, was he not? The hunters preferred his place to Le Roy. By the time they came in the autumn he would have the showers installed in every bedroom. Hunters liked to shower in the evenings.

'*Bonjour,* Madame Marmot,' he said, 'Give them my regards when you write. And also to your brothers-in-law when you see them.' She couldn't be too proud of *that* set-up.

'*Merci bien.*' She shook her head. 'Poor Maurice. He hasn't his troubles to seek with that brother of his.'

'We all have our troubles.' He decided not to mention the two cartons she had not charged for.

His spirits were at an even lower ebb that evening as he stood behind the bar. He had persuaded *Maman* to go to bed early and found her amenable since she had enjoyed the salmon loaf and the accompaniments—he hadn't told her they were a gift—he had kissed Bernard and told him to be good while Martine helped him to have his bath and he had giggled, suspiciously like her—he had frowned at that—now there was nothing left for him but the dreadful sameness of every evening, the same people, even worse, he thought, seeing that bore Weezard Prang and Sachet who was paying one of his rare visits. He caught a sight of his own face in the mirror as he turned and took a deep breath, consciously lifting the corners of his mouth. He was still François Delouche, the son of the owner, he had a beautiful son, maybe not much luck with women but things were bound to improve. They couldn't get much worse.

Prang, he must be careful not to call him that. Monsieur Henri, was at his most obnoxious, prattling his usual drivel about the war. The *pétanque* crowd were ignoring him as usual, bored out of their minds, and looking at them grouped together François wondered if there was a hint of envy in their dislike since they were all, to a man, fugitives from the *foyer*, while Monsieur Henri was free and unencumbered.

Barbie had liked him, strangely enough. They had been in the habit of exchanging London place names like a conversation game, 'Grosvenor Square,' 'Hyde Park', 'Tottenham Court Road', 'Berkeley Square', many strange-sounding names which he would never be able to check. If he and Barbie had been married they could have gone to London, seen some of those places, watched the Changing of the Guard—ah, what was the use...?

'Do you know Ayr in Scotland, Monsieur Sachet?' Henri was saying. 'In your line of business, is it not?'

'*Comment?*' Sachet said irritably, 'Ayr? Ayr? *L'Ecosse?*'

'Yes. I ask because I flew my first Spitfire there with the Squadron. *Vay-bay.* Jolly good chaps, I found them.' Sachet, who had spent his war years behind the counter of the Post Office, looked disdainful and studied his glass. Henri was not to be put off.

'Ah, but le *Jour Jay.* D-Day they called it! Four operations covering landings and escorting gliders, sweeps over enemy air fields. All the time we laughed and sung, even when someone was sitting dead in the cockpit. That was the way of it, the joke all the time, weezard prang, jolly good show!' There was stifled laughter from the card players, and someone in the *pétanque* crowd echoed, 'Weezard prang!' François tried to keep his face straight.

'I admit,' Henri said, looking down his

306

nose at the card players, 'that I was uniquely privileged to fight at the side of that great man, General de Gaulle. Agreed, Monsieur?'

Sachet, raising his head from his glass, bayed like a sad bloodhound, 'One serves one's country in different ways.' And seeing that his remark had fallen on stony ground, he added, 'I volunteered, as a matter of fact, but I was turned down on medical grounds, as you well know.'

'Fallen arches,' Monsieur Henri said, twirling one end of his blond moustache. No one laughed this time. If you annoyed the postmaster, he could keep you waiting for an unconscionable time for your *l'Allocation*.

François' irritation, not only with the silly pair, exploded like a small bomb in his brain. Normally he had no time for Sachet who could make one glass spin out all evening. He said calmly, 'Everyone realizes the work of the Post Office must go on. Monsieur Sachet is well respected in the village, never a day off in all the years he has been with us.' Why am I supporting the bugger, he asked himself, but instead of appearing gratified Sachet waved him aside.

'You may have flown with the British, Monsieur Henri, but that was no better than, say, the brothers Marmot who both were in *le Movement de l'Intérieur!'*

'Maquis!' Monsieur Henri twirled the other end of his moustache disdainfully. 'Holed up in the Causse smoking Gauloises half the time, ridiculous messages, secret codes, Boy Scouts! General de Gaulle was where he could be *seen*, striding the world like a colossus, the saviour of France!' He took a drink of wine, and the bottom edge of his moustache turned pink, making him look like a clown.

There was a murmur of assent around the bar and at the card table.

'When he asked for volunteers for the Free French Forces in April 1944,' Henri was in full flood now, 'there was no holding me back. I had been evacuated from Dunkirk as you all know. I knew England. What wonderful camaraderie there was with the British officers, the Chasseurs Alpin, even the Foreign Legion! Those expeditions we went out on in the early morning, our fur-trimmed leather jackets to ward off the cold, the good British breakfast of the bacon and eggs inside us! "Come on, you chaps!" "Right-o, old man!", Then catching a Do2l7 in our sights high over Eindhoven...the *politesse!* "Mine, I think, old chap!" "Weezard prang!" '

What a sight he was, François thought with that yellow and red striped moustache and his one watery eye (he had lost the other one while providing cover for HMS *Warspite*—God knows how often he had heard that tale!) Pity he hadn't got lost too. 'Does it ever strike you, Monsieur Henri,' he said calmly, 'that we are bored to *death* with your anecdotes!' He *heard* himself saying that. 'Look at Christian there. He's white, not with flour but with sheer boredom!' Some of the *pétanque* crowd laughed uneasily. The card players raised their heads. This was a new development.

'Am I dreaming this?' The man put his glass down, looking around as if to reassure himself. 'I come here to have a peaceful drink, to chat to my friends—and let me tell you, François, we are doing you a favour since the hotel is empty except for us—and you choose to insult *me*, a customer!' He breathed in and out noisily. 'Insult *me*, after years of custom freely given as I gave my service to my country...'

'He is only joking, Weezard Prang,' Christian interrupted. His face fell. He clapped his hand to his mouth. He took it away. *'Je vous demand pardon.* A joke. Weren't you, François?' He gave a nervous laugh.

It was a let-out, and he refused to take it. Henri, alias Weezard Prang, represented everything he hated today, senseless talk ringing in his ears, Madame Marmot patronizing him with her two cartons slipped in beside the salmon loaf, *Maman* silent, brows drawn—all he wanted to do was to retreat to his own room with his black cloud of misery.

Why had he chosen hotel life with the necessity of always being there, no matter how one felt, of having to listen to ridiculous clowns like Weezard Prang? He should have gone to Paris and worked at something interesting, gone out on the town in the evenings, met some smart girls...

'No, I wasn't,' he said. 'Even if *you* weren't, Christian, I am bored, *bored* with the tittle-tattle that goes on around this bar, the boasting, the gossip, the same old stuff night after night...' He swept his tea towel over his shoulder and noisily clattered some glasses together. He still didn't believe he was *saying* those things.

Monsieur Henri seemed transfixed. His striped moustache wobbled in disbelief. His eye had become pink, red, it had merged into his face which was a bursting fuschia colour. He suddenly banged his glass I down on the bar like an exasperated child, so hard that it smashed into fragments which flew in every direction. François felt something like a sharp wasp sting in his hand, looked down and saw a bright red incision which was pulsing out little gobs of blood.

'Look what you've done, you fool!' he shouted. 'Christian told you it was only a joke! I was pulling your leg!' He felt ashamed when he saw how the man trembled, his shaking hands lifted in apology. Maybe he *had* been affected by the war, the glass eye, everything...

"*Je suis desolé*. I didn't intend...' his moustache bristled, 'but you started it, François, whether it was a joke or not, with your insults. You have changed, I'll tell you that!' He looked around for confirmation. 'Everyone liked you once for your gaiety. And was sorry for you... This place has changed. If it weren't for us, you would have no one...'

'What are you talking about, you miserable old fool!' He could have bitten his tongue out, but that intense irritability was there again, not to be borne, the wish to hurt. And he didn't want Weezard Prang feeling sorry for him. Barbie... He knew his fists clenched. 'Always you and de Gaulle! Did you win the war between you? Did you get into bed with him as well? "*Ici Londres. Ici Londres.*" My Papa used to hear it, he told me...'

'*Doucement, doucement,*' Christian said. He looked uneasily between the two. The card players had stopped to watch. The *pétanque* crowd were staring at the mirror behind François as if it were a television screen.

A needle-like pain shot through François' hand. He looked down. The wound was still spouting gouts of blood in little jerks, thick blood which didn't flow but made him feel sick. 'Look at the damage you've done, Monsieur Henri, Monsieur Weezard Prang! It isn't a joke now, is it? Look at my hand!' He shouted the words. 'This is a serious business!' His irritability burst like an abscess in him and drove him round to the other side of the bar. He took the man by the lapels of his jacket. 'You're seeing real blood now, aren't you? Probably for the first time in your life if the truth were known! We don't all believe those marvellous exploits you are always telling us about, Weezard, Weezard...!' He even managed to *sound* like an Englishman, he thought.

He felt hands on his shoulders, dragging him away. He saw Monsieur Henri being conducted towards the door by two other men from the card table. They were talking to him in consolatory voices. A third man came over to where restraining hands had forced him to sit down. He was elderly, someone from the next village who was working on the roads here. He had the face of a judge.

'What has come over you, lad?' he said. His voice was kind but reproachful. 'That was a serious thing to do to a customer. He'll tell the police, you know, and you will not have a leg to stand on. You will have to apologize.'

'Yes,' he said, passing an arm over his forehead, 'yes, I'll have to apologize...'

Christian had come out of the kitchen with water in a basin, and a towel. He looked pale, but then he was always pale with his long hours in the bakery. 'I'm going to bathe your hand and bandage it. Have a rest, and if it gets worse, I'll take you to the hospital.'

'It's nothing.'

He watched while Christian bathed the wound. It was purple round the edges, but there was no glass in it. A long piece must have acted like a stiletto. The blood was still oozing but it would seal itself.

'Thank you, Christian,' he said. He heard his voice far away. 'I'll go upstairs. Don't come with me. I'm all right. I haven't been sleeping...get off home to Marie-Thérèse.' He had the feeling that the place was empty. His voice echoed.

He lay open-eyed for a long time. His heart was beating rapidly in his chest as if a bird were trapped there. Tears slid from his eyes, ceaselessly. I am crying like a girl, he thought. I have become like a girl, soft, emotional. What has happened to me?

He went downstairs after an hour or so and found the place dark. Christian must have put out the lights although it was only nine o'clock. *Maman* couldn't have heard anything, thank God. She had retired to her room after their meal. He took his jacket off its peg and went out and along the dark village street to apologize to Monsieur Henri.

Chapter Nineteen

As if there had been any hope of keeping it from *Maman!*

'What on earth's wrong with your hand, François?' She greeted him with the words as he slid in opposite her at the kitchen table. Coffee he needed, black, black coffee, strong. He got up again and poured himself a bowlful, thinking as he did so what he would say.

'A little accident, *Maman.*' He spoke with his back to her. 'Nothing much.'

'I can't hear you. Come and sit down.' He took a deep drink, feeling the coffee's black strength slide down his throat and fortify him. He went back again.

'A little fracas at the bar. That fool, Weezard Prang, talking his head off as usual, broke a glass. A fragment cut me. *C'est tout.*'

'It's difficult to see how...' she looked doubtful then seemed to accept the explanation. 'Is it properly bandaged? Who did it for you?'

'Christian Grinaud. Don't fuss, *Maman.* I am not a child. Has Bernard gone to school?'

'Yes, I allowed him to go on his own, otherwise he would have been late. Didn't you sleep well? You look terrible and why can't you shave before you come downstairs? It creates a bad impression.'

'When we have guests I will...'

'We must talk about that.' She bit her lip, looking worried. 'The truth of it is I'm not in good shape since Jean-Paul died.' Why did she never say 'your father?' He missed the old man, a kindly, shrewd presence always, not saying much but providing a tranquil background, an antidote to *Maman's* acerbity. 'The doctor doesn't hold out much hope of me ever really being well because of my heart. That means I shan't be able to help you much when we start having guests again. I doubt if I'll be able to stand at the stove.' She looked at him. 'Do you still want to carry on the hotel?'

'I must,' he said. 'What else is there?' He had a swift picture of himself in Paris working in a high-class *hotel*, his evenings free, going out with smart girls on high heels with bouffant hair-styles, crowded boulevards, cafés glassed in against the cold, laughter, music... 'And there's the hairdressing salon.'

She didn't look impressed. 'Custom there seems to be falling off. Or perhaps they are going to a Gramout hairdresser when they shop there.' Trust *Maman*.

'Well, if the hotel is busy it doesn't matter. Don't you worry about helping, *Maman*. It's time you had a rest. I'll go this morning to the Employment Agency and see if I can engage some staff. I have great plans...and there's your bungalow. I'll hurry Cavel along with the plans.'

'Isn't he waiting for *you*?'

'Well, perhaps...anyhow, I'll see him when I'm in Gramout. Don't worry. *Tout s'arrange.*' She gave him a strange look, shook her head slightly. He knew she was disappointed in him, as he was in himself. He would like to have laid his head on her breast and said, 'Help me...' Laughable, at his age.

'Martine is late as usual,' she said. 'If only I had my legs again! And I've promised Bernard you will take him to the Marmot's farm this afternoon for eggs.

316

Don't let *him* down.' Did she emphasise the pronoun?

'It's all fixed.' The draughts of coffee were making him feel better. 'Gramout in the morning, Marmot's in the afternoon. Meantime, you rest and let Martine do what is necessary when she comes.'

'If she comes...' Martine came bustling into the kitchen at her words.

'*Bonjour, tout le monde!* I got held up. How do you like my new blouse, François?' She giggled and he smiled thinly, thinking, looking at her, that anyone with such dangling boobs should have bought it two sizes larger. Perhaps Charles Bezier, one of the *pétanque* crowd, liked it. The two of them had been seen at night in the shadow of the buttresses of the church. One always knew it was Martine because of her insane giggling.

'*C'est charmant,*' he said, '*le dernier cri.*' At the time of the Revolution.

'You are a naughty boy, you know,' she said, waggling a thick finger at him. 'The whole village is talking about it.'

'Talking about what?' Madame Claire said.

'*Ah, Madame, quel catastrophe!* Haven't you heard? Your son lost his temper with Monsieur Prang and shook him like a rat. Isn't that the way of it, François?'

'Rubbish,' he said, 'it was a game. He

banged his glass down and I pretended to be annoyed.' He saw his mother's grim mouth. 'We're the best of friends, *Maman*. I had an amicable talk with him afterwards.'

'Well, if it shuts him up, you should do it again!' The girl's burst of giggling grated on François' ears like a saw. 'Do you know what Weezard Prang's next caper is? He wants to have an annual parade through the village every August to celebrate when that old man—what's his name—walked down the Champs-Elysées in Paris. A *re-enactement*, no less. The Maire wasn't having any of that. He was a *military* general, de Gaulois, you know.'

'De Gaulle,' François said, in disgust.

'*De Gaulle*.' She pronounced it slowly, separating the two syllables, mocking him, 'and the Maire says it was the military lot who gave us all the trouble and how do we know that he wasn't mixed up with all that! Charles Bezier told me...'

'...behind the third buttress?' Her giggle made him wince.

'You *vilain!* You're all the same. But that monsieur, I mean Prang, do you know what he's always asking of me? To go into his cottage to see his old wireless! I know what *that* means. I wasn't born yesterday. He's becoming an old goat, that one.'

And you'll become an old tart, François thought. He stirred his coffee, watching how the oily iridescence on the surface swirled into pleasing patterns. He felt an unutterable sadness. Another day to go through...*Maman* was tapping her stick impatiently.

'We've listened to you long enough, Martine. Get upstairs and do the beds and then come down and start the vegetables. Monsieur François has business in Gramout today so keep yourself tidy for answering the door, if you please. And button the top button of your blouse, if you please. *C'est tentant.*'

François got up thankfully. Gramout first. And he would take the Peugeot to Michel on the N20 and get it filled up. Michel had an Alsatian called Bruno but no wife and seemed perfectly happy without one. They had gone to school together, fished together in the *tributaire*. His open, unquestioning attitude always did him good. God knows, he could do with some of that after *Maman*.

Bernard was delighted to go to the Marmot farm. 'It is quite my favourite place,' he said as François drove him through the village, past the Tabac and the football field, past the lake, which, unlike in summer when the fishermen with their knitting wives on deck chairs gave it a *plage*-like air, was grey and sullen, like the day. 'No ducks, François.'

'They are probably hiding in the sedges. It is too cold for them to swim.'

'Sitting with their bottoms in the water behind the sedges must *make* them cold. I would truly like a tame hen like the Marmots have,' he said as they drove over the little stone bridge which spanned the sluggish *tributaire*. François had never known its proper name all the years he had fished there with Michel.

'I don't think your Mamee would like it walking about the table.' He smiled, glancing down at his son. His heart filled with love for him. He was the only one who could chase away the black dog by his innocence and trust.

'I could keep it in my bed and make a nest with the blankets. She would be pleased if I gave her some nice warm eggs.'

'It would do more than lay nice warm eggs.'

'Oh, Papa!' He covered his mouth with his hand. 'You mean...?'

'*C'est ça.* We have enough difficulty getting sheets washed now that Simone has gone.'

'Everything smelled nice with Simone. The sheets and the towels. And so did she. Now, ugh!' He made a face. 'That

Martine! And she cuddles me close and tickles me! I still think Simone would have made a good *Maman* for me, François. I should snap her up if I were you.'

'Where do you get such sayings?' He laughed this time. 'Snap her up indeed! Not from Yvette Levrault, I bet.'

'No, it was Martine. She says she can't understand why all the ugly girls in the village get snapped up.'

'And she's one of the beauties, I suppose.' The laughter was good for him. He felt sane, a father with his son on an expedition.

'She's a good giggler anyhow. Her *tetons* shake up and down when she giggles.'

'Don't use that word, please.' He straightened his mouth. 'It is not *comme il faut* for a boy of your age.'

'The *pétanque* crowd use it.'

'They're grown up, and don't say "the *pétanque* crowd". It's disrespectful.'

'*You* say it.'

'They are my *copains.*'

'Martine is my *copaine*. We giggle together when she tickles me.' He was beginning to have his doubts about Martine.

'Keep quiet. Here we are.' He steered between the broken tractor and the great pile of ordure which was a disgrace so near the door. Maurice said René would not let him move it, that he 'turned nasty'. It could be true.

He saw a change in René when they went into the cluttered kitchen. His face seemed thinner, the mouth had fallen in so that the lips were drawn back wolfishly from the gleaming teeth, but the smile could be interpreted as welcoming.

'*Ah, bon!* Here is my little *camarade!* I know what brings you here. It is the boudoir biscuits, is it not?'

'That and the hens,' Bernard said. 'We don't have them walking on our table at home.'

'*Quel dommage,*' he said absently. 'Sit there, my little sir, where I have cleared a space and I shall attend you while Maurice looks after your father. There, now we are quite like Le Roy.' He had cleared the table of some of the rubbish on it with a sweep of his hand, then reached to a shelf for a packet of biscuits which he placed in front of Bernard, while Maurice, at the same time was producing a bottle of Mombazillac and glasses from another one. 'But we need *sirop* for the little gentleman, Maurice! Ah, here it is.' He took a bottle from a clutter of dishes at the sink and dumped it down too.

François saw a dead fly sticking to its rim, and leaning forward, he flicked it off with his nail. '*Pardon,*' he said.

322

'You know Simone is home, do you?' Maurice gave him a full glass. 'They're being married next month, so she will be busy with her trousseau and making arrangements for the wedding. Everyone thinks they will make a fine couple. What a pity that English beauty of yours didn't settle, François.' There was genuine pity in his eyes.

'*C'est la vie,*' he said. The Monbazillac helped. It soothed the sore places.

'You will be receiving your invitation to the wedding before long. My sister-in-law is helping Simone with the list.'

'We'll see...' He changed the subject. 'I have chosen the site for my mother's bungalow. On the other side of the ravine. I hope you will have your rolls of wire netting removed by that time, René. They are unsightly. They will spoil the ambiance.' He laughed, then wished he hadn't. The man's face, which had been gleaming at some remark of Bernard's, had changed. And the eyes.

'It is a good cache,' he said.

'I told you before, René.' Maurice spoke sharply. 'They will deteriorate there. You should have moved them into the barn long ago. We don't want litter lying around the place, spoiling it...' François concealed a smile.

'Outside Louvière there is a big dump for old motor cars,' Bernard said. 'We saw it when we went with Mademoiselle Yvette for our school picnic last summer. She said it was a blot on the landscape.' René's head was bent. Maurice met François' eyes.

'Shall we go and get your eggs, François? You will want to get back.'

'Certainly. Come along, Bernard.' The boy got off his seat obediently. The hen which was pecking about the table squawked and flew down too.

'*Au revoir*, Monsieur René,' Bernard said. 'Thank you for the boudoirs and the *sirop.*' The man waved his hand in dismissal but didn't raise his head.

In the car Bernard didn't mention the incident to François. Children never took umbrage, he thought. 'Shall I go with you to Simone's wedding, Papa?' They were going down the hill past the ravine.

'If you are invited, and if I go.' He saw the boy was playing with the matchbox again. He had noticed that he took it out of his pocket if he were distressed in any way. The primary colours of the confetti inside gleamed momentarily as he opened and shut it time after time. The sight irritated François. 'Why do you hang on to that old thing?' he asked. 'It is a silly toy.'

'I don't have many toys.'

'What's wrong with your beautiful new bicycle?'

'I can't ride it. You said you would teach me.'

'So I shall. I've been very busy in the hotel. And your grandmother doesn't keep very well...' He saw the boy's lower lip sticking out and felt ashamed.

'Pascal has this lovely gun with a repeater mechanism. You should buy me a gun, François. Fathers buy guns for their sons. Pascal says, "Ask your father for one." '

François glanced sideways. He saw the downbent head, and again the rush of love was immediate, cleansing, banishing his misery. Barbie was gone, now Simone was getting married. He must try to reshape his life, build up the hotel, settle *Maman* in her new house, and devote more time to this son of his, Barbie's gift to him. No bitterness he thought, no searing of the soul. 'Tomorrow,' he said, 'after school, we will go to Gramout and buy a present for Simone and Luc and a gun for you.'

'With a repeater mechanism and caps?'

'With the lot.'

'*C'est bon.*' He put the matchbox back in his pocket and sat up. 'I wonder if the ducks will have come out from the sedges,' he said, 'with their cold bottoms.'

This was to make him laugh, François knew, but the lake was still grey and sullen and the wind blew drearily across it.

Chapter Twenty

The visit to the Gramout store was successful, the best one in town which specialized in household equipment of all kinds from clothes-washers to cutlery, and had a separate children's department for clothes and toys. Bernard got the gun he wanted. The assistant, a part-time *chasseur,* demonstrated all its capabilities, its telescopic sights, its trigger guard, its chamber for caps, its overarm sling. Bernard was respectful, *'Oui, monsieur,'* he said as yet another facility was revealed, *'Oui, je comprends absolument,'* but was enchanted by the leather stock engraved with Indian tepis.

'It's a good thing it doesn't fire real shot,' the young man said to François when he was wrapping it up, 'otherwise there would be no *sangliers* left for the hunters.'

'It's finer than Pascal's, François,' Bernard assured him when he came out clutching his parcel (he had called him 'Papa' in the shop as a mark of respect), 'and the monsieur where he got his didn't give him a sheriff's badge.'

'Don't boast too much or you will spoil your friendship,' François said. 'He'll see all its attributes without you pointing them out.' He thought that Pascal's father wouldn't bless him for having paid more for Bernard's shot-gun than he had paid for Pascal's. It was the leather stock engraved with tepis which had put the price up.

Simone and Luc's present had been bought in the same shop when the assistant had casually mentioned that they had been honoured by their wedding present list. His choice was a set of crystal wineglasses, remembering his mother's injunction to get half-a-dozen of the finest quality rather than a dozen of cheap rubbish. He felt fairly confident with his purchase the following evening when he dressed himself carefully and set off for Simone's farm.

She herself opened the door to him, and all his new-found peace of mind vanished at the sight of her. In the few months she had been in Paris she had acquired a new poise. She was dressed in jeans and a sweater, but both had a Parisian cut, and her hair was shining and well-groomed. Expert scissors had been at work. 'François!' Her smile was nervous.

327

She was obviously surprised to see him. 'How lovely to see you!' She held up her face to be kissed, turning her cheek as he drew near. 'Do come in.' He followed her into the farm kitchen.

'I hope I haven't come at an awkward time.'

'Not at all. As it happens I'm alone, preparing dinner. Sit down. Yes, that chair there. Keep away from the flour bin.' She laughed, still nervous, he thought. 'Madeleine is upstairs with the children and Marcel has gone to fetch mother.' Her speech was rapid. Even that had changed. 'Luc will be here any minute.'

'I wondered whether to go to your mother's house...I shan't stay. I only called to bring you a wedding present. Nothing much.' He had been carrying the parcel in its plastic bag (she would see that it came from a good shop), and he put it down on the table. 'It's fragile,' he said, 'something for your dinner parties, if you get time to have them.' He laughed.

'Oh, you are kind.' She came over and kissed him on the cheek, briefly. Her perfume, Parisian, surely, enveloped him for a second. She hadn't worn it when they had been in bed together. 'So kind.' She had coloured. 'We'll write our thanks, of course, when we open it.'

'*De rien.* You're looking marvellous,

Simone. Different. I missed you when...'
He stopped himself. He musn't ask for
pity. She had gone back to the stove and
she turned to face him.

'Paris changes one perhaps. I missed
you...but I thought it was right to go.
You understand.'

'Yes.' He looked at her. 'I kept on
hoping...'

'It's finished, François. I'm so sorry...'
He didn't speak. He shouldn't have come.
All the old regrets, the longing for Barbie
transferred to this girl had returned. She
spoke brightly. 'Life is speeded up in
Paris, I can tell you. It seems to suit
me...but it's not the same.' Her voice
was uncertain, hesitant, 'Not the same...'
She waved her hand at the window, at the
gentle farmland rolling towards the small
cluster of red roofs with the church spire
on the horizon. 'The village. I'm a country
girl at heart.'

'You don't look it.'

She smiled. 'When in Rome...tell me
about yourself, François. How are things
with you?'

'Not so good.' His pretended insouciance
had left him, the black dog was there again,
its weight on his shoulders, bowing him
down with the old feeling of despair. One
should fight... 'We don't have guests at the
moment. There's a dullness...and *Maman's*

health doesn't improve. Help is difficult to get, and so Bernard suffers too...it's hopeless! There's never been anyone like you, Simone!' The words burst from him. 'A stupid village girl to do the chores whose laugh goes through me like a saw. *Maman's* nagging. Why did you leave me? Why?' He was appalled at himself, sitting there at the scrubbed table, whining and cringing like a beggar for scraps.

'I had to do it, François.' She looked at him with deep dark eyes. 'It wouldn't have worked. We weren't suited.'

'But that night? It was good for you, wasn't it?'

'I don't regret it.'

'Or was it just a bit of amusement for you? A way of preparing yourself for Luc?' He saw her whiten.

'You're cruel.'

'I don't know what I'm saying half the time...'

'I'll answer you.' That was the secret, he thought, to be able to make decisions. 'It wasn't amusement, and Luc doesn't know. I've decided not to spoil the wedding and afterwards for him. I'll find the right time to tell him that he wasn't the first. *I'm* not cruel.'

'You always work things out so neatly for yourself.' He was bitter. 'Don't you lose sleep, ever?'

'Oh, yes. I lost plenty of sleep thinking about you, of being with you, the pleasure...the *intensity* of the pleasure. I nearly came running back to you, but...'

'But what?'

'I had had a talk with your mother. Oh, I didn't tell her, but I'm sure she guessed what was between us. Don't look so surprised. I could see it in *my* face in the mirror. She's not a fool.'

'Did she advise you to walk out on me? It's hard to believe. She was always singing your praises. She thought you could have been my salvation.' He laughed.

'No one is anyone's salvation. You have to find that for yourself. She might have *liked* me—well, I know she did—she might at one time have wanted us to marry—but she took Luc into account. We talked frankly. What we said was between us, as two women. But I think I would have made up my own mind in any case. Although I'm independent, I still need to be looked after. Luc can do that. He makes me feel...secure.'

'How exciting!'

'Don't sneer. There are different kinds of happiness. I wanted one that would last.' She shook her head. 'It's over between us, François. It was difficult—deciding that...lying in bed night after night longing for you. I'll never forget that night, the love, the special kind of love...'

'Thanks very much.' He got up and looked out of the window. Everything seemed to be over in his life. There was nothing ahead...

'Tell me, how is my little *copain?*' Her voice was falsely gay. 'Is he doing well at school? Is he top of Yvette's class?'

'I don't know.' He moved his head from side to side. He was distraught. 'If you knew the extent of my misery at times...it is impossible to convey. I don't sleep, I never want to eat, and I drink...to forget.'

She came over to him and gently turned him round, put her hands on his shoulders. The sophisticated perfume was there again, finding ways through his head, making him sway slightly. 'My heart aches for you, François. Believe that. I wish I could do something for you. Could I help you to look forward, to you and Bernard becoming our dearest friends, visiting us in Paris? Luc would take you about. You would see life from a different angle...' There was a noise outside of the farm dogs barking, a car door shutting. Simone straightened and they both turned as Luc came into the kitchen.

There was a subtle change in him too, the patina of Paris, he thought. He had always been a suave bastard, even as a schoolboy with his sleeked fair hair, but now there was an air of authority about him. His eyes were shrewd, with small lines etched round them, but his smile seemed sincere.

'François! *Quel surprise!*' He came over and shook hands with him vigorously, then kissed Simone. He noticed his face softened. 'Has Simone been entertaining you?'

'He's brought us a wedding present. Isn't that kind?' She pointed to the box lying on the table. 'And I haven't even offered him a drink. He hasn't been well, Luc.' She looked at François. 'You don't mind me saying that? We're all old friends.' He shrugged, embarrassed.

'I'm sorry.' Luc's face was concerned. 'What's been wrong?'

'Nothing much.' To patronize him like this, the great hotelier back in the sticks with the girl *he* had wanted... He felt his hands curl into fists at his side, his back become tense. The terrible irritability invaded him again. like a thousand needles, making him want to hurt as he was being hurt. 'You have a sympathetic fiancée, Luc,' he said. 'Has she told you we used to be more than friends?' He couldn't believe he had said the words. They hung between them, like hovering poison darts. He saw the man's face whiten.

'Simone and I have no secrets from each other.' 'Liar!' he wanted to shout, then shame overcame him.

'I'm sorry, Luc. Pay no attention to me. Perhaps Simone is right. I'm not well, far from well. Of course, Simone and I became, well, close, when she worked for us, but that's all there was to it. Who wouldn't admire someone looking as she does? You're a lucky man.'

'I know it.' His eyes didn't leave François' face, as if he were watching for something. And waiting... There was a silence now. He hung his head, wondering how he could move away, get out from this situation he had created. Then he heard Luc's voice, pleasant, calm, as if nothing had happened. 'When is dinner, Simone?'

'In about an hour.' Her words tumbled over each other. 'Marcel has gone to fetch Mother but I know she wants him to fix a table lamp for her, and Madeleine will be having a rest until I call her...yes, in about an hour.' She slowed down. 'Won't you stay, François? They would all love to see you.'

'No, thank you.' He shook his head. 'I'm sorry. I don't know what I'm saying these days. I get...confused. But I must be getting along. *Maman* will be waiting for me to serve our meal. It's difficult for her to get about the kitchen now.'

'Poor Madame.' She looked at him. 'You make me feel guilty leaving you both in the lurch, but...'

'Don't feel that. I understand. You have your own life.'

'Well, an hour gives us time to have a drink at Le Roy before you go back,' Luc said. 'You won't eat before eight.'

'No, but...'

'Then I insist. Simone will telephone your mother and tell her you'll be home in an hour. She would like to have a talk with her in any case.'

'Yes, oh, yes.' She brightened. 'I've been meaning to call her.'

'That's settled, then. You will follow me in your car?'

'Really, I'd rather...' The idea of having a tête-à-tête with this man who was going to marry Simone did not appeal to him. This is Luc Marmot, he reminded himself, not, 'this man', you've known him for years.

'I won't have you refusing me after your kindness in bringing us a present.' He was smiling. 'Simone wants to get on with the meal in any case. She tries out her Parisian recipes here. You've been longer at the hotelier game than I have, François. I want to pick your brains. *D'accord,* Simone?' The look they exchanged made him feel excluded.

335

'*D'accord.* On you both go.' She put her hand on François' shoulders and kissed him on either cheek. 'We both love you,' she said, 'don't forget.'

'*À toute a l'heure, coquotte.*' Luc's arm went round her briefly. There was plenty of time later for more.

He led him with confidence, each in their own car, through the busy streets of Gramout, waving once to a passer-by, another time to someone sitting at a table outside the Café du Centre. The triumphant hero returning...he parked in the smooth tarmacadamed space in front of the hotel where the cars proclaimed the type of clientèle: two Mercedes, a clutch of big Citroëns, a Jaguar, no Deux Chevaux. The menu was displayed in an impressive wrought-iron stand, and the chairs and tables in the glass-enclosed patio were white with coloured cushions in a Toile du Jouay print. The hall was gleaming. There must be plenty of staff to achieve that well-polished look in the parquet and on the panelled walls. The sconces were rose-shaded, the flowers were professionally arranged. There was an obsequious waiter who became familiar when he recognized Luc.

'Luc Marmot! Well, well! Come to visit the scene of the crime, eh?'

'If I'm allowed to darken the door. This

is a friend, François Delouche, who runs a hotel nearby. Come to criticize.'

'I know it.' The man didn't look impressed. 'I think I've seen you when I've dropped in to have a drink.'

'We prefer not to open to guests in the winter,' François said. 'The hunters keep us busy up to the late autumn.'

'We'll go and have a drink and you can see what it's like here.' Luc put a hand on his elbow. 'See you later, Raoul.'

'Sure. Remember, I want a job in Paris if you can swing it for me.' The man turned away, dapper in his starched white bolero and black trousers.

'I wouldn't give Raoul a job in a month of Sundays,' Luc said when they were in the dimness of the bar and ensconced in a corner seat, 'He has sticky fingers.' He had put a cognac in front of François. 'I was glad to get out of this place.' He sipped his own. 'The graft that goes on! I can't tell you. If I ever went back it would only be as manager, and then there would be some wholesale sacking.'

'But you're happy where you are?'

'Oh, yes. It's ideal, for the present. But I could pick myself up and move at any time. I don't put down roots easily. Meantime I like the speed of Parisian life and yet we are in a neighbourhood. Paris is made up of little villages because people from villages have come to live there and they recreate them. The only thing I miss, strangely enough, is the *Causse.* It's...cleansing somehow, those high arid spaces. The Luxembourg Gardens aren't the same with buildings all around.'

'Simone seems to like Paris. She looks wonderful. I'm sorry for that outburst back there, Luc...'

'*De rien.* Yes, she's grown there. She assimilates easily, a rare gift. I tell you, François, I consider myself lucky beyond words, but, then, she has always been the only girl for me. Don't mistake me. I knew she was in love with you when she came to Paris and I suffered...' he blew out his breath. 'Let us leave it there. But I didn't pressurize her in any way. I didn't want a reluctant bride. She worked through her problem and I left it to her. We both suffered, by God. But I knew that whatever she decided I would have to accept. Well, she came to me willingly in the end. I give you my word.'

'I loved her so much.'

'I know. It's hard. Life's hard. The "if only". Somehow one has to learn to manage one's affairs...here, your glass is empty! Another cognac?'

'Thank you. I shouldn't drink so much.'

'We do a lot of things we shouldn't do. Believe me, I don't sit in judgement.

338

Tell me,' he paused, 'did you love Simone more than Bernard's mother?' Even in the dimly-lit bar he saw the piercing gleam in Luc's eyes.

'Barbie? Well, differently.'

'Did you ever...compare them in your own mind?'

'Perhaps. I never intended to, but, well you know how it is.'

'I'll tell you, François,' he had raised his hand and the waiter was at his side, 'Give my friend another cognac, please.' He was still only halfway through his. 'I'll tell you,' he had waited until the waiter had gone away, 'Simone and I have always been frank with each other. When she was able to talk about it she said that the thing which decided her—yes, we were contestants, my friend, and believe me I felt murderous at times towards you—the deciding factor for her was that she felt she could never take the other girl's place.'

'Barbie.'

He nodded. 'Barbie. That she knew she came first with you, always would. Simone was very young when she first met you. I realized she had to get you out of her system somehow because I knew *I* was the one for her. Does that sound pretentious? Maybe so. I don't think you have ever realized the extent of Simone's pride. I've known her since she was a little girl. I've watched her, her craving for excellence. She has to be first with everything. She is competitive, even with herself, she sets herself targets. She has helped me to run my hotel as if her life depended on it. We made a team. I don't think you and she did. She has taught herself to cook professionally, she is up at five in the morning to go to Les Halles, she has to *achieve*, she has to be first.' He found himself nodding in agreement. That was Simone.

'She couldn't be more unlike Barbie. She was...easy. She had only one aim, to get away from the situation she had got herself into, which included me. And her son. Can you imagine how that damages one's self-respect?'

'In one way, yes. But she would never have been any good to you.'

'She was Bernard's mother.'

'She left him.'

'That's what I mean.' Instead of making him feel better, the second cognac, now that it was finished, had only depressed him further. The black dog was there again, he could feel its weight, and with it a kind of agitation, even of muscle weakness, as if he was imprisoned against his will in this warm brown alcove with this self-assured man who got everything right. He felt his head swim, his eyes blur, and forced himself to rise.

'I think I'll have to go,' he said.

'Sit for a minute, please.' Those piercing eyes missed nothing. 'I'm going to order coffee. I always drink it after cognac.' He lifted his hand and the waiter was again at his side. 'Two black coffees,' he said, 'strong.' And to François, who had resumed his seat, 'Bad for the liver. Simone and I watch we don't drink too much of it.' You would, he thought. 'Life's tough, eh?' Luc smiled at him.

'Don't pity me for God's sake.'

'I don't mean especially hard, but hard for you. I remember you at school, although I was in a higher class. In sports you took things badly. You were vulnerable.'

'Is that so?' He felt suddenly deathly tired.

'You've had a dreary winter, and your mother,' he grinned, 'Well, she's a character! Still, you've had a basinful, Mademoiselle Barbie, the responsibility of a child, it can't have been easy. Simone worries about you.' The coffee came. 'Sugar?'

'I don't take it. I'm putting on weight, and don't for God's sake tell me to do something about that!'

'Is that how I come over to you? Bossy? No, it's a pose. And if I remember correctly, it was always you who was

341

getting into trouble at school, things we admired you for, getting the cigarettes we smoked behind the toilets, gettings away ahead of us with girls. They all adored you.'

'I matured earlier.' He was pleased, briefly.

'And how!' He laughed, then sobered. 'François, don't take this amiss. We'd like to help you.'

'I don't need...'

'Let me finish. We would really like to help you in any way we can. You need a break. Come and stay with us after our wedding, and bring Bernard.'

'I just walk out of the hotel and leave *Maman* to hobble about on her own?'

'No, it wouldn't be like that. When we've finished our coffee we'll go and see the manager here and he'll recommend a couple for you. He's got a list.'

'I intend to engage staff for the start of the season.'

'When do you open?'

'After the Easter holiday.'

'There's still time to have a week or so with us. Monsieur Hermant will know a couple who would take over for you, the man in the bar, the woman cooking and looking after your mother. Can you afford it?'

'I suppose so. We don't spend much,

except for me drinking the profits.' He was able to smile. The coffee had cleared his head, the trembling had gone, even the black dog had slunk away for the time being.

'And I should see a doctor if I were you,' Luc said casually.

'If he would give me something to make me sleep I might even consider it.'

'I'm sure he would. Does the idea of coming to Paris appeal to you? We could do the sights. Think how Bernard would love it.'

'You don't want me, come on, admit it.'

'I'll tell you the truth, it's Simone's idea. But you're a friend of mine from away back. I don't have one in Paris, too busy. You're from my home town, part of my background. We'd like you to come. I mean it. Have you finished your coffee?'

'Yes.'

'Come along, then, and meet Monsieur Hermant. This is a good time to catch him. He's always approachable when he's had a good dinner. They eat before the guests.'

He drove home half an hour later, feeling that his life had altered, or that he must believe it had been altered. There was still a core of misery, but Luc was sure Doctor Theopile would be able to help him there. People who ran hotels often got low.

It was like being an actor. You were on the stage every night. Sometimes you got encores, sometimes you played to empty houses.

For once, he had something to look forward to, a visit to Paris, the arrival of Monsieur and Madame Rambeau, an experienced elderly couple fit as fiddles, Monsieur Hermant had assured him, who revelled in 'helping out' for a limited period. And when he came back fit as a fiddle himself with Bernard, there would be the new season at the hotel. While he was in Paris he would pick up some new ideas, discuss his plans with Luc and Simone...Luc had said it would be a new life.

Chapter Twenty-One

Maman didn't look angry and ask him why he was late, which he had expected. On the contrary, she had an air of pleasure and there was even a tenderness in her expression.

'Can you imagine,' she told him as he began bustling about the kitchen, 'Simone telephoned me.'

'Yes, she said she was going to do that.

Would some cold chicken and salad do, *Maman?*'

'Of course. Heat up the soup. We can start with that and there is some *cabecou*. And why don't we have a bottle of Cahors?'

'I have one in the bar.' When he returned with the bottle he said, 'She must have put you in a good mood.'

He went to the sink and ran the tap as he separated the leaves of the lettuce.

'She was very sympathetic. But then she always was.'

Encouraged, he took the bull by the horns.

'They would like me to visit them in Paris with Bernard when they are married. Just for a week before we open here. I went with Luc to Le Roy and met Monsieur Hermant, the manager there. He would arrange for a couple to come in. Of course, you would be in charge.'

He waited for the storm.

'It's not a bad idea at all.' She was nodding slowly, 'not bad at all. It would be a change for both of us. And Bernard would love to see Paris.'

'That goes without saying.' He shook the lettuce in its wire basket, hiding his surprise at her acquiescence. 'Did he go to bed himself?'

'Yes, I sent him upstairs at eight o'clock.'

'You wouldn't really mind me going?' He turned round to face her.

'No.' Her expression was equable. 'Simone thinks you could learn a lot being in Paris. You would see how other places are run. She is such a sensible girl, and sounds happy with Luc.'

'She is.' He put the salad in a bowl, shook some walnut oil over it, some salt and pepper, and carried it to the table, placing the wooden spoons beside it. *Maman* always did the mixing. Now the platter with the pieces of chicken arranged on it. She had managed to set the table and cut the bread. He went back to the stove and ladelled out two bowls of soup, ready ravioli with left-over vegetables cut up small, a constant in the kitchen. 'Ready, *Maman.*' He assisted her from her chair, taking her weight, got her to the table and seated, then brought the bowls to each place. He unfolded her napkin with a waiter's flourish, *'Bon appetit.'*

She was hungry. She spooned the soup with relish while he watched her. He took a few sips himself, but he had no appetite. He poured some Cahors for the two of them, and tried not to gulp his. He felt its warmth like a dark red lake spreading round his heart, leaving it like an island of soreness in the centre.

'You would be better advised to take

346

your soup than empty your glass.' She missed nothing.

He shook his head. 'I'm sorry. I'm not hungry.'

'Simone says that if you go to Paris she will tempt your appetite with some new dishes. She and Luc experiment in their kitchen. Their hotel seems to be a great success.' He had had enough of Simone and Luc.

'Since you think so much of her, I wonder why you didn't manage to make her stay instead of deserting us?'

'That was her choice.' She was turning over the lettuce with the spoons, grinding more pepper over it. She liked lots of pepper.

'But you approved of her choice.'

'I knew what would make her happy.'

'Why did you do that to me, *Maman?*' He reached for the bottle, refilled his glass. 'I loved her. She loved me...'

'It was a girl's infatuation which had lingered. Oh, don't think I didn't know what was going on...but in the end she came down on the side of common sense.'

'Common sense being what makes me unhappy.'

Amazingly, she was eating during the conversation, helping herself to lettuce, taking up a piece of chicken on her fork. She pointed it at François. 'Don't relate everything to yourself. You must get out of the habit of thinking the world revolves round you all the time.' She ate the piece of chicken, sipped her wine, considered, head on one side, 'Too rich for white meat.' They were both silent. He didn't try to break the silence, but drifted into a miasma of memories, the light freshness of Simone like the *églantines* that summer, the heavy dark richness and beauty of Barbie, potent like the Cahors. *Maman's* voice came softly to him, changed. 'I knew someone like that once, who only thought of himself...'

'Who was that?'

'Your father.'

'My father! He was self-effacing, the opposite of what you say!'

'Jean-Paul was not your father.'

The wine saved him from having a brainstorm. He was sure of that. And the previous cognacs. What she was saying didn't concern him. The warm glow inside him made him sympathetic towards this man who was being told that after so long the gentle soul whom he had loved was not his father. That must be terrible, a shock beyond speaking about.

And then, like cloth tearing, it became *his* situation. *His* father who wasn't his father. Blood hammered in his ears, coloured his vision red.

'You are saying that Jean-Paul...and you...were not...together...my parents?'

'That is so.' Her eyes were very black in her pale face. She was no longer eating. 'Your father was an Englishman called Joseph Delaware. He came here...and left before you were born...'

'Just a minute, just a minute!' He knew he was shouting. 'You are telling me that there is someone in the world, going about, in England, who is my father! It is...incomprehensible!' His voice had shot up the register, become a scream. He saw fear in her eyes.

'I am telling you that. Lower your voice.'

'Lower your voice she says! Lower your...' He did, swallowed, 'And why have you kept it from me? Wasn't I entitled to know?'

'How can I explain? Or expect your forgiveness. It was a question of priorities. Certainly you were entitled to know, but Jean-Paul was entitled to have you believe that he was your real father. He married me when I was pregnant. He never reproached me. All he wanted was my respect for him if I couldn't give him my love. But he needed yours. It meant everything to him. I decided it was the one thing I could do to repay him.'

'So why are you telling me now?' The

349

scream had left him hoarse.

'Because I told Simone, and today on the telephone she said I ought to have told you too. I didn't think it necessary after Jean-Paul died.' She looked at him. The pain in her black eyes made him wince. 'She made me see it was necessary, that one shouldn't hide the truth. She convinced me that there had to be honesty, that it was too big a burden to place on her alone. She is older than her years, that one.'

'My mind is whirling. I don't know what to think...' He put his hand out to the bottle.

'Try thinking without that. Or at least listening. I should have told you. I regret that bitterly. Telling Simone made it possible. I had broken the silence of many years...now I want to tell you what he was like so that you may know where you sprang from, so that you can explain yourself to yourself, perhaps readjust your life. I know it's gone wrong for you. I've watched it, my heart breaking for you...'

'My...real... father came from England? Like Barbie?' The coincidence was like a bitter taste.

'Yes, like Barbie. I wonder, if she had known...'

'No, it wouldn't have made any difference.' He waved his hand. 'It was the place she detested even more than me, "the closed little village," she called it.'

'In that case she was no great loss.'

'How can you say that! She was my first love. My great love. You don't know what you're talking about. She ruined my life.'

'I'm sorry I said that. I *do* know, that agony...Joseph was *my* first love. And at the time I thought *my* life was ruined, even after I married Jean-Paul and you came. But there was still life. One hangs on to that.'

'Is it worth hanging on to?'

'You owe it to Bernard, as I owed it to you. You're so like Joseph in appearance.' She smiled. 'Now I can tell you. The golden *mèche*. I wasn't young when I met him, at least not as young as you were when you met Barbie, but the passion...but then you know that passion, son. Think yourself lucky that you have experienced it. Perhaps it is your inheritance.'

The shock was still there, but with it the beginning of curiosity about this man who had come here, impregnated his mother and gone away again, disappeared out of her life the way Barbie had disappeared out of his. 'Tell me about him.'

'He was different, strange, to me. Do you think that is the first excitement, the strangeness? He wore corduroys and a white shirt with rolled-up sleeves like a workman. He had brown forearms and white teeth. Workmen rarely have white teeth, or one doesn't see them, I don't know which. He was an engineer employed by the *Conseil Municipal*. And he was a birdwatcher.' She seemed to speak with pride.

'What is that, a birdwatcher?'

'It is an English thing. One watches birds. One has to be prepared to sit for a long time with binoculars in the hope of seeing them. Sometimes when we were making love he would stop and turn his head and stay very quiet. Once when he did this he said in a hushed voice, like being in church, "By Jove," that is English, "By Jove, a golden oriole!" Then...he went on again.' He turned away. It was distressful for him to sit and listen to this old woman's tales about making love. That was only for Barbie and him, or Simone... 'He let me look through his binoculars. He was like a boy, excited...you remind me of him the way your face lights up and you look as young as Bernard. The golden oriole was his "quest", that was the word he used. He would recite strange words out of a little book he carried, reading them like a litany...' she paused, 'Let me see...yes, "Habitat deciduous", and "lowland woods"—that was another one, "thickets...*mouilles...les buissons fourrés...*" ah, it's a long time, "*le nid...le nid...*well-hidden near ground in brambles and nettles..." ' She finished with a rush, smiling like a young girl. 'I remembered most of it! He taught me English words!' It was all too much for him.

'I cannot comprehend. Tell me, where was this place where you met...this man?' How could he say, 'my father'?

'Didn't I tell you? At the *chateau d'eau*, beside our land. All that summer we had only a trickle of water from the taps at the hotel—this hotel—I worked here then—and the *patron* was forced to send to Gramout for someone. Your father—don't wince, your real father—was doing what he called a "stint"—I remember still so many of his words—with the Municipality here because of this interest he had in birds of our region. His French was good, you see, so he could take the job. I remember he said making love was the same in any language.' He turned away, wishing she wouldn't make remarks like that.

'Go on, *Maman,*' he said.

'We had an Englishman in the hotel who complained all the time that there was never enough water for his bath. "Spare me from the English and their eternal baths," the *patron* used to say. Joseph stayed here while he was mending whatever he had to mend at the *chateau d'eau*. In your room. I couldn't believe in his beauty at first, his strange beauty. I was almost thirty and still a virgin, a write-off in the village...'

His heart was bursting with sadness as she talked. Just when he thought he was on an even keel with his life arranged so neatly for him by Simone and Luc, there was this impossible blow, an assault on his whole being. What was it Luc had said of him? That he was 'vulnerable'. Well, by God, who wouldn't be if they were presented with a new father at the age of twenty-six? 'I was getting things worked out,' he said, 'and now, this.'

'Simone said you ought to know, that you could never make a fresh start if the ground weren't cleared. You have to open your mind to the fact of your father, your real father, François, because there is a lot of him in you. He was moody, and he left me with you, still to be born. Unreliable. Sometimes he came down in the morning with a shining face, other times he wouldn't talk at all. You're the same. He drank like a fish at the bar. But he was liked. He won over the men who came here. He had great charm and I loved him, utterly and completely. I won't ever forget him, as you won't ever forget Barbie, and there you're like me. That's our cross. Who knows where the attraction lay? Perhaps the strangeness...'

He got up, swayed on his feet as he straightened. 'I am going to bed. Can you manage to get to your room?'

'I can manage. Come and say goodnight to me.' She held out her arms.

He went round the table, and as he bent over to her the sensation was as if his brains slid to the front of his head. He kissed her cheek. *'Maman...'* he said. He shook his head slowly, his heart too full.

'Go to bed, son. Everything is straight now. You know who you are, who you came from, it will explain a lot to you, although it may not make it any easier. Tomorrow we will plan for the opening of the hotel, how you will come back from Paris, a changed man full of ideas.' He straightened and she caught his hand. 'You forgive me?'

'What is there to forgive?' There was a loud beating in his temples. 'We're straight now. That is the main thing.'

Upstairs, when he passed Bernard's door he pushed it open and went in. His son was lying neatly, his head on the pillow. The foreshortened child's face made tears spurt from his eyes. The twin barrel of the gun lay neatly on the pillow beside him, the covers tucked round it, as if it were a body.

In his own room he tumbled into bed,

only kicking off his shoes. He lay awake until the beating in his temples steadied and he could think of his new father. On the face of it he would have made a better one than Jean-Paul who had always been too old to play games the way Pascal's father did with him.

But for Jean-Paul to die with that secret! He searched his memory, remembered how often he had passed the old man in the yard, too busy or too careless to give him a greeting. He groaned, turning in the bed. But there had been love between them surely? Remorse gripped him, his heart physically ached.

He would never sleep, he knew that. He took two aspirins, then another two, but they seemed to stick in his throat. He coughed and spluttered, got up and drank some water, then swallowed two more in case he had spat them out. He lay on the bed again, his eyes stretched wide, sleepless.

Sometime later, driven to despair he got up and went downstairs, went to the bar and poured himself a glass of whisky, an English drink, he thought. He preferred wine, but at least it seemed to clear his throat of the powder residue of the tablets. He poured some more and drank it to make sure.

He tiptoed upstairs again, and threw

himself on the bed. This time his mind was giving him some peace. Everything was at one remove. He seemed to be in a green wood, dark, mysterious, so dark that the sun couldn't penetrate it. Suddenly he slept.

Chapter Twenty-Two

He awoke suddenly with the damned beating in his temples again. The black dog was now lying on his chest, suffocating him. He heard the sound of its breathing. He threw himself upright and off the bed, then sat on its edge. Tried to think.

His father. His new father. His real father. Joseph Delaware. As strange as Barbie Sinclair. *That* was what was troubling him. And strangely enough, *Maman's* bungalow. That too suddenly seemed important. Perhaps now that he knew about this Joseph Delaware it would be better to face it towards the *chateau d'eau* instead of the ravine where those ugly rolls of wire netting lay. If she looked onto the water tower it would revive pleasant memories of her lover—and his father.

Yes. It seemed so right. He would give her binoculars as a gift when she moved in so that she could look for the golden oriole with them to remind her of this Joseph. Everything was falling into place. And perhaps Bernard would become a birdwatcher as well. That was much more suitable and less belligerent than shooting with double-barrelled shotguns...

Although it had that *feeling* of rightness, he still didn't believe what he was thinking, about the *chateau d'eau* and *Maman's* house facing towards it, nor golden orioles, nor Bernard becoming a birdwatcher, nor indeed the new father. It was too strange...

But it must be important, otherwise he wouldn't have wakened in the middle of the night. He *had* to go and see where exactly *Maman's* house should be built. Now. He saw he was still wearing his jeans and shirt. That saved time. He bent and scrabbled for his shoes under the bed, put them on, found a jersey there too and pulled it over his head. It would be chilly at this time of night. Best to keep warm.

The Peugeot was parked on the hill on which the War Memorial stood, and so he was able to slip in behind the wheel and run down the slope away from the hotel without switching on the engine. He did this as he passed the Tabac, its windows shuttered. Thank God that was not a vice of his. He had enough with drinking...and mad ventures in the middle of the night.

He laughed out loud.

The football field was a luminous green, the goalposts shone bone-white in the moonlight. He had enjoyed football at school. It was a pity he hadn't kept it up. Christian was Captain now of the former pupils' club, and Pascal's father was goalkeeper for them. He had asked him once or twice if he would like to take it up again and he had said he would see.

The English played football. He remembered a strange saying of Barbie's father when he had been talking of a cup game he had watched. 'Their brains are in their feet.' But they were altogether strange. And it was strange how his father, his real father, had been English, and then he, François, had fallen in love with an English girl. Or *was* it strange when he was half-English himself?

Now over the little stone bridge spanning *Le Tributaire*. Tomorrow when he was buying stamps from Monsieur Sachet he would ask him what it was called. He was an expert on local history, although he didn't have to be so glum about it. But how absurd that *he* should have lived here all his life and never thought to ask.

And now, change gear and up the steep incline leading past the ravine. Fortunately the road to their land branched off to the left before he got close to the Marnots' farm, otherwise that madman René would hear the Peugeot. He would be another one who couldn't sleep.

The night air through the open car window refreshed him. Soft night airs, the purring sound of the car...relaxing. How good it was to feel decisive, to have made a decision to choose the site for *Maman's* house once and for all and to get the building started before the Easter holiday. He wouldn't take any excuses from old Cavel. Really, things worked out for the best. If *Maman* hadn't told him of his real father and the *chateau d'eau,* he might have built the bungalow facing the wrong way.

He felt good, and with the good feeling tender thoughts filled him of Barbie, her dark appeal, her white, voluptuous flesh. How happy they had been that summer, close-lipped in his room, loving through the warm nights. He would never feel like that again. Simone...well, she had been a release but she hadn't had the *wildness* in her of Barbie. She would never have surprised him as Barbie had done. It was the strangeness, the English strangeness. The tears were running down his face as fresh as if she had left him yesterday. He caught them with his tongue.

But there was still life. One hangs on to that, *Maman* had said. There was this new house, and Paris with Simone and

Luc. He lifted his head and saw the tall shape of the water tower, a silver pencil against the skyline, he saw it now as Joseph Delaware's *chateau d'eau*, the watcher of birds, his father. Yes, it was a good idea to turn *Maman's* house to face it, away from that mess René Marmot had left at the foot of the ravine despoiling the countryside. God knows when he would shift it. This year, next year, sometime, never. He was crazy.

It would help him to go to Paris and see some reasonable people for a change, smart friends of Luc's and Simone's, sit in cafés and watch the Parisian crowds go by. In a way, hearing about his father had been like a watershed. He would go on from there now, an interesting person who had led an interesting life, rather strange, really, an English father, an affair with an English girl who had given him a beautiful son, good friends in Paris where he could spend an occasional weekend—he might even fly from Toulouse—this new house for *Maman*—really, life was opening out for him, he had, to put it crudely, kicked that black dog in the backside.

The dark maw of the ravine was on his left. He stopped the car on an impulse and got out to peer down into its depths. God, what a shambles! And most of the netting was rusty, as far as he could see, in the small amount of moonlight which penetrated its fastnesses. Brambles and nettles had grown through it, rampant, as if to cover its ugliness.

An English father! The beating started up in his temples again. He still could not accept it. Had he inherited some adverse traits from his strangeness? *Maman* had said so, his moodiness, the drinking, but at least coming here in the middle of the night finally to choose the site for her bungalow had been a good thing. Joseph Delaware had been able to make decisions too, to clear out without saying a word to the woman who was pregnant with his child. And so had Barbie. Clearing out. Was it an English trait?

No matter. Everything was straight now. It was a sorrow that Jean-Paul had been obliged to keep his secret, but then he had wanted it that way. As long as he had been given love...he winced, turning his head because of the pain in his heart. Had he taken him too much for granted? Simone had loved Jean-Paul. Often she had chatted to him when she was hanging out the washing, and Bernard had shown him love, running to Papee with all his tales, climbing up on his knee...

Far down in the darkness, in the tangle of vegetation he thought he saw a gleam. Had the moonlight caught the wire netting, making it silver? But the gleam he had seen was golden. Was he sure about that? Wasn't it the rust on the netting which had given it a golden sheen?

No, there it was again, a moving glint of gold among the thickets...he heard *Maman's* voice repeating the strange words of the strange man, your father, he reminded himself, 'Habitat deciduous...*les buissons four...*', no, he couldn't remember, ah...*'le nid caché...près du sol...'* the gold was dazzling him, there were darting prisms in front of his eyes.

He began scrambling down the side of the ravine, feeling exultant. This was how one felt when one lived a life of decisions, having an idea, putting it into practice. He would rescue the bird, the golden oriole, but, of course, that was what it was, trapped in that stupid wire of René's. It would bring him closer to his new father, make him seem real.

Loose stones rolled under his feet and he tore his hands on the brambles he grasped to prevent himself from falling. Once he went down on his back and slid a few yards, grazing his shoulders and his calves, hearing the ripping of his jersey as the juniper bushes caught it.

Now he was at the foot, trying to find a flat space to enable him to walk amongst the rolls of netting as he searched for the bird. His foot rolled on something. An empty bottle. But the golden gleam was no longer there. No wonder, he consoled himself, with the noise he had made slipping and sliding down the slope, the bird had somehow managed to free itself. Or at least hide somewhere in the darkness. If he sat down quietly and waited, he was bound to see it. They were shy, solitary birds. How did he know that?

Ah, there it was again, the glint, like his hair, like the English father's hair, the moon had slid from behind the clouds that was why...he half-rose, his limbs tense, his heart beating quickly. The noise in his head was tremendous. It blew his body to bits as it reverberated round the bowl of the ravine.

The silence afterwards was like no other silence, but he didn't hear it.

Chapter Twenty-Three

It was June again, an *églantine* summer. Simone saw the open pink blossoms climbing through the hedges as Luc drove swiftly out of Gramout and along the narrower road to the village. How verdant everything was after Paris which remained grey and silver throughout the summer except when one had a moment to walk in the Luxembourg Gardens. She would not like to die in Paris. Luc had promised her that.

She had been unable to come and see Madame Claire earlier because of morning sickness—that was the excuse she made. In fact the news of François' death had made her physically ill, an almost unknown state for her. She kept from Luc the full extent of her grief. She would have been no use to François' mother in such a state of longing and misery.

'Are you glad to be back in the countryside?' she asked him, admiring his neat profile. He drove the way he did everything, quietly and efficiently. His love-making was the same, no heights, but then, no depths. The only abandon she had ever known had been with François, but she doubted if she would ever have grown fond of him, the way she had grown fond of Luc. He was her anchor. Already she could not imagine life without him. People were as they were. She was beginning to accept that, and that marriages were broken by women trying to change their men. How did she know that she hadn't fallen short of *François'* requirements? There was no doubt with Luc. He was steadfast in his love.

'It is home,' he said. 'We will come

back. Do you smell the *églantine?*' He said softly, 'the fragrance of summer.'

'Yes, I smell it.' Yet her heart ached.

'You are all right, my darling?' He was the type of man who concerned himself with every detail of her pregnancy, who would be part of her discomfort as well as her happiness. It was *their* child. That was what he had said when she had asked him not to fuss. He was discerning. She didn't doubt that he had noticed the extent of her grief over François' death however much she had tried to hide it.

She was trembling when she went up the few steps to the verandah and into the *salle-à-manger* when Luc held open the door for her. The hotel rested in its afternoon silence. She knew how every hotelier looked forward to that hour or two of peace.

They went towards the kitchen. Would Madame Claire be there, or confined to bed, broken by the shock of her son's death? Still, it was three months ago now. She might have known. Madame Claire was seated at the table busily chopping mushrooms. She seemed engrossed in her task. Simone had never seen her hands idle, even at this time of relaxation. She was thinner, paler if anything...'Madame!' She went towards her.

Simone!' She had turned at the sound

of her voice and was holding out her arms. 'At last! I've been counting the days! Why didn't you come earlier?' She made to rise as they embraced. Her stick clattered to the floor.

'No, don't get up. I came as soon as I could. Oh, Madame! How good it is to see you!'

'And you. You look well. And so *chic*.'

'That's Paris. But you? How are you?' She knew there were tears in her eyes. 'Does it begin to be easier?' Madame Claire waved away the question to greet Luc.

'*Ça va*, Luc? You look prosperous. Things go well for you in Paris?'

'*Extrèmement bien, merci*, Madame.' He bent and kissed her on both cheeks. 'How could they be other when I have Simone at my side?'

'*Bon*. Sit down, please. I'm sorry I can't stand to receive you. But first, there is coffee on the stove, Simone. Perhaps you will pour it. Madame Rambeau rests in the afternoon. She and her husband are treasures. I couldn't have done without them. Monsieur Hermant did me a good turn there, thanks to you, Luc.'

'I did nothing. But you have other help?'

'Yes, a girl who comes from Gramout to wait the tables. She has a car so she goes home at night. And Martine, who grows on one.' She smiled, pulling down her mouth. 'That is for you a pleasure deferred. However, Madame Rambeau is a good reliable cook, not imaginative, but I can still supply some of that if needed, eh, Simone?' There was a hint of sad mischief in her smile.

'As far as I remember.' She laughed in relief. Her fears had been groundless. Here was no broken woman. In a way the tragedy of François' death had changed her, made her calmer, ennobled her, even. It was evident in the way she held her head, her careful coiffure. Who looked after her hair now? François had enjoyed dressing it, had commented on its rich blackness. Now there were wings of white above her ears, the only apparent sign of her grief.

She opened a cardboard box she had brought with her after she had poured the coffee. 'A sample of *my* work. Not much imagination there.'

'*Les réligieuses!*' Madame Claire's hands went up in pleasure. 'My favourite, as you well know. And quite perfect, as one would expect from you.'

'They're nothing. The work of an amateur, but I thought...' She had been painstaking in their preparation, slicing off their caps neatly, piping the cream. She had put love in them.

'She's too modest,' Luc said. 'And she hasn't mentioned that the plate under the silver doiley is for you.' Madame Claire lifted a patterned silver edge.

'Sèvres,' she said. 'Ah, no, Simone, it is too much.'

'Luc bought it, so you must chide him.'

'Far too much, Luc.' She put a hand out to both of them. 'You are too kind, but thank you, thank you.'

'*De rien*,' Luc said. 'If I may boast, Simone has become well-known for her *confiserie*, but, naturally, Sevres plates don't accompany them every time.'

'Shush, shush!' Simone smiled at him. 'The proof of the pudding is in the eating. Try one, Madame Claire. I remember you had a sweet tooth.'

'That's true.' She examined closely the *patisserie* she held. Simone had provided a plate. 'This shows the difference between us. You have the attention to detail, I used to go in for the grand gesture, hit or miss. If it came off it was good, if not, it was a disaster.'

Luc laughed. 'There's room for the two of you.'

The conversation had run to a halt. They had exhausted the irrelevance of cooking, considering the circumstance, but it had been useful in filling in the first few minutes. Should she now say something about François? She and Luc had discussed often how they would behave. They mustn't ignore the subject, however difficult it was to broach it. See how it goes, Luc had said. The *réligeuses* had been a *divertissement*...

'We have thought of you so...' She began and stopped. Bernard came running into the kitchen, and she held out her arms to him, half-relieved. 'And here's Bernard! What a big boy!' He allowed himself to be kissed then wriggled out of her arms.

'I listened for your car for ages, then I went round the back to play with Mou-Mou's new kitten and didn't hear it.'

'*Quel dommage.* You have grown into a regular schoolboy, hasn't he, Luc?'

'Yes, indeed. I expect you can read quite well now, Bernard?'

'*Naturellement.*' His look was scornful.

'We brought you some books from Paris.' Luc handed him a parcel which he had laid on the table. 'I hope you like them.'

'We have books at school.'

'Bernard!' His grandmother reprimanded him. 'Open your present from Luc and Simone and say, "Thank you", if you please.'

He tore off the wrapping paper and looked at the bright covers, at first quickly, almost nonchalantly then taking more time as something attracted his attention. *'Merci bien!* We don't get books like those at school, certainly. I shall show them to Mademoiselle Yvette on Monday.' He read out the title of one, 'The Naughty Cat.' He peered. 'It looks like Mou-Mou.' He looked at another. 'The Town Mouse. Is there a difference, I wonder? Ah, here is one about cowboys! I like the cowboys. *Merci bien.'* Simone noticed he was wearing a toy gun on a strap over his shoulder and that there was a sheriff's badge pinned on his shirt. They should have brought a leather-fringed jacket for him instead of books. Well, when he was with them in Paris they would remedy that.

'Are you looking forward to coming back with us for a holiday, Bernard?' she asked him.

'Yes, thank you. I have made a list of the places I wish to visit. Perhaps there will not be time for them all...'

'We will make time.' She said deliberately, 'François would be pleased to know you were going to Paris. He had intended to come...' There was a silence. She wished now she hadn't mentioned his name. The boy looked uneasy. Madame Claire sat at the table, not moving.

'Shall I tell them how I knew about François, Mamee?' The boy's voice had

371

gone higher. There was a defiant edge to it.

'*Si tu veux.*' Her face was rigid. This was not what she and Luc had envisaged. There should have been tears and embraces, and expressed sorrow and reminiscences of François who had died in such a terrible way.

'She was funny, Martine.' Still the excited, high-pitched voice, the bold stance. 'She was giggling but she had her hands over her face and the tears were running out.' He looked from Luc to Simone. '*C'était bizarre.*' Simone felt cold with apprehension.

'I remember Martine giggled,' she said. François had told her.

'Everyone was talking in the village about it,' he said, 'running about and talking. She cuddled me but this time she did not tickle. Monsieur René—you know, Simone, where they have the tame hen—had come to the ravine when François was there in the middle of the night and shot him with his gun.' His mouth quivered and he repeated even more loudly, 'Shot him with his gun.'

'We heard,' Simone said, 'it was a terrible accident.'

'Martine said he should be locked up and he *is* now. When he gets out of prison I'm going to shoot him,' he let out a high

372

giggle, 'just see if I don't.'

Luc was the first to speak. 'There is no need for that. He has been punished, and he will never be let out for the rest of his life. He is sick. Simone was right. It was a terrible accident but it is finished.'

'I have told him that,' Madame Claire said. Her face still had no emotion in it. 'Perhaps he will believe you.'

Simone went over to her and put an arm round her shoulders. Had she wept so much that there were no more tears left? She looked at the boy. 'Yes, it is true, Bernard. To be locked up for the rest of one's life is nearly as bad as being shot.'

His lip stuck out. He scraped his foot on the floor. He didn't believe her. 'Anyhow, when you came Mamee said I could ask you if you would take me to see the ravine. She says you would know what was best.'

Luc looked at Madame Claire. There was surprise in his face. 'If you think it is wise, we could take him.'

'I didn't mean you,' Bernard said. 'It was Simone.' She saw the bravado in the child's face, imagined his troubled nights upstairs with no one to run to except an elderly Madame Rambeau or her husband. No mother...

'I think it would be best to go,' she said. Madame Claire put her hand up and covered Simone's.

'I knew you would say that.' Her eyes went to Luc. 'She was always one for decisions.'

'Let's go, then,' Luc said.

'Only Simone.' The boy looked at him. 'I don't know you well enough.'

'That's reasonable.' Luc took the car keys out of his pocket and gave them to Simone. 'I'll stay with Madame Claire and keep her company. We have a lot to talk about.'

Simone knew what that was. They had decided that in a year's time, or at the most two, they would offer to buy the Hotel Delouche. Their hotel in Paris was a going concern. It should be easy to sell. If she accepted, they would invite her to stay on and build an annexe for her. The idea of a house beside the place where her son had been shot was now impossible. Bernard would be their responsibility. They had plenty of love to give, even with children of their own. 'My altruism is not boundless,' Luc had said. 'I believe I could make it the best hotel in south-west France. Regional cuisine is big business.'

'You must learn manners from Monsieur Marmot,' Madame Claire said to Bernard. 'Apologise before you go with Simone.'

'No, no,' Luc said, 'I like frankness. And

I am not Monsieur Marmot. I am Luc.'
The boy smiled hesitantly. Luc would win
him over, Simone thought. Everyone liked
him. 'Have a *réligieuse.*' Luc was holding
out the box. The boy's eyes widened and
he took a cake eagerly.

'*Merci bien,*' he said. He took a bite,
leaving a trace of cream round his mouth.
'*Bon!* I'm ready, Simone.' He hitched the
strap of his gun on his shoulder. There was
a bright spot of colour on either cheek.

'Quick march!' Simone said. She smiled
at him. 'You lead the way.'

Everything reminded her of François, the
village roads they had driven about on
many of those early morning trips, to
Christian Grinaud's bakery for the *tourtes,*
to the Tabac for newspapers, to the *boucher*
near the old chateau for the steaks Madame
Claire liked but which she always grilled to
the consistency of old boots. Simple grilling
was too simple for her. She remembered
the unalloyed happiness she had felt before
Barbie Sinclair came to stay.

And then the *églantines.* The perfume
came through the open window of the
car as it had done when she had driven
with François to the ruined mill. She
remembered her tremulousness because
she had felt she was on the brink of
something wonderful. First love. Nothing

would ever be like that, not even with Luc. She accepted that, as she accepted that today she was not the same girl who had adored that young handsome man with the golden *mèche* who had arrived from Toulouse and changed her life, but whose love she'd had to wait for so long. He had been the first for her, but not she for him. 'Barbie, Barbie...' he had said in his sleep that night.

It had taken her three months after they were married to tell Luc. He hadn't spoken to her for the rest of the day, going about the hotel with a stony face. But at night in bed together she knew he was weeping and she had gathered him into her arms. Her love for him became strong because she had seen his weakness. 'Of course it's male pride,' he had said at last. 'You are my wife now. That is what matters.' They had never talked about it again.

'This is an expedition you and I are making,' she said to Bernard. He had been very quiet. She had felt his body rigid beside hers.

'*C'est ça.*' He didn't turn his head.

'I think you are wise to make it.' She spoke casually. 'Best to see for yourself.'

'Martine says Monsieur René thought he was shooting a Hun. I asked Mademoiselle Yvette what a Hun was and she told me. It was a German in the war. I ask

376

Mademoiselle Yvette many things.'

'You have some good friends. Pascal...'

'Yes, Pascal.' He sounded uninterested in Pascal. 'Mamee says Monsieur René may have thought he was shooting a golden oriole because of François' hair. He has this...' He made a backward movement with his hand above his forehead. 'He has this bright golden bit.' He speaks as if he were still alive, she thought. 'Mademoiselle Yvette showed me a picture of a golden oriole in a book. It is golden, that is true.'

'Perhaps it is better to think of a golden oriole than a Hun.' She breathed deeply to prevent the tears. 'And one doesn't say "Hun" nowadays. It is not *comme il faut.*' Would they ever know why François had climbed down the ravine in the middle of the night, and why he had been there in the first place? 'You will learn to forgive Monsieur René in time,' she said. 'He is wrong in the head. He would not have harmed François.'

'But he did.' The boy's voice rose. 'With a gun! I am going to keep my gun at the ready in case he ever escapes.' Luc and I will have to work hard with this boy, she thought. They crossed the stone bridge.

'The name of this little river is the Gregogne,' Bernard said. 'Our latest project at school is to draw a plan of the whole village. I got first prize.'

'Good for you. Here is the ravine. Shall we get out?' She spoke calmly and he scrambled out of the car, hoisting the strap of his gun onto his shoulder. They stood at the edge and looked down where the netting still lay. Only glimpses of it were visible. In time it would be completely covered with rioting juniper and no one would know it was there. She saw the sun glint on something lying at the foot. Perhaps a bottle.

They would never know whether François had climbed down because he saw a trapped bird, or whether René Marmot had shot him because he thought he was a Hun. Luc's mother had said he wandered about half the night, that his brother had grown tired of keeping an eye on him. She must ask Madame Claire sometime in the future if she had told François about his real father and his interest in the golden oriole. She had thought it was the right thing to do, that night they had spoken together on the telephone. Madame Claire had agreed, had said she had thought of it often.

Luc had said to her one night a few weeks after François' death. 'There is something else beside grief troubling you,' and had comforted her when she told him of her fears. 'Who knows whether you were wrong or not? Some things you have to live with.' His arms had held her closely. 'I will live it with you.'

'I am going to shoot my gun,' Bernard said. 'Three shots. I have loaded it with caps. Mademoiselle Yvette told me that was what they did sometimes at funerals.' He raised the gun to his shoulder and the sharp small reports didn't even raise a bird. They would scarcely be heard by the boy who tended the goats round the *chateau d'eau* where once she had cried her heart out. She saw the slim tower rearing against the horizon beyond the ravine. A memorial, she thought, to François, to my lost love, to his mother's. *'Bon!'* Bernard said. 'It is quite a good gun, don't you think?'

'It seems to be.' François must have bought it for him.

'Would you hold it for me, Simone?' He handed the gun to her. It was ridiculously light, meant for a child. She remembered when she used to go over the fields with Marcel to shoot pigeons how heavy a real gun had been against her shoulder when she pulled the trigger. Bernard was searching in his pockets, first one, then the other. She saw he had a matchbox in his hand. She remembered it.

'You have kept that all this time?'

Children were strange how they clung to some objects.

'Yes.' He was shamefaced. 'François hates it. I can make him angry if I bring it out.' She shivered. He slid open the little drawer, inviting her to look. 'See.'

She peered in and saw the small figure of a woman made of rubber lying on a bed of confetti. She felt a sickening stab at her heart. 'What is it?' She drew back.

'It is a key ring. One of the *pétanque* crowd gave it to me long ago to keep me quiet. I like to play with it. Or I *did.*' He shook his head. 'But not any more. It was when I turned the spindle that François hated it most. Like this.' He put a finger tip on the top and the rubber figure moved convincingly. He turned the spindle faster and it writhed as if in an agony of sexual desire.

'That's enough,' she said, turning away. The pain was between her legs. 'It's a strange thing for a boy to have.'

'Yes.' He nodded. 'Perhaps a gun is better.'

'So, what are you going to do with it?' She tried to speak normally.

'Watch. I have finished with it now.' He stepped back a few feet, took schoolboy aim, his head on one side, his arm lifted, and the matchbox flew over their heads and dropped into the depths of the ravine.

She thought that now he might throw himself against her in tears, at last, in realization of his father's death, and she stood ready to comfort him, but when she looked at him his face was adult in its sternness.

'Shall we go now?' she said. He didn't reply. 'Bernard, shall we go?'

He turned to her, a child again. His eyes were clear. 'I expect so. I have finished now.'

'Poor Monsieur Maurice without his brother. My mother-in-law, that is, Luc's mother, tells me he is failing.'

He considered that, calmly, then, as if he were conferring a favour, 'If you wish we could go and see him. They have a tame hen which walks on the table, and boudoir biscuits.' He smiled upwards at Simone. 'You remember?'

She nodded. *'Bonne idée.'* They walked back to the car together.

This Large Print Book for the Partially sighted, who cannot read normal print, is published under the auspices of

THE ULVERSCROFT FOUNDATION